His body reminded her she was a woman...

The battering he'd taken earlier, evading the sheriff, only made him that much more dark and dangerously appealing. Her pulse throbbed.

Matt was in her space, breathing the same scarce air. The more he looked at her, the more powerful he became and the deeper in his thrall she fell.

"I'll be back in the morning," he said. "You'll need to go along with whatever I say or do. Clear?" When she didn't answer, he continued, "You don't want to cross me, Fiona. The sheriff will be back in the morning and they'll be saying you're the one who murdered Kyle Everly."

She swallowed hard. "I don't believe that."

"You don't have to believe me, Fiona. Just wait and see." He stepped closer to her, and in the frigid night air she could feel the warmth emanating off his body, smell the scent of hay and horseflesh on him. He touched her cheek. "I want you to know this," he said, his voice low. "I want you to know you can tell me anything."

He just didn't know. That was the one thing she couldn't do.

Dear Harlequin Intrigue Reader,

All the evidence is in! And it would be a crime if you didn't "Get Caught Reading" this May. So follow the clues to your favorite bookstore to pick up some great tips.

This month Harlequin Intrigue has the distinguished privilege of launching a *brand-new* Harlequin continuity series with three of our top authors. TRUEBLOOD, TEXAS is a story of family and fortitude set in the great Lone Star state. We are pleased to give you your first look into this compelling drama with *Someone's Baby* by Dani Sinclair. Look for books from B.J. Daniels and Joanna Wayne to follow in the months ahead. You won't want to miss even a single detail!

Your favorite feline detective is back in *Familiar Lullaby* by Caroline Burnes. This time, Familiar's ladylove Clotilde gets in on the action when a baby is left on a high-society doorstep. Join a feisty reporter and a sexy detective as they search for the solution and find true love in this FEAR FAMILIAR mystery.

Our TOP SECRET BABIES promotion concludes this month with *Conception Cover-Up* by Karen Lawton Barrett. See how far a father will go to protect his unborn child and the woman he loves. Finally, Carly Bishop takes you out West for a showdown under a blaze of bullets in *No One But You*, the last installment in her LOVERS UNDER COVER trilogy.

So treat yourself to all four. You won't be disappointed.

Sincerely,

Denise O'Sullivan
Associate Senior Editor
Harlequin Intrigue

NO ONE BUT YOU

CARLY BISHOP

HARLEQUIN®

TORONTO • NEW YORK • LONDON
AMSTERDAM • PARIS • SYDNEY • HAMBURG
STOCKHOLM • ATHENS • TOKYO • MILAN • MADRID
PRAGUE • WARSAW • BUDAPEST • AUCKLAND

ISBN 0-373-22616-0

NO ONE BUT YOU

This edition published by arrangement with Harlequin Books S.A.

® and TM are trademarks of the publisher. Trademarks indicated with ® are registered in the United States Patent and Trademark Office, the Canadian Trade Marks Office and in other countries.

Visit us at www.eHarlequin.com

Printed in U.S.A.

ABOUT THE AUTHOR

Carly Bishop's novels are praised for their "sensuality, riveting emotional appeal and first-class suspense." She was a RITA Award finalist in 1996 for her Harlequin Intrigue novel *Reckless Lover,* and she's won numerous awards and critical acclaim throughout her ten-year writing career. Carly lives in Colorado and regularly uses the great Rocky Mountains as the backdrop in her stories.

Books by Carly Bishop

*Lovers Under Cover

Don't miss any of our special offers. Write to us at the following address for information on our newest releases.

Harlequin Reader Service
U.S.: 3010 Walden Ave., P.O. Box 1325, Buffalo, NY 14269
Canadian: P.O. Box 609, Fort Erie, Ont. L2A 5X3

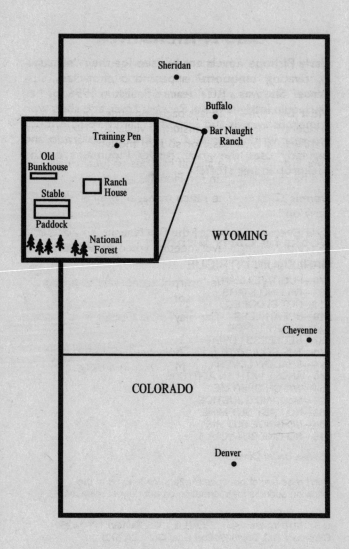

Sheridan

Buffalo

Bar Naught
Ranch

Training Pen

Old
Bunkhouse

Ranch
House

Stable

Paddock

National
Forest

WYOMING

Cheyenne

COLORADO

Denver

CAST OF CHARACTERS

Fiona Halsey—She spent her time gentling wild mustangs on the ranch her parents once owned. Would she tame Matt's heart, or set him up?

Matt Guiliani—The last bachelor undercover agent in operation against an insidious vigilante organization, Matt was all business...or so he'd thought.

Dex Hanifen—The sheriff had ties to local thugs, and he really had it in for Fiona.

Dennis Geary—The ranch manager went AWOL early on.

Kyle Everly—Owner of the Bar Naught, he was set to conduct a high-level meeting when someone shot him in the back.

Elliott Braden—The Interpol agent wanted a clean sweep of *all* the conspirators.

Pascal Lariviere—The playboy in Fiona's past was a very careful man.

Garrett Weisz and J. D. Thorne—Top undercover agents, they worried that Matt was in deadly, unforeseen danger.

In memory of
Boyd D. Adsit

I miss you dearly

Chapter One

At six minutes past eleven, Matt Guiliani rode into view of the main house on the Bar Naught Ranch. The deep irony of his own timing didn't escape him. Nothing much ever did.

The window of opportunity had reached its own eleventh hour. The time to move on Kyle Everly was now.

Matt reined the sorrel to a halt and dismounted, dropping silently to the freezing earth. He could smell winter coming in the frigid night air. He could almost smell his own anticipation. He'd been preparing for nearly seven months to go after Everly. The wealthy Wyoming rancher, never dirtying his own hands, made the shadowy vigilante organization known as the TruthSayers look like a bunch of local yokels trying to get up a lynch mob.

Under cover of the moonless night Matt tethered his mount to a patch of scrub oak at the edge of national forest land. He crouched low and pulled a pair of high-tech night-vision binoculars, no larger than a deck of cards, from the breast pocket of his heavy flannel shirt.

He dropped to one knee and began to familiarize

himself with every detail of the landscape below—
the yard, the hedges, the barn, the residence. And he
allowed the thrill of the chase to seep into his awareness… Everly had so narrowly escaped their notice.

Matt had arrived here tonight on an undercover assignment for the U.S. Attorney in Seattle. The Department of Justice wanted the TruthSayers dismantled, once and for all. This business of vigilante
extremists doling out their own brand of justice had
to be stopped. No one would have made the connections between Everly and the TruthSayers but for one
arrogant mistake.

Scrutinizing the main ranch house once more for
good measure, Matt turned his focus upon the barn.
Inside the upscale, heat-controlled, state-of-the-art facility Everly kept his horses: six polo ponies, three
Thoroughbred studs, a couple of working mounts—
and the ruined show-quality Arabian that belonged to
Fiona Halsey. Soldier Boy, she called him.

All the stable doors were divided in two. Only one
had the top half open. From satellite reconnaissance
photos, Matt knew that stall housed the viciously
claustrophobic stallion. Word had it that everyone in
town had warned Fiona the horse should be put down
before he killed someone.

She had grown up on the Bar Naught. The land
had been passed down through her family for five
generations, but her parents had lost it all eighteen
months ago. She resided now in a small apartment at
the west end of the barn.

If there was a wild card in the deck Matt was about
to shuffle, it was this woman. A long-stemmed beauty
too perverse or sentimental, or both, to do what had

to be done with a horse that had survived the fiery hell of a rollover in one of Everly's trailers.

As far as the neighbors were concerned, poor Fiona kept to herself, broke feral mustangs on a government contract program to adopt out the horses, oversaw the breeding of Everly's Thoroughbred studs, and spent her evenings alone sitting with Soldier Boy. The local princess, descended from the landless younger son of a nineteenth-century British earl, brought brutally and unfairly low.

But Fiona Halsey had a dubious past with a French playboy who had too many ties to a group of international thugs Interpol had dubbed The Fraternity. These men brokered illegal weapons, assassins, guns-for-hire and mercenaries. They fostered and gave away arms and services to vigilante groups like the TruthSayers.

Kyle Everly was one of them, almost certainly in command, and here was Fiona Halsey, living on the Bar Naught by his leave.

Coincidence? No one knew for sure.

Satisfied with his survey, Matt snapped shut the binoculars, tucked them away, shouldered his duffel bag and began to pick his way down the mountain-side.

As he drew nearer and approached from a westerly angle, Matt saw flickering candlelight within the curtained windows of the ranch manager, Dennis Geary. The ramrod could be counted upon to be entertaining a lady friend in his bunkhouse quarters. Probably one of the clerks from the local convenience store.

The main house was lit up in a couple of rooms. Matt knew Everly himself was away for a regular Friday night poker game that always lasted into the wee hours of Saturday morning. Everly was said to lose a lot, currying favor of the locals.

Which left only Fiona's whereabouts to account for. Her four-wheel-drive vehicle was parked beneath a pair of old cottonwood trees just outside her apartment. It took Matt thirty seconds to satisfy himself that she was inside.

He had his doubts about her as well. Devil or angel? Player or patsy? Everly's dupe or a woman who simply loved the Bar Naught and would live on it as an employee if that was her only option?

Not knowing left Matt edgy. He didn't like it, but there it was. Everly was his target. If Fiona Halsey got in his way, Matt would have his answer.

He crouched low and circled around to the back of the main house. Vaulting easily over the pristine white picket fence at the perimeter of the lawn, he crossed to the back door of the ranch house. There on the porch he knelt to open his duffel bag. He took out a small flashlight and shone a narrow beam on the doors and windows, then disabled the security system.

He opened the back door of the residence, slipped inside and hung his bag by its strap over the inside doorknob. But as he turned around to get a sense of the place, he had an almost visceral feeling of a plan about to go very wrong.

Matt let the feeling spread through him. He stood there in the kitchen listening for the smallest sound, the barest hint that he was not alone. Hearing nothing to alarm him, he began a stealthy room-to-room search of the house, in the end satisfied that he was alone. Still, the feeling of something badly amiss persisted, like a distant siren that went on and on without fading away.

A sudden memory rose up in his mind, of another night he had experienced just such a chilling, powerful presentiment—the night the TruthSayers had snatched his best friend's young son, Christo.

Matt dragged in a deep draught of air and blew it out slowly, letting his breath carry off the adrenaline rush and the tension the memory evoked in his body. At least no child's life was at stake this night.

He took a couple of powder-free latex gloves from the back pocket of his jeans, pulled them on and began going through the house, taking it apart, studying the interior and furnishings in earnest. He wanted to become as familiar with Everly's possessions as if they belonged to him. As if *he* were Kyle Everly.

Tension lingered inside him. He sat down at Everly's computer at twelve-thirteen and set to work against the subtle ticking of an antique grandfather clock.

He spent half an hour at the computer, finding detailed maps. He suspected these would match up perfectly with the shipments of illegal arms Interpol had meticulously tracked. In spreadsheet format he found timetables he knew would match thefts and bombings and murders carried out all over creation.

All of these files could be explained away by a defense attorney, but the information gave Matt the leverage he needed to blackmail his way into Everly's affairs. Tomorrow he would be back, a dangerously renegade cop, formerly of the Anti-TruthSayers squad, ready now to go on the take. Matt Guiliani would become Everly's new best friend and partner in crime.

He printed key files, then a household inventory as well. One never knew when it would come in handy to know the exact worth of the Renoir on the bedroom wall or the bronze sculpture in the living room. An eagle in flight, clutching its prey in fearsome claws, it was a perfect metaphor for Kyle Everly, the predator who owned the bronze.

The psycho profilers described Everly as a narcissist sociopath, a blond, blue-eyed pretty boy that no one had ever given nearly enough credit for having a brain.

A mistaken prejudice, Matt thought now, that physical beauty such as Everly's inevitably went unmatched by intellect. Everly sat out here in the middle of big Wyoming thinking himself safe. Thinking he slipped with ease under the radar of law enforcement. He expected to get by with whatever pleased his twisted fancy because he always had.

But Everly hadn't met Matt yet.

He checked his watch. He had no more than five minutes before he needed to clear out. He had one last task, just in case Everly balked at taking the renegade Matt Guiliani on as his new best friend.

He took a floppy disk from his pocket and planted on Everly's computer documents that would make it appear that Everly had conspired against his brothers in The Fraternity. That with the brilliant assistance of a powerful Phoenix attorney, Everly had siphoned millions of dollars off the deals The Fraternity made providing illegal arms and hired killers. The guy in Phoenix routinely played such undercover roles for the Department of Justice.

Everly was about to find himself between a rock and a very hard place.

ELLIOTT BRADEN BOARDED his flight at Heathrow, brimming with a certain bonhomie. The Americans had already deployed their undercover cop into international affairs that did not concern them. Braden had been assigned the watchdog job of Interpol "liaison." Surely the most glorified term for the thankless and impotent position of making sure the Americans did not screw it up.

In fact, he knew they would. He knew they didn't know when to quit. Americans prided themselves on their never-say-die attitude.

In a haze of contempt, both for his superiors in Interpol and the necessity of involving the Americans, Braden took his first-class seat, graciously accepting the crystal goblet of Chenin Blanc from the flight attendant. The aircraft took off after a delay of only seven minutes.

He had no desire to embroil himself in the Americans' doggedness, but he supposed his sacrifice might pay off handsomely in the not-too-distant future. Very soon now he would meet them.

Garrett Weisz. J. D. Thorne. Matt Guiliani.

These were the players, the heart of the U.S. Attorney's Anti-TruthSayers task force, the men running the current undercover operation against Kyle Everly. And as touchingly loyal to one another as blood brothers, all incapable of minding their own petty, provincial business, even when their loved ones were threatened.

The small son of Garrett Weisz, for instance, a child named Christo. He'd been kidnapped by leaders of TruthSayers when Weisz, Thorne and Guiliani's undercover operation threatened them. The threesome prevailed and the child was restored to the bosom of his family. The TruthSayers were left without much leadership.

Months later, their numbers greatly reduced, the rabid TruthSayers made an attempt on J. D. Thorne's life. And then on the teenage son of Thorne's girl-friend, a Seattle detective named Ann Calder. Enter Kyle Everly. The wealthy local rancher and Truth-Sayers sympathizer had, for some inscrutable, arro-gant reason, lent his considerable resources to the straightforward attempted assassinations of J. D. Thorne and Ann Calder.

The trained killers failed. Guiliani rescued the teen-ager. Everly, however, proved untouchable. That fact had done nothing to faze the dogged investigations of Weisz or Thorne, least of all Mateos Guiliani.

Such a hero, Braden thought.

But Braden was stuck. Interpol had enough to move on a few of the other suspected members of La Fraternité but nothing concrete on its wealthiest and therefore most powerful member, the wily, wealthy, twisted rancher. To make a clean sweep and put an end to their scattered reign of terror, Everly must be caught up in the sting, and the other unconfirmed members with him. But he was an American citizen, and it was Guiliani who could, if all went as expected, force Everly's hand.

Such an unexpected bit of luck, Braden reflected.

He allowed himself a vinegary little smile. Perhaps the stars and the planets had aligned themselves in just the most pleasing configuration. Perhaps Guiliani would give him the most amazing coup de grâce.

He blinked, and lifted his goblet in silent salutation.

SATISFIED WITH HIS night's work, Matt shut down the computer and turned soundlessly in Everly's leather chair. Staring off into the night, he took a few moments more to visualize his first face-to-face meeting with his quarry. In his mind's eye, he watched Everly's trademark, guileless smile fade dead away.

Matt left the computer and started toward the back of the house when he heard a vehicle approaching. His senses went on high alert, his pulse slowed. He had no fear of being caught. He could still slip away unseen in a matter of seconds. But his thirst for the chase had been whetted.

He decided to go back and let the sting begin. To let Everly find him here *now* rather than in the morning. He moved silently as a ghost back into Everly's study and took up a position to the side of the picture window looking out, within several feet of the front door.

It was Everly who had driven into the yard. Matt watched him turn toward the garages, cut the engine, get out and shut the door on his shiny black Lexus four-wheel-drive. Deep in conversation, he had a cell phone plastered to his ear.

He turned back momentarily, clearly expecting Geary to have appeared by now to put the Lexus away. Still talking, his breath making puffs in the freezing air, he strode back to his vehicle, jerked open the passenger door, leaned in and laid on the horn.

Interesting, Matt thought, that Dennis Geary still didn't come running.

Everly must have decided to ignore it. He left the Lexus with the door open, reached the first riser and kicked the dirt off one boot and then the other as the motion-detector turned on the porch light. He took the next two steps in a single stride, landing him on the veranda.

He cast a look over his shoulder, grimaced, then snarled into the phone and moved out of Matt's sight. He had only cracked open the door when a shot rang out in the valley of the Bar Naught. The cell phone went flying onto the floor of the entry, and Kyle Everly fell with a sickening thud to the floor of the foyer.

A powerful shudder roiled through Matt's body. Seconds passed in its grip. He thought he heard another shot, but revised his opinion in a split second. What he'd heard was the cell phone crashing onto the parquet floor, and behind that, an echo of the gun blast. He moved swiftly to the front door, careful to stay concealed. A massive amount of blood had already pooled on the hardwood floor. Too much loss to survive? Matt laid a finger at Everly's carotid artery. He felt nothing.

Everly lay dead in his tracks.

A chill train wreck of emotions rose up in Matt. To see a man dropped in cold blood without warning, shot in the back like that, crossed the line. *Jesus, Mary and Joseph.* He crossed himself with the motions his mother had taught him when he was too young to know what he was doing. *If I die before I wake, I pray the Lord my soul to take…*

He wasn't sure he believed any of that anymore. He knew if there was a hell, Everly deserved to be set on that path. But shooting Everly in the back had never occurred even in the stark revenge fantasies Matt had harbored.

The freezing night air rolled in through the open door, but failed to carry off the stench of blood. Aware of the commotion the shot had caused in the stables, of horses half-frenzied, he fought the over-whelming temptation to return fire blindly just to draw it again. He might get a fix on the direction the shot had come from or the direction the shooter had moved. There was no other noise. No sounds of a retreating vehicle. But even if the ruse worked, how would he explain his own presence?

The murder of Kyle Everly changed everything. It didn't take a lot of imagination to see that Everly's death opened the door to a huge power struggle among the members of The Fraternity. That someone would move in soon to fill the vacuum of power.

Matt made the split-second decision to reinvent himself and his mission. He could not be seen here tonight. He moved out of range of Everly's bloody corpse, stood and began to move soundlessly away. He snatched up the papers he had printed and shut down the computer.

When he left there must be no hint that anyone had been inside the mansion at the moment of Everly's demise.

No more than sixty seconds had passed. Still no one appeared in the yard to check out a shot in the dark, but the turmoil in the stables escalated.

Six months ago what Matt knew about horses could have fit onto the head of a pin, but even then he'd have recognized the high-pitched whinnying and the sounds of hooves crashing against barriers for what it was. The edge of stampede behavior in what amounted to a lockdown situation. A disaster waiting to happen to very pricey animals.

Was it the gunshot, or the scent of death permeating the frozen night air that incited the panic?

Fiona Halsey had to have her hands full.

Matt moved through the silent house toward the back. Through the open front door where Everly lay dead, Matt heard a male voice bellowing. "What in Sam Hill's going on? Fiona!"

Geary, Matt assumed. He stripped off his gloves and stuffed them along with the printouts into his duffel bag, then let himself out through the back door. He reversed his earlier sabotage to the alarm system and then, hugging the exterior walls of the ranch house, circled round to its southwest corner. There, crouched out of sight at the base of a box-elder hedge, he watched.

Geary came out of the bunkhouse, stuffing his arms into a heavy parka as Matt took up his position.

"Halsey!" His hair tousled, indignant as hell, Geary hunched down into his coat and started for the Lexus with its interior light burning and the passenger door still hanging open. Some realization must have kicked its way through to his foggy head.

Geary stopped bellowing for Fiona, whose hands he had to know were full-up taking care of the horses. He froze in his tracks. He turned slowly and stared hard at the front door gaping wide open under the porch lights. A siren began to wail in the distance. Geary's girlfriend popped out of a door in the bunkhouse. "Dennis, what's going on?"

"Get back inside, you idiot!" he barked, bellowing again for Fiona as he ran to the porch.

Then Fiona Halsey let herself out of the barn. Her long, dark blond hair hung heavily down her back; tension rode her hard. "Geary, I swear, if you don't cut it out—"

She never finished the sentence. The siren grew more and more shrill, and she forgot whatever she'd been thinking about the blaring horn and gunfire and Geary's subsequent bellowing.

Geary had launched himself up onto the porch and out of Matt's line of vision. "He's dead, Halsey! Everly's dead!" he shouted over the shrill noise of the oncoming siren. "What the devil? D'you do this?"

Focused now on her, Matt watched disbelief replace the irritation on her face. His knees stiffened and the cold brought on a shiver. He watched her lips shaping the answer to Geary's question, *Don't be an ass, Dennis,* but what Matt supposed must be the sheriff's SUV, brakes screeching, turned off the highway and up the country lane. The siren drowned out the sound of her voice.

Belatedly, maybe goaded by the shrill approach, she ran toward the porch herself as Geary's girlfriend closed herself back into the bunkhouse.

Matt snapped shut his binoculars and shook his head in disbelief over the unlikely speed of the local law enforcement arriving on the scene. Was it the sheriff Everly had been talking to when he was gunned down?

Matt drew a deep, silent breath and faced the crucial decision—stay or go. He had only seconds to conceal himself in a better position to observe what went on, or to head back up the mountainside. He could observe perfectly well from the spot where his horse was tethered, but he wouldn't be able to hear what was said.

He scanned the gabled roofs of the house, the barn and the bunkhouse, then backed around the length of hedge, keeping his options open for those few seconds as the sheriff's vehicle slammed to a stop and two men piled out.

The larger of the two, clearly in authority, was Dex Hanifen, the Johnson County sheriff. "Fiona? Geary? What's going on here?"

His deputy, Crider, scurried up to the porch at the front door where Everly's body lay collapsed. "Oh, my God, Dex! It's Kyle! Deader than a doornail."

Hanifen stared. "No way—"

Crider began to moan, cutting him off. "Yeah, boss. He's shot in the back. Jeez, Dex, the blood!" He swore, and then gagged and retched and threw up.

Hanifen cut loose a blue streak about contaminating a crime scene and all but flew up the steps and as quickly hurled Crider off the porch. He shouted at Geary, ordering him to his side. "I need some help here."

The man stalled. "You want me to look around, Dex? I could see—"

"Sure, Geary. I've got a moron deputy woofing his cookies in the middle of a crime scene, and I'm *dead* certain the murderer's waiting around to be discovered," Hanifen snarled. "Now get your butt over here and give me a hand with this freaking mess."

The moment Geary stepped reluctantly forward, Matt moved out. He chose the roof of the barn so that if he slipped, the noise would go unnoticed. He circled around, far outside the perimeter of the yard lights.

At the west end of the barn he climbed onto the paddock fence and gripped the edge of the roof. He swung forward hard and jackknifed his body onto the rooftop, landing with a lot more noise than he'd hoped.

"What the hell was that?" he heard Crider shout.

"The horses, you ninny." Hanifen's voice. Wildly

grateful for the sheriff's preoccupied impatience, Matt nevertheless plastered himself to the roof. Scraped raw in the maneuver, his hands felt on fire, but he didn't move, hardly breathed.

Matt heard Hanifen get on the radio and order in help to seal off, search out and protect the evidence. "And the horses are getting whacked out, so whatever you do, don't put on the siren."

Matt gauged his position on the roof and moved crabwise to situate himself before Fiona went back into the stables. He just glimpsed her entering below him as he molded himself to the asphalt shingles to watch what was going on.

Not another five minutes had passed before a second vehicle with the county sheriff's logo pulled into the yard. If the killer had made any tracks, if the shell casing had been left on the ground, if any number of possible clues to the killer's identity remained in the drive or yard, Matt thought the sheriff's crew was doing one hell of a job laying waste to the evidence.

He stayed on the roof growing stiffer, colder and more irritated by the moment for nearly two hours. Photos were taken of Everly's position when he fell over dead. Hanifen conducted a cursory search of the house and ruled out the necessity of bringing in crime-scene technicians.

The murder, after all, had taken place on the front stoop by a shooter outside the house.

One would think, if one didn't know better, Matt thought, that the sheriff didn't give a damn about preserving the integrity of the evidence. Matt had to wonder if there was any percentage at all in staying on the roof, observing, listening.

Then, just as he'd decided to move out, Matt got

his payoff. Hanifen and Crider wound up virtually beneath Matt's position, leaning in against the stable wall, lighting their smokes.

"I'll bet you anything the princess killed him," Hanifen's underling was saying.

"Maybe," the sheriff returned, "but I'm not taking her in tonight."

"But—"

"But what?" A cloud of smoke chased the sheriff's abrupt interruption, wafting upward toward Matt.

"Well, she's a flight risk for one thing—"

"Oh, stifle it, Crider," Hanifen snapped. "This is not New York and you are not on *NYPD Blue*. Fiona Halsey has motive up the ying-yang, she had opportunity, and—"

"And more than enough firepower to arm a small nation, let's not forget…" Crider trailed off.

Matt could almost feel through his frozen senses the quiet wrath coming off Hanifen. His words dropped out like chunks of glacier. "What firepower would that be?"

Exactly, Matt thought. What firepower? Was Crider blabbing about an armory in existence on the Bar Naught? And one Fiona Halsey knew about?

But Crider cleared his throat and backpedaled like a demon. "You know. Just what's stashed…in the inside. And Fiona's gotta have a rifle herself."

More glacier shedding. "You're a fool."

"I know when to keep my mouth shut," Crider protested.

"Like now?"

"But, Dex, it's just you and me out here—"

"I don't ever want to hear a word that even rhymes

with 'firepower' out of your mouth again. You got that?''

"Yeah," Crider answered, sullen-voiced.

Hanifen went on. "I don't want to hear any disrespect in regard to Fiona Halsey, either."

"You gone all soft on her, Dex?"

"Shut your trap, Crider. That little girl and I go back a long way."

"She's not a little girl anymore." The fool dug his hole deeper. "You gonna just let her get away with it?"

How, Matt thought, did the guy dare taunt Hanifen? But to his utter disbelief, Hanifen let the ridicule go.

"She's not going to get away with anything." He tossed his cigar butt into the yard. "Here's what's *not* going to happen. I am *not* gonna have the whole damned county down on my head for railroading the local princess."

Chapter Two

The first time he met Fiona Halsey face-to-face, Matt found himself staring up the barrel of her cocked, .30-30 lever-action rifle. The Remington was a beauty, powerful enough to fell a moose from several hundred yards out. And it still had the faint acrid scent of burnt gunpowder.

"Back away from Soldier Boy," she commanded, "and keep your arms in the air."

He raised one arm but left the other on the scarred, discolored withers of the Arabian.

It was already some kind of natural miracle that Matt had survived the standoff with Soldier. He'd had about two seconds' warning when, apparently for no real reason other than to amuse himself, Crider had elevated the searchlights attached to the sheriff's second vehicle and started the beacon rolling.

Who knew? It was possible the fool still would not have caught sight of Matt even with the searchlight glaring full on. It was just as possible that even in the sweep of the beacon halfway up the mountain, Matt might not have been spotted.

He'd reacted as if his body weren't stiff from the cold, crabbing his way back over the rooftop, expecting to hang out on the dark side of the roof for a while. The only trouble was, the floodlights on the paddock side of the barn had been turned on in the exhaustive search for clues, and now lit up not only his escape route, but the slant of the roof as well.

He had only one decent chance to escape detection and that was to duck into the stall of a killer horse named Soldier Boy. He estimated where he had to be to turn himself off the roof and into the stall and then he prayed for a second time in one night.

He positioned himself, gripped the icy edge of the roof and somersaulted off into space. His legs cleared the half door of Soldier Boy's stall, but he'd thunked down so hard on his middle that every last molecule of air in his body was pounded out. He twisted in pain and landed on his butt, his back up against the stable door.

The stallion had wheeled around, his ears flattened, his hooves scraping with an incredible menace along the floor. If an animal could breathe fire, it was this one. Dropped to the floor, Matt couldn't have moved to save his life.

Head lowered, legs stiffened, his mane bristling with wrath, Soldier had snorted, and come as close to foaming at the mouth as Matt ever wanted to see. His own mouth had gone as bone dry as his lungs were empty.

Over the past months he'd spent countless hours around horses in preparation for this assignment. He wasn't going to go onto the Bar Naught without knowing his way around. In those weeks, he'd been bitten, kicked and thrown. He'd deliberately sought out the meanest critters he could find so nothing he might later encounter on the Bar Naught would take him by surprise. It was just the way he worked. He had to know it all.

He'd learned to ride and keep his seat in a dead run. He'd learned a few stunts and dislocated his shoulder, half mangled his hand when he got caught up in twisted, unforgiving reins.

But Soldier's fiery temper made all Matt's weeks of preparation seem useless. The pitched battle of wills between him and Soldier was oddly silent. A scene without sound except for Soldier's wrathful breathing.

Matt had to establish dominance, but for too long a time he couldn't get his lungs functioning to send oxygen to his muscles. For long seconds he could only sit there and cower, inviting his own destruction.

He fought for every breath, praying for the second time in one night. *Just let me get out of this one....* Then Soldier let out an eerie sound and gathered his powerful muscles to rear back and rain down death with a killing lunge.

Beyond conscious thought, Matt brought his legs under himself and sprang at the horse, aiming his shoulder at Soldier's head with every shred of strength left in his battered body. The blow connected, jarred even his own teeth, ricocheting through him as if he'd hit a brick wall. But Soldier hauled back and a grudging respect set in.

In the intervening hour, while the sheriff and his men departed and Halsey and Geary went about turning off all the floodlights, Matt had barely moved. By now, he'd smooth-talked himself into a guarded truce with Soldier Boy, managed to get back on his feet and even get a steadying hand on the stallion's flank.

Now, facing Fiona Halsey's rifle, Matt had zero

inclination to give up the uneasy rapport he'd achieved with a stallion that would still as soon stomp him into a mud hole and kick it dry.

"Put your hands in the air and move away from the horse." The sensual grit in Fiona Halsey's Brit-cultured voice plucked strings Matt didn't even know he had, made him weak-kneed.

He didn't cotton to the sensation at all, which immediately put him out of a mood to do her bidding. Even to save his own hide.

If the tall, lush, lanky blonde with the complexion of an English rose had murdered once—and the stench of gunpowder clinging to the gun she still held gave the theory credence—then she had it in her to do it again.

His ribs ached like all billy hell. His shoulder was so stiff he could no longer feel it. Still and all, perverse as it was, maybe he was also a bit turned on by the fact that Fiona Halsey had his disbelieving heart in the crosshairs of her scope.

He left his hand resting where it was, in physical contact with the stallion, and gave Fiona Halsey his most charming grin.

He really didn't want to die. "Suppose you disarm, and we'll talk."

"Suppose I don't, and you do the talking."

"I don't do so well under the gun." He smiled, stroking Soldier's flank again. "So to speak."

"Too bad." Flinty-edged, her tone still struck him as powerfully seductive. He wondered, did that particular combination come with the royal genes, a couple of generations removed?

His nose itched from what seemed like protracted hours in the softly lit horse barn, but his eyes were attuned to the semidark and his focus homed in on Fiona Halsey's splintered attention.

Riveted to the motion of his hand, she was equally unrelenting and steady in her dead-on aim. But for an instant he thought he saw confusion in her, jealousy flashing in her shadowed eyes—not for want of his hands on her, he thought, but because her beloved, wrecked Soldier Boy allowed his touch.

Everyone knew Soldier tolerated her least of all.

She tossed that silky curtain of deep blond hair without altering her aim one millimeter off dead center of his heart. "Are you mocking me?"

"I wouldn't dream of it," he answered, solemn as a judge. Not a woman in possession of a deadly weapon he had no chance of taking from her. Standing outside Soldier's stall, on the other side of the stall door, she could blow him to kingdom come before he could get anywhere near enough to disarm her.

His survival mechanism, the instincts by which he lived so as not to die, kicked into higher gear for the second time that night. He shook his head slowly. "The grandniece of an English peer, distant cousin to the queen herself?" He shook his head again, and discovered a splitting headache to go with his jammed shoulder and bruised ribs.

Her aim faltered for half a second. He'd succeeded in unnerving her, tossing off her obscure royal connections. He pressed this narrow advantage by using her name. "C'mon, Fiona. We both know you won't pull the trigger."

Her chin went up. "Try me."

"Oh, I don't doubt you'd kill me, but..." He

shrugged. "You're not going to do anything that would upset Soldier."

"Soldier *Boy*," she answered, the grit in her voice turned more lethal than sensual, "is already upset."

"You should have seen him an hour ago." But it occurred to him that provoking Soldier to a frenzied rage might serve her purposes. The thought congealed into a nasty suspicion that he must be very careful not to underestimate Fiona Halsey. "It wouldn't take much to send Soldier over the edge, would it?"

"No." She cocked a hip forward, agreeing…softly. Bitterly. Choked. "It wouldn't take much at all."

He found his weak-kneed self, the one reacting to her voice, suffering. What man wouldn't want to spare her the turmoil of loving a horse who would never again return her emotional investment?

Fool. He should be baiting her into the stall, disarming her. What was he doing? What was the point of playing her—or letting her play him? Soldier's flesh skittered under his hand, and the stallion threw his head up.

But there *was* a point in goading her, he knew. The smoking Remington made her suspect. The scope made it even more likely. She could have gone five hundred yards up the tree-lined lane leading into the main ranch house with the rifle, picked Everly off and made it back to her quarters in time to make it look as if she had never been gone. He went on stroking the massive animal she loved, subtly stoking her resentment that Soldier tolerated him at all while he offered up his theory.

"Here's how I see it. You have to be worried about the possibility that I saw what happened. That I saw you do it."

She stared at him, unblinking. "You think I shot Kyle?"

"Yeah. I do." He nodded, appreciating her quickness, leading her farther down the path. "And I can appreciate your dilemma. Should you shoot me next, and have to call Hanifen back, or—"

"Or," she interrupted, anticipating him, "maybe fire off a round and cause Soldier to trample you to death." Her chin went up. "It would be a little less efficient than a bullet through the heart."

"But really, not a bad trade-off in terms of explaining everything to Dex."

She blinked. "It wouldn't do to leave alive a witness to the murder."

He nodded. The flint in her voice was backed by tempered steel at her core. If she'd decided to murder Everly, she was capable of it. If she had, Matt was toast. Somehow, in spite of the solid possibility, he doubted that she had done it. "You'd get away with all of it. Plays nicely, I think."

"Except that your premise is fatally flawed. I didn't shoot Kyle."

"Really? Is that your gun?"

"Yes."

"When's the last time you used it?"

"Months ago. What difference does it make?"

"Then someone else shot Everly with your gun, princess."

Her eyes narrowed. He knew them to be a stunning hazel-blue, but all he could see was an angry darkening. "Who—"

"Check it out, Fiona. You may have been the local debutante, but you're not green. Are you telling me you can't smell the spent powder?"

Whatever color there was in her face drained away. "I didn't shoot—"

"I think you did." But he really didn't know. Her reaction could be taken in two completely exclusive ways. Either she'd shot Everly in the back and was now caught red-handed with the murder weapon, or she had only just now figured out that someone had neatly framed her.

It struck him that if Kyle Everly had an arsenal of weapons stashed somewhere on the Bar Naught, which was what Hanifen's deputy had seemed to imply, weapons Fiona Halsey knew about, she would have been smarter than to used her own Remington.

She swallowed hard. He watched the pitching of her throat beneath the delicate, luminous skin of her neck in the low lighting of the stables. Rustling sounds, scrapes and hooves and clanking of the other Bar Naught horses, filled the silence.

"Who are you?" she demanded, her chin thrust forward.

Her question was more complicated than she knew. Matt answered more honestly than he'd had any intention of doing. "Whoever I need to be."

He watched the shadows alter on her face, knew that her jaw tightened. "What were you doing hiding out in here?"

"Basically, I thought I'd be better off staying out of Hanifen's way."

"Just shy, I suppose."

He cracked the smile, but the image of Everly dropping dead of a bullet in the back was not far from his mind.

She lowered the rifle a bit. If she truly wasn't the one who had shot Everly in the back, then she had at least to suspect that she had the murderer in her sights. But she had a problem, he knew. She wasn't willing or inclined to kill him, or she'd already have pulled the trigger. But if she turned her back on him to call Hanifen, he would either kill her or get away.

Why was she willing to stand here jawing with him?

Then the thought occurred to him that she had known all along that there was someone hiding out in the stables. She'd kept an eagle eye on the horses during the last few hours. He'd heard her come and go a couple of times before Hanifen and his men cleared out, making the rounds of stalls, calming the valuable animals by her presence and her soft, sultry reassurances.

She hadn't come near Soldier's stall. He'd sensed her nearby, smelled hesitation on her, but in his oxygen-deprived head, he'd chalked it up to Soldier's inhospitable attitude. Now he had to wonder. He took the stab in the dark. "You knew before Hanifen and his boys left that someone was holed up in here with Soldier, didn't you?"

Her chin pitched up. "That's ridiculous."

"Why didn't you turn me in when you had the chance, Fiona?"

Her trigger finger flinched almost imperceptibly. Her shadowy eyes narrowed. "Maybe... No, you're wrong. I didn't know anyone was in here."

"Maybe?"

"I wasn't sure."

"I think you were."

"You think?" she mocked him.

He turned his head slowly, minutely, back and forth. "You knew." *He* knew, now, without a doubt.

His stab in the dark had struck a nerve. He still didn't get it. What possible reason could she have for not exposing an intruder's whereabouts to Hanifen? For that matter, why wasn't she persisting till he gave her straight answers as to who he was and what he was doing at the scene of a murder?

"All right, then," she tossed back, at last releasing the firing pin, lowering the rifle butt-first to the ground. "Why do you think I kept my mouth shut?"

"It's a mystery to me." More so with every moment. Why put the rifle down now? "Maybe you aren't at all sorry that he's dead."

"Hmm." He heard heavy derision in that noise. "Maybe I wanted to find out who hated Everly more than I do." She tossed her head, sent her long hair flying. For the first time he saw uncertainty edging in. She gritted her teeth "Maybe I wanted to help whoever did it get away. Maybe I wanted to kiss you—"

She cut herself off awkwardly. Her mouth clapped shut. "I mean—"

He knew what she meant. She knew what she meant. Maybe, she'd have kissed anyone who got rid of Kyle Everly for her. A sort of bounty. But in Matt's perceptions—and hers, he thought—the meaning expanded, time slowed, and the air between them all but blistered.

His heart boomed. His blood pooled deep down. He'd spent his life keeping not only his passions but visceral reactions like this under impenetrable wraps, but he knew his gaze sharpened in spite of him, intensified, locked on her lips.

She couldn't let her mistaken meaning go uncorrected. Her tongue swiped at her lips and she tried to take it back.

"Kiss whoever—" She swallowed. "I meant…not you."

"I know what you meant." He tried to put a stop to the slippery slope of sexual awareness sucking the air out of them both. "Did you hate him that much, Fiona? Enough to kill him?"

"Yes. But I didn't."

Stricken and still pale, shaking now, she fixed her gaze on Soldier Boy, avoiding the threat of a kiss between them. Then she turned and gave him a withering look. "When is the last time you had a tetanus shot?"

"Beats me. How long do those things last?"

She rolled her eyes. "Come with me. Or forget it. Take your chances. It really doesn't matter to me."

But he had the distinct impression that it would suit her very well if he if walked away and took his chances with a fatal case of lockjaw.

He followed her instead.

FIONA TURNED ON HER HEEL and led the way from the barn into a room outfitted with an examining table and stocked with veterinary supplies. Aware that he was following her, she switched on the glaring overhead lights. Her hands were shaking. She set the safety and put aside the rifle, then opened a gleaming white cabinet door and pulled out a vial containing a dose of tetanus booster.

Dear Lord, what was she doing?

She began to go through a drawer in search of a small syringe when he boosted himself up onto the small-animal exam table.

"That's meant for animals under a hundred pounds."

"Must not get a lot of use." He pulled one arm out of his coat and began rolling up a sleeve.

"That's not the point." He didn't belong there. Didn't belong on the Bar Naught at all. In fact he didn't have any business looking at her the way he was looking at her.

"It's fine."

"It's not fine." He meant that the table would hold up. She meant much, much more. Nothing was fine. Nothing had been fine for her or the Bar Naught in a very long time.

"Fiona—"

She looked straight into his dark brown eyes, noting the fringe of thick black lashes. "Don't bother sweet-talking me, Guiliani."

His pupils flared, otherwise she would not have known she'd caught him off guard. He was that good.

He blinked slowly. "If you know who I am, Fiona, then what was that all about in Soldier's stall?"

"I didn't know at first. Not for a while. Now that you're under the lights—" *Now that you made a fool of me, broke my heart cozying up to Soldier Boy—* She cut off the thought and shrugged. "I know. That's all."

"How?"

"Kyle."

"Kyle? What about him?"

She turned back to her search for supplies, still so shaken by Kyle's murder and the timing of Matt Guiliani's appearance on the Bar Naught, and what the fallout would be to her own purposes, that she couldn't think what lie to tell or how to deliver it.

She combed unnecessarily through the drawer full of syringes to cover her delay in answering, then plucked out an unused eighteen-gauge syringe.

He grabbed her other forearm. "Look at me, Fiona. What about Everly?"

She jerked her hand away, but he held tight and all she accomplished by pulling so hard was to bring his naked wrist into contact with her breast.

An intensely sexual awareness, keen, fierce and unexpected, hit her, a flash flood of mutual suspicion crashing down through canyons of barren, thwarted desire. Her mouth watered. Her nipples tightened unbearably. *Another slip, Fiona?* she thought, like the unintended mention of a kiss in Soldier Boy's stall?

What was it about him that had her reacting this way?

She swallowed.

He released her wrist.

Their eyes met, and she backed away, one step.

"I want you off the Bar Naught. Now." She knew he wasn't any less affected by her slip than she was. Her breast still tingled. However unwitting, he stroked the part of his wrist that had touched her with the tips of the fingers on his other hand.

She couldn't do this, couldn't *be* here, be in a situation where a man made any difference to her. Or made her feel. Or made her tingle, wanting more.

He had to get off the Bar Naught and stay off it. She had made the worst mistake of her life by not betraying his presence to Dex. If she had, Dex would have hauled Matt Guiliani off to jail, and then she could try to decide what to do. What Kyle's murder meant. How her own future would go now that her excuse for being on the Bar Naught was dead.

But Guiliani still wanted to know how she knew who he was. "I'm not leaving till you tell me what Everly said."

The part of her that flawless composure had been drilled into responded with the necessary lie. "Kyle showed me your photo. It had come up in a conversation about bodyguards." She joked to neutralize the tension, to defeat the stirring of attraction to this intruder into her life. "Kyle was skeptical, making fun of the possibility, but he told me that you would try to kill him one day."

The implication that Kyle might actually need a bodyguard was the first time he came close to revealing what she already knew. He dealt with men who dispensed illegal arms, guns, bombs and rockets to half-baked causes, dangerous men—and profited hugely in doing it.

Her ears had perked up, her attention snared. He never told her in so many words what his international business dealings were about. He avoided the subject all the time. She'd asked a few questions, trying to make her curiosity seem without any particular motive behind it. Kyle had only stroked her chin between his thumb and forefinger in a way that repulsed her, and he told her not to worry her pretty little head.

He would always have things under control, and when he needed her to know more, he would tell her.

Guiliani was the last man alive to whom she would confess what she knew, and why she was really back on the Bar Naught, enduring Everly's arrogance, fending off his mocking advances all these months. She had made her deal with the devil. She would be the necessary ears and eyes on the Bar Naught, reporting every move Kyle Everly made in exchange for the chance to regain ownership of the ranch.

He wasn't moving anymore, but it was still faintly possible that she could prove useful enough.

Her situation was already tenuous. Matt Guiliani would make it worse if he knew what she was doing here. She'd be off the Bar Naught faster than she could pack her meager belongings—and her chance would be lost forever.

The Bar Naught was far more to her than a symbol of the pretensions to a privileged, polo-playing country-manor lifestyle of distant royalty, which was what the ranch represented to her idle parents. Much more.

She loved the work.

She loved the land, the freedom, the responsibility, the beautiful wild mustangs that she gentled. The love and respect and care of horses made people into better people. She knew that firsthand. Personally.

The Bar Naught was her safe haven, and she was willing to do whatever unsafe things she had to do to have it back.

"You didn't believe him?" Matt asked, interrupting her thoughts. "That I'd try to kill him?"

"I don't know what I believed. What does it matter now?"

"It matters." His eyes fixed on hers, but she averted her gaze, searching for the alcohol swab for an excuse to look away.

She was easily as tall as Guiliani, but his male dimensions, his sheer presence, befuddled her wits, and she needed them all operating at a perfect pitch. "He's just as dead no matter who did it."

Matt craned his neck till he trapped her gaze. "It matters to me."

She shrugged. She doubted very much that Matt Guiliani was the kind of man who would shoot another man in the back, but she couldn't afford to reveal to him all that she knew. And Matt might have changed, might have turned killer.

Soldier Boy had. Anything was possible.

She decided that must be her tack. Deny everything. "I don't really know you. How could I know if you would gun a man down?"

His eyes tracked her. "One never knows."

"Have you killed anyone?"

His expression left out any hint of excuses. "Yes."

"What if someone betrayed you?" Because if he wouldn't stay off the Bar Naught she would lie through her teeth to make sure he did. She would swear to Dex Hanifen that she had seen Guiliani pull the trigger.

"Is there a point to this?"

She swallowed, feeling as if he had read her mind, knew of her intention to pin the murder on him. "Yes."

"Are you asking if I would kill you if you betray me?"

He shook his head slowly. "I wouldn't advise it, Fiona."

"Is that a yes?"

His brows drew close together. "Is that what stopped you from turning me over to Hanifen? The fear that I would come after you next?"

Lie, she told herself. *Just do it.* "Yes. All right? Yes. I was afraid I would be next."

"Now you know better."

"I don't."

"Of course you do." He didn't believe her, and

why would he? He reached for a packet of cedar sticks from his breast pocket, broke one off and stuck it in his mouth.

The lie had been a mistake, which only made him more suspicious of her, not less. Would a woman fearful that he would kill her have turned her back on him? Would she lead him docilely into her treatment room to administer a shot before he did her in?

What made her think he could not have turned into a killer?

She watched the cedar splinter travel over his lower lip from one corner to the other, shoved by his tongue. Her mouth felt parched as bones dried in the sun, and she licked her own lips as she aimed her gaze in another direction. She couldn't be attracted to him. *Could not.*

"Fiona," he said, his voice so low its tones thrummed inside her, "what's going on?"

Her tongue swiped again at her dry lips. "Nothing."

"Maybe I can help—"

"I don't need any help." He was the last man alive whose help she needed.

"You want to change your answer?"

"No." She busied her hands, forcing the syringe barrel through the paper.

"Fiona," he snapped, "let's just cut the crap, okay? You're not stupid. If you're telling the truth, you didn't know who was in the barn. I could have been the one who shot Everly in the back. Why would you take that kind of risk?"

"Kyle had enemies," she answered. "I didn't want to get involved. I don't want to *be* involved."

She cleared her throat and clamped her lips tight.

Emotions like some vicious animated kaleidoscope of feelings—jealousy, resentment, even hatred for the way he was able to strike a truce with Soldier Boy—turned inside her.

Not only a truce, either. Soldier Boy *permitted* this man's touch.

She *had* seen him swing down into Soldier Boy's stall. She'd seen him fall to the floor. But her reasons for leaving him there, for failing to mention his presence to Dex Hanifen, for coming at him with her rifle, had nothing to do with the murder at all.

The point was that Soldier hadn't killed him. In a deathly still way inside her that she really didn't understand, that was all she needed to know.

She trusted Soldier Boy's instincts more than her own. That was the last thing she would admit to anyone, Matt last of all. She dredged up her maddeningly stiff-upper-lip upbringing and buried that messy kaleidoscope of emotion.

"If you knew what kind of man you were dealing with, then what are you doing back on the Bar Naught at all, Fiona?"

"Because I want it back."

Chapter Three

The Bar Naught was all Fiona Halsey had ever wanted. Ever. "My parents lost it. I want it back. It's really just that simple."

"Even if it meant tangling with Everly?" Matt asked. "What am I missing? How did you think you were ever going to get the Bar Naught back from him?"

She met his eyes directly. On this point she was more prepared to lie. "I thought he would eventually get bored. He talked like that. He was a liar, you know. Pathological. Kyle Everly would as soon tell a lie as the truth when the truth would serve him better." She took hold of her long straight hair and shoved it behind her. "All to prove, over and over again that he could get away with it. To see if he could ride the crest of his charm right on by common sense one more time."

She popped the metal lid off the vial and swabbed the rubber stopper with alcohol, uncapped the needle, drew up the dose of booster and recapped. She turned away and put down the syringe on the countertop, then plunged her icy hands beneath a rush of hot water at the sink. "Months ago, Kyle offered me the chance to come back to the Bar Naught. He said that I could have it all my way, that— I didn't know what a liar he was. At the time, I didn't know.''

She withdrew her hands and the electric eye shut off the water. She grabbed a couple of paper towels from the dispenser and turned around when she thought she could finally manage her own emotions well enough. What she saw in his face encouraged her. ''Any other questions?''

''Just the one.''

She flashed on the image of him crashing down into the stall. A dark, unrelentingly handsome man, a stranger breathing the same air as Soldier Boy, gasping for that air like a fish out of water, and Soldier...not moving in for the kill. There was no satisfactory answer she could give him as to why she hadn't turned him over to Dex.

''Shall I tell you why I want to know?'' he asked.

''I don't care, but listen. Why don't I just take care of that now so you won't have to explain yourself?'' She tossed the spent paper towels into the trash. ''You wait here, and I'll just go make the call.''

His eyes darkened. ''Fiona, I have to know if someone told you I would be here tonight. Answer the question. Yes or no.''

''No.'' Whatever other lies she had told him, whatever she had to keep from him, this much was true. ''No one told me you were coming. Did you know Kyle was going to be murdered?''

He had the look of a man who thought even a distant cousin of the Queen of England ought to be plucked from the fray and planted back in Kensington Gardens. If he knew the fire she was playing with,

everything she had ever wanted would be lost in one
fell swoop of alpha-male whim.

No way.

She picked up the syringe again and uncapped the
needle. "Roll your sleeve up higher."

He shoved the flannel as far as it would go, but the
long underwear he wore beneath it wouldn't be
pushed higher. She cut him a look and stepped back
again. He pulled both shirttails out of his jeans, stuck
his hand beneath them and shoved the fabric high
enough to free his arm, baring his muscled shoulder
and half his torso as well. "Okay?"

She simply refused to be affected by all that powerful masculine flesh, the swirls of dark hair, but it
was impossible not to notice. Not to imagine her fingers there. Not to linger overlong with her eyes as if
she were preoccupied with her observation of the
deep bruises.

His body reminded her she was a woman, and the
battering he'd taken only made him that much more
dark and dangerously appealing. She swiped his biceps with an alcohol pad and drove her needle in
deep.

Nary a flinch, but he made no move to get back
into his shirts, either. She made the mistake of meeting his knowing eyes, and she could no more look
away than move out of his orbit. Her pulse throbbed.

His heart thudded till she could nearly hear it.

He was in her space now, breathing her same
scarce air, and she had stabbed him with her needle
to punish her own longings, and the more he sat there
taking it, watching her, seeing her, the more powerful
he became and the deeper in his thrall she fell.

Somehow she found herself stepping back.

He writhed his way back into his shirts. She turned hurriedly away. "I'll be back in the morning," he said. "You need to go along with whatever I say or do. Clear?"

She pitched the syringe into an impervious container. "I understand you, if that's what you're asking."

"You don't want to cross me, Fiona." He looked at her as if to say she could take his threat any way she wanted, except to defy him. "Hanifen and his boys will be back in the morning. And they'll be saying you're the one who murdered Kyle Everly."

The possibility, the rightness of it, the inevitability struck her. She swallowed. "I don't believe that."

"You don't have to believe me, Fiona. Just wait and see. I'll be a gentleman. I won't say I told you so."

She followed him from the treatment room and ushered him out the sliding door that opened onto the paddocks.

The temperature had dropped. She wrapped her arms around herself and thought she heard the nickering of a horse in the stark, distant silence.

Guiliani turned back to her, so close that in the frigid night air she could feel the warmth emanating off his body, smell the scent of hay and horseflesh on him. He was looking at her again, but she looked past him. She wanted him to go.

"Fiona—"

"Go. Just go!"

He turned fully toward her and touched her cheek. She saw it coming and could have turned away. Somewhere inside herself she must have wanted his touch, must have needed a comforting gesture so much that she would stand still for one from him.

"I want you to know this," he said, his voice low and quietly reassuring. "I want you to know you can tell me anything."

He just didn't know. She really couldn't.

She watched him jogging off into the dark, up the hillside where Bar Naught land bordered the national forest. He was dressed all in black, as one might expect of a trespasser in the night, or a sniper.

He had never denied being the one who had pulled the trigger. Had he intended to leave open the possibility? Intended to keep her unsettled and uneasy in his presence? She didn't believe he'd killed Everly, either. But someone had, and if he was right, her rifle would prove to be the murder weapon.

Shivering hard, she turned around and went back into the stable, securing the door behind her, and returned to the treatment room where she had left the Remington. Not bothering to turn on the light, she took the rifle from behind the door. The gun metal barrel felt cool in her hand.

She brought the end of the barrel to her nose. The scent, faint but unmistakable, put her doubts to rest. Her rifle had been fired tonight, and if there had been prints on it from the shooter, she'd obliterated them by handling the gun herself.

With the gun weighted perfectly in her hand, she walked down a hall to the gun rack.

There were spaces for half a dozen firearms, but since she'd returned to the Bar Naught, only her Remington had been kept there. Anyone could have taken her rifle, used it to kill Everly and then put it back.

She stood looking at the empty gun rack, trying to

see in her mind's eye the last time her rifle had been billeted there. She so rarely had reason to pick it up that it was possible she might not have missed the rifle if someone had taken it days ago. But no matter how long she stood there imagining the rack empty, she couldn't believe it had happened that way. The gun hadn't gone missing. She'd have known.

Whoever had taken her rifle had been in the stable some time in the hours before Everly was shot.

Her throat clutched tight and horror, the weight of the night's events, Kyle's murder, all that blood, settled in her chest. She couldn't breathe. The mewling noise that came out of her shredded what was left of her nerves.

She'd seen two of her grandparents laid out in their coffins, and a high school boyfriend who'd shot himself after he rolled a Jeep and emerged from the accident paralyzed from the waist down.

She'd seen her share of horses put down, dying pets put to sleep, and butchered game. You didn't grow up on a ranch in Wyoming, even if you were the great-granddaughter of English royalty, a revenue man, without being exposed to death. But she had never seen anything like Everly's body collapsed in a pool of his own blood.

She shook her head to banish the images. *Breathe, Fiona.* Through the nose, deep. *Breathe.* She had to clear her head, decide what to do about the gun.

She didn't believe Dex Hanifen would be back to arrest her for Kyle's murder. He knew her. He'd known her all her life. But Dex would have to know about the gun.

How could they have missed it in their search if it had been put back after Kyle was shot?

It was two-thirty in the morning. Should she call the sheriff or wait until morning to call? Wait until he came back?

Would he even be back? Of course. A murder had been committed here. He'd be back. She could tell him then, explain everything then, how she'd—

No. Her breath felt stifled again. If she told Dex she'd only taken her gun down from the rack when she heard an intruder in the stable, when she'd *known* there was someone hiding out, after Kyle had been killed… Dex would demand an answer to the same question Matt Guiliani wouldn't let go.

Even if Dex Hanifen never accused her of Kyle's murder, how could he avoid the inference that the killer had been hiding in the stable all along and she'd let him get away?

Surely Dex wouldn't believe her capable of that, either. But her uncertainty began feeding other doubts. A chill racked her body. She took hold of herself, stepped forward and replaced the rifle, then took it down again.

She would keep the rifle with her for protection, and in the morning hand it over to Dex.

She returned to her rooms and headed through the darkened, spartan quarters filled in every nook and cranny with all her old treasures, then stripped in the dark and stepped into a hot shower.

She got out only when the hot water ran cold. Bundled in a threadbare terry robe with the faded family crest embroidered in gold above her breast, her hair bound up in a towel, she sat down at her computer. She needed to relay the news of Everly's murder to her father. She typed Guiliani's name, then deleted it and sent the simple missive, short and to the point with no mention of his presence on the ranch after the murder.

She had to remind herself over and over again that she wasn't guilty of anything. At least, nothing that could be prosecuted. She had to fight now, to salvage whatever she could. The Bar Naught was all she had ever wanted, the only place she wanted to be.

She thought of the complications of Matt Guiliani on the ranch. There must be no more slips. No more lapses in her vigilance over her self. He was just an ordinary man and he had no power over her. God help him if he got in her way.

But as she lay in her bed, willing herself to fall asleep, she realized that in the aftermath of Kyle's murder, there would likely be no party of big game hunters from around the world, gathering on the Bar Naught next week.

She sat bolt upright in the dark, her fist held tight to her lips. Kyle's murder changed everything, like a fire breaking out across the landscape of all her sacrifices and her dreams. It would all have been for nothing that she had come back, only a torment to wake up every morning on the ranch she could never have back.

MATT RODE UP to the small ramshackle barn at a quarter of three in the morning. His mount was in a nasty temper. He understood. He was in one himself. The pain that racked his body made him want to puke.

He didn't have to urge the mare into the barn. He followed instead, pulled the saddle off her back and threw it over its resting place, drew off and folded the sweaty blanket, then freed the horse of the bit and reins. He forced himself to give the sorrel a quick brushing down. He doled out a coffee can's worth of oats, then shouldered his duffel bag and let himself into the back door of the widow Aimee Carson's cracker-box-size house.

His plan to reinvent himself and his assignment was going to take some fancy footwork. If Sheriff Hanifen lost interest in pinning Everly's murder on Fiona Halsey, he'd start nosing around for other suspects. A stranger arriving in town within twenty-four hours of the murder would provide the sheriff an interesting alternative.

It could have been worse. In the early planning stages of Matt's operation to bag Everly and ultimately to destroy The Fraternity, he had planned to book a suite at a fancy dude ranch resort in the area. The idea had been to send Everly the kind of arrogant, in-your-face message that, even as a rogue cop, Guiliani's significant resources could not be easily discounted.

At the end, the use of a resort had been rejected. Instead, every resource had been used to find Matt a discreet and anonymous place to stay this first night.

Aimee Carson's little spread fit the bill. She knew nothing and wanted to know nothing of what was going on. She couldn't guess why anyone would pay her to put up a man for one night. Legendary in these parts for keeping to herself, she lived on a tiny homestead outside the town of Kaycee. Her niece was the best friend of Garrett's wife, Kirsten.

Staying with the Widow Carson gave Matt room to maneuver. No one, save Fiona Halsey, would ever know he had been within five hundred miles of the murder.

Matt waited to see if the old woman would get up.

After a few moments, he switched on a small tasseled lamp sitting atop a crocheted doily and stripped out of his clothes in the middle of her living room. He didn't have room enough to turn around in Aimee's bathroom. He would have preferred a shower, but all she had was a hose to attach to the faucet.

As he ran the claw-footed tub full of hot water, he caught sight of himself in the tiny mirror over her sink. Even in the dim light and patch of mirror he could see a massive, angry purple bruise stretching beyond the breadth of his lowest rib. But he'd been lucky. He could as easily have punctured a lung.

He soaked for an hour, listening to the water gurgling down the drain, adding hot water every ten minutes or so. When the dried blood had soaked off his hands, he saw that they were not quite as badly scraped up as he'd feared. It occurred to him that he should at least have washed his hands in the sink of the treatment room.

It occurred to him that Fiona Halsey might have offered to tend to his hands.

It occurred to him that his brain had unaccountably migrated south, and the thought didn't sit well.

He got out of the tub onto a sweet pink throw rug and took himself off to the living room to towel dry. He pulled on a fresh pair of long underwear, then turned off the light and lowered his aching body onto Aimee's sturdy baby-blue tweed sofa. He lay there, eyes wide open, thinking through his options until daylight broke.

The threat Matt Guiliani posed to Everly was as a renegade insider cop gone over to the other side, clever and resourceful enough to have fabricated evidence ruinous to Everly's reputation among The Fraternity members. He believed it would still work. He had to do two things: first, convince Dex Hanifen that the deal Matt had planned to extort from Everly, to make Matt his partner and heir-apparent, was already signed, sealed and delivered. Second, he had to portray himself through the ether of electronic communications as the man who had eliminated the thieving traitor from the rarefied ranks of The Fraternity.

He would step fearlessly forward to usurp control of Everly's empire.

A deal worth millions was imminent. The summit of international badasses Everly had himself called was set to take place on the Bar Naught in a few short days in the guise of a big-game hunting party. Matt had to act quickly to ensure the meeting came off as planned despite Everly's sudden demise. The vacuum of power had to be filled, and Matt's would be the preemptive claim.

He combed again through the possible suspects in Everly's murder. He couldn't entirely rule out random motives or a killer unrelated to Everly's operations—the woman scorned, an old score now settled. But he still believed the odds were that some local pretender to Everly's throne, a sharpshooter in his stable of killers, perhaps even Hanifen himself, had taken the shot.

His own odds of surviving had taken a dive. In seizing control, Matt made himself a far greater target than he would have been with Everly alive.

Sheriff Dexter F. Hanifen was the big unknown. Where Dennis Geary had served as manager of the Bar Naught and occasional bodyguard to Everly, Hanifen was believed to be Everly's true lieutenant. The analogy had been drawn more than once to a Mafia don and his consigliere, but Hanifen was more of a

functionary than adviser. Everly would never abide a
lieutenant so powerful as the consigliere role implied.

The men expected to gather for the big-game hunting party were the ultimate targets of Matt's operation. Even their true identities were at this point unknown or unconfirmed.

Matt believed they would still come, like the heads
of all the Mafia families assembling to evaluate the
threat and perform their damage control. More likely
still, to stop cold the incursion of Matt Guiliani into
their death-dealing consortium.

But behind all his careful planning, his thoughts
returned over and over again to Fiona Halsey. He
couldn't displace her for long. She played into every
scenario just by her presence on the Bar Naught.

But he was lucid enough in those sleepless hours
to know that on a certain level, it didn't matter to him
where she fit into the mix or what her secrets were.
He was caught. His attention was arrested. He wanted
to follow the gleam in his own inner eye. He could
imagine making love to her, not giving a solitary
damn what else went on.

He would have to be very, very careful.

AT 5:00 A.M. HE CHECKED his e-mail on his handheld
wireless device and found a message from his friend
and partner, Garrett Weisz, who had headed up the
TruthSayers task force in Seattle for the last five
years. The message stated only that Fiona Halsey had
e-mailed her father the news that Everly had been
murdered. No mention of the fact that Matt had been
there.

Garrett didn't waste a lot of words, didn't even ask

for details. What he wanted to know he put into two words. *Go? Abort?*

Matt returned: *Going live, arrival on Bar 0 by 0800.* He knew Garrett and J.D. would know he planned to proceed as if his partnership with Everly had been long-since sealed.

At six-thirty he got up and ate the beefsteak and eggs Miss Aimee prepared for him. Afterward he shaved closely in front of the tiny bathroom mirror, splashed on a rich, wickedly scented and expensive aftershave and changed clothes. He chose clothes befitting his upgrade from rogue cop to Kyle Everly's partner. Dark designer jeans, a very light green silk shirt requiring cuff links and a pricey black cashmere sport coat tailored to accommodate both his shoulders and shoulder holster. He added the cuff links and watch, and then, turned away from Miss Aimee's reluctantly curious eyes, he shoved the ammunition clip into place in the butt of his automatic pistol, holstered the piece and threw on a tie.

He grabbed up his duffel bag and a leather suitcase, then flirted shamelessly a moment with the ancient, birdlike Miss Aimee while she played with the knot in his tie, and kissed her on her flowery-scented, powdered old cheek.

"Mmm. White Linen?"

"Go on," she scolded. "You peeked."

He shook his head solemnly. "My grandma wore White Linen. She had to make a tiny little bottle last a couple of years, and by then—" He broke off, having sucker punched himself with the memory of Anna Disorbio. "Thank you."

She shooed him out. He went into the old toolshed, where he'd reorganized twenty-five or thirty years'

worth of newspapers and *Harper's Bazaar* magazines
in order to park the Ford Bronco out of sight. He
reached I-25 from the country road and headed south
to the Bar Naught. He got off the highway on the
access road, drove another couple of miles. Beneath
a gate that announced the ranch, he signaled his turn
and waited for an oncoming vehicle to pass first.

Instead, the Johnson County sheriff's vehicle, Hanifen's, turned off in front of him. Matt made the turn
as well. Hanifen pulled over and got out, leaving Crider in the passenger seat, and approached the driver's
window of Matt's Bronco. He held down the button
to roll the window down.

Hanifen tossed a butt on the ground. "You lost?"

Matt shifted his weight forward on the seat and
slouched, his arm resting in the open window.
"Nope." He directed his focus toward the ranch
house, on the other side of a couple of acres of spruce
and lodge pole pine, wondering how long it would
take Hanifen to remember him. "How's it going,
Dex?"

The sheriff frowned. "I know you?"

"We've never met face-to-face. But I'm sure you
remember me. Name's Matt Guiliani. I'm the one
who rescued the kid your buddies in the TruthSayers
framed for firebombing his parents' house last winter."

The sheriff's expression turned stony. "That vigilante pack aren't any friends of mine."

"No? But you do remember."

"Like I said—"

"Yeah, Dex. You're as innocent as a newborn
lamb. But see, here's the deal. I know better. But
don't worry. I switched sides recently. I had no idea

what a market there is for defectors. Kyle made me an offer I couldn't refuse." Matt watched a glint of fear give way to disbelief in the sheriff's eyes. "In fact, Kyle was expecting me this morning."

"*Was?* What do you know—"

"Save it, Dex. Kyle was murdered last night," Matt stated flatly. "Or have I been misinformed?"

The sheriff scowled. "Where did you come by that information?"

"Sources. The important thing for you to know, Sheriff, is that with Everly dead, I'm the guy in charge."

"Whoa, wait—" Hanifen thumped the brim of his hat up. The barely visible, threadlike veins crisscrossing his nose seemed to sprout crimson. "Just you wait a gol-darned minute. You think I'm buyin' into that shine, you've got another think coming—"

Matt cut him off. "What do you say we drive on up to the house and sort this all out. I'm going to be wanting some answers, Sheriff." He stepped on the gas, churning up dirt and chunks of gravel as he drove off down the road, missing Hanifen's toes by no more than a couple of inches.

GARRETT WEISZ WOKE at the first light of dawn. It had always been his habit, but it was easier these days. In Kirsten's bedroom in the house on Queen Anne Hill, their home now, the first rays of sunlight shot across the ninety-three million miles to nestle on their bed.

As it did every morning, gratitude filled his heart. Abed with the woman he loved, his very pregnant wife, he settled in closer to her and let his fingers stray close enough on the mattress that, as she slept, he could almost feel the weight of the babies in her belly without waking her.

Twin girls.

When they learned that, he and six-year-old Christo had made a secret pact. The boys would be outnumbered in the Weisz household when the babies were born, and the menfolk would have to stick together to keep their girls safe.

Picking the babies' names now preoccupied their older brother. He'd allowed as how Hannah might be one of them, but couldn't decide between Madeleine and Irene for the other.

Garrett smiled, deeply content, more comfortable in his skin and in his life than he had imagined he would ever have a right to be. Kirsten had been confined to bed for toxemia problems since last week. He'd joked that he finally had her where he wanted her, and the poignant part of it was that it was true. True in the sense that he pretty much had the care of Christo to himself.

The timing wasn't the greatest. The day her doctor ordered Kirsten to bed was the day it had been decided Matt would go to Wyoming within the week. Garrett's hours were crammed with planning sessions for Matt's undercover operation with J.D. and half a dozen other interagency cops, including their new Interpol liaison. He'd taken Christo along several times, so his son didn't wind up at day care too long after his kindergarten let out.

From Christo's point of view, life was sweet. One swell adventure on top of another.

Kirsten turned a bit in her sleep. Garrett feasted his eyes on her swollen breasts as he heard wee feet tiptoeing into their room.

Christo was good, a chip off the old block, but the tiny squeak of a floorboard gave him away. Garrett knew exactly what Christo was after. The electronic pager-cell phone Garrett kept on the nightstand. Christo knew he could expect a message from his Uncle Matt, who was off in Wyoming doing his undercover agent thing.

This was too cool for Christo to bear. He wanted to be the one who got the message, the one to tell his dad the secret communiqué had been received. Garrett lay utterly still and let Christo take the device off to his room. There was not one chance that his son would let a message from Matt go wanting.

Stirring restlessly, Kirsten shifted the weight of her belly, brushing Garrett's fingers. Her eyelids crept open, and she gave a soft smile tinged with her discomfort. "Copping a feel again, Daddy?"

God. His heart just flooded. He loved her to the ends of the universe, smart mouth and all. "Shh. The babies aren't old enough to hear that kind of talk."

"Naughty Mommy." She slid her hand down over her belly toward Garrett and he knew what was coming. Knew she'd find him with his straining, telltale flesh. She stole his breath away and asked, "Have you heard from Matt?"

Though the pleasure of her touch spread through him like molten gold, he kept his eyes open, playing her game. How long could he keep up a normal conversation under the onslaught of her caress? "Not yet." He paused, let a wave of pleasure sidle through him. "Christo was just in."

Kirsten smiled. "Did he get away with your pager?"

"He did." He moved his leg to trap her fingers in a particular place.

"Clever boy."

"Who, me?"

"No. Christo. Are you sure—"

His lips tightened. His whole face. "I'm sure."

She whispered, "Surrender, Weisz."

"Uncle." But he didn't close his eyes, chose instead to let her see his naked emotion, the pleasure welling up inside him.

They lay together for nearly an hour. Her back ached, and she begged a massage. He kissed her nape after she had managed to roll over, then applied his hand to the task of easing the twinges in her lower back.

They must have looked asleep to Christo. From the door came his best shot at a whisper. "Dad! Dad!"

Garrett sat up thinking this was it. "It's okay, Christo-man. Mom's awake. What is it?"

"Uncle Matt. It says *Go!* and something else." He launched himself across the room and onto the bed. "What's it say, Dad?"

Garrett looked over his son's shoulder at the digital display and then at Kirsten who struggled to sit up as well. "You were right, Christo. It says, *Go!* It says, *Going live, arrival at Bar 0 by 0800.*"

Kirsten swallowed. Garrett nodded grimly over Christo's head. Things had already gone awry, and the danger to Matt was multiplied a hundred times.

Chapter Four

Fiona had just finished turning out Soldier Boy when she heard a vehicle barreling into the yard. She crossed the central stable corridor and craned her neck to see Matt Guiliani wheeling to a stop in the yard. Dex Hanifen came roaring in after him, and braked so hard that the rear tires of the oversize vehicle spun out just as Guiliani stepped down from the Bronco.

She felt herself stiffening with anxiety, half ridden with guilt for what she was about to do.

Dex got out snarling, rushing at Guiliani and stabbing a finger at him in the air. "You pull that kinda stunt again and I will personally—"

"Settle down," Matt ordered peremptorily. "I want to talk to Fiona."

"Oh, you know Fiona now, too," Dex challenged, his voice notching up.

"Matter of fact, I do."

"I don't think so. See, I know the people that folks around here associate with, and you are not one of them. And you are no more in charge around here than the little man on the moon."

She'd never seen Dex taking any crap off anyone, and though he clearly had no intention of taking it now, he'd already been knocked off his pins, reacting in knee-jerk fashion rather than taking control of what went on.

She shoved hard and the stable door glided smoothly open. She was wearing jeans split at the knee, an ancient mauve mohair sweater with a fairly grubby down jacket over it, but from the way Guiliani's eyes lit up, she might have been wearing a ball gown. As if it had been a too long a time since he'd seen her. Had her.

Her guilt evaporated. For his insolence alone he deserved to be locked up. She had to stop him now.

He was dressed to kill, looking somehow nothing like last night's trespasser. Powerful, yes, but in a different way that commanded the attention of everyone in his orbit.

She lifted her chin, fighting off the unmistakable thrill, and looked at Dex, who was flushing angrily, and Crider, who was being so closemouthed that she thought Dex must have ordered him to keep his trap shut. If it had been Matt's intention to goad Dex, he'd succeeded. "Dex, Crider. This is the man you're looking—"

"You know him?" Dex demanded, interrupting her. "You know what kinda delusions of grandeur he's spouting? He thinks he's stepping into Kyle's shoes."

She walked right up to Matt, daring herself to do it, to go through with pinning Kyle's murder on him. She looked him right in the eye. He gave her a wink, a jolt of such intensely sexual energy that she forgot to breathe. "I know him, all right." She tore her gaze off Matt and turned to Dex. She didn't want to see

Matt or face his wrath when he heard how she betrayed him. "He's the one who shot Kyle."

"Oh, Fiona," Dex hollered over a gritty gust of wind. "Let's not be muddying up the waters with that kinda horse-hockey."

"That's all right, Sheriff," Matt soothed. His hand fitted itself to the small of her back. She felt wildly distracted, somehow incapable of moving away from Matt's possessive touch. "Fiona and I have had a bit of a spat. I'm afraid she's just angry enough with me at the moment to pin the murder on me."

For a second, Dex looked completely fuddled.

She spun around and knocked Matt's hand away, demanding Dex's attention. "Dex, listen to me. I'm telling you the truth. He used my Remington to shoot Kyle in the back. I caught him holed up in Soldier Boy's stall after you left last night"

Dex squinted. "How'd you do that?"

"With—" *Oh, God.* "With my gun," she answered firmly. "He must have put it back in the gun rack afterward, and when I—"

"Oh, I see," Dex interrupted. "And you say you caught him holed up where? Soldier's stall, was it? Because, see, Fiona, that is just flat impossible and everybody knows it! No one gets close to that animal and lives to tell the tale."

Her heart sank. Her mouth went dry as dust. She should have seen, should have known. No one but Guiliani had ever gotten so near Soldier Boy, and no one, least of all Dex, was going to believe Guiliani had been there, either.

She hadn't believed it herself. Her face felt on fire. "I'm telling you the truth, Dex. He was there."

But he looked at her as if it hurt him to listen to

her making up such desperate, inept lies. ''You know what chaps my butt, half-pint? You didn't hand over your rifle last night. And here I am thinking I made myself clear when I told you I had to take in every firearm on the Bar Naught.''

''How could I have handed it over, Dex, if he still hadn't put the gun back where it belonged?''

''Are you saying, Sheriff,'' Matt broke in, ''that you believe Fiona had anything to do with Kyle's murder?''

She couldn't let Dex answer that. ''Please just listen to me. If I wanted to lie, would I say I'd caught him in Soldier Boy's stall? Wouldn't I make up a better lie than that? I could have just said I saw him shoot Kyle!''

Guiliani stuffed his fingers into the front pockets of his jeans. ''She has a point, there, Dex. On the other hand—''

''Stifle,'' Dex interrupted, turning a scathing look on Matt. ''I'm gonna want to talk to you later. Right now I'm taking Fiona inside for a little chat.''

''I don't think so,'' Matt said. ''Not without an attorney, Dex. C'mon. You know better than that.''

''Excuse me, but I don't need a lawyer!'' Fiona cried. ''I didn't do anything, I—''

''Not another word, sweetheart,'' Matt warned her softly.

Dex bit off a curse. ''I'm cold. I'm moving this inside. Fiona—''

''Do you want me to escort this jerk off the property, boss?'' Crider asked.

''Ever hopeful,'' Matt murmured.

Florid, Crider hitched up his belt and backed off.

Fiona glared at Matt. "Don't you ever stop? This is not helpful."

"Hush, princess."

Hanifen ordered them inside. Matt held out a hand signaling Fiona to precede him, then fell in line.

Inside, Hanifen blew off a frustrated breath, turned away and shrugged off his coat. "In the library."

The entryway, thirty feet in height and in length, absorbed every bit of light coming in through the beautiful clerestory windows Everly had added. The darkly stained hardwood floor gleamed beneath turquoise silk carpets imported from the finest Persian weavers.

Dex hung his coat and hat on the coatrack, then took a deep breath to calm himself. Hooking his thumbs into his belt, he took up a position behind the settee.

Crider stood gawking around the corner at the bronze eagle. Fiona took the antique Queen Anne chair, removed her coat, then draped it over her shoulders. She was chilled far deeper than the biting wind outside could account for.

She watched Matt helping himself at the wet bar as if he had done it a hundred times before, popping the tab on a can of tomato juice he'd taken from the concealed refrigerator.

Unnerved, watching the incredulous look straining Dex's features at Matt's easy familiarity in Kyle's house, she sat up very straight. She had the feeling that Matt knew the house and its contents down to the last book of matches. Had Matt been trespassing last night with the sole intent of gaining entry to learn his way around?

But what would be the point, unless he knew Kyle

would be dead by morning? Unless his real intention had been to waltz in the day after and take immediate, convincing control of Kyle's affairs?

But he hadn't known. Guiliani was every bit as shocked as she had been that Kyle had been shot to death.

She set the issue aside. She knew more about Guiliani and what he was doing on the Bar Naught than he had any idea of, but she was in too dangerous a position herself to reveal what she knew. "About my rifle, Dex—"

"I want to hear about that, Fiona, but I'd first like to clear up what the hell it is Guiliani thinks he's doing here." Dex had never seemed so ungainly to her. His lips twitched, and she knew he was far more concerned over Matt's presence on the Bar Naught than by who had killed Kyle and what had become of her rifle.

She watched Matt pouring the tomato juice into Baccarat crystal as Dex went on.

"You got here awful quick. How did you know Kyle had been murdered?"

Matt splashed an ounce or so of vodka into the glass, a dash of Tabasco, then took a mixing stick out of the drawer in the service bar. Delaying, she thought, with no other purpose in mind than to get under the sheriff's skin. "How did I know?"

"That's what I said. How did you know?"

"Kyle was on the cell phone when he was shot in the back."

Matt's answer blew her away. What was he doing? Like a wily old fox on the scent of some wounded prey, Dex jumped on Matt's answer. "How do you know that, Guiliani? Are you telling me you were on the horn with Kyle when he died?''

Matt shrugged idly. ''I was—''

''That would be a flat-out lie.''

Matt took a drink without ever breaking eye contact. ''Well...let me ask how you know that, Dex?''

The sheriff glared back. ''Let's just say I know.''

''Because you were the one on the phone with Everly?'' Matt suggested. ''Is that what you're saying?''

She thought of soft-spoken men carrying big sticks, but his strategy in goading Dex, whatever his purpose was, wasn't helping. She didn't need him provoking Dex Hanifen.

''*I'm* not saying anything.'' Hanifen cleared his throat and swallowed. ''*I'm* the one asking the questions.''

''You want to lawyer-up, too, Dex?'' Matt asked in the same respectful and still powerfully subtle mocking tone. ''See, in my experience, it's always the ones scrambling to avoid answering the simple questions who—''

''You're coloring way outside the lines, boy,'' Dex warned. ''You're in Wyoming now and I'm the one in charge of this investigation. Maybe—'' his jaw thrust forward ''—maybe you didn't just show up this morning. Maybe you were here last night. Maybe you're the one that set Kyle up to be blown away.''

''Now, there's a promising path.'' Matt sucked on his drink, letting his words sink in. She had the uneasy feeling that he wasn't goading Hanifen at all, but congratulating him for a brilliant deduction. ''It makes at least as much sense as Fiona pulling the trigger.''

Dex barked, "Where were you last night between eleven and midnight?"

"Here and there."

Dex glowered. "When did you get here?"

"You mean, this morning?" He shrugged. "Or last night?"

"If you were here, why didn't you let Everly know you were in town?"

"Why would I want to do that?"

What was he doing? His cavalier attitude invited Dex to draw the conclusion that he hadn't phoned Kyle because it made no sense to warn your intended victim that you'd arrived.

Was it possible he was trying to shield her by casting suspicion on himself?

Dex came around the settee. "You want to answer the question?"

Matt shrugged. "I thought I had. Kyle knew when I expected to be here. Besides, Dex, when I got in, he was probably playing poker with you. Last Friday of the month, right? I know he had his cell phone on him, but you don't interrupt a man's poker game. Not where I come from."

Dex sat back down on the settee. "What's the cell number?"

Matt gave a pitying look. "You know it off the top of your head, Dex?"

"No, but I've got it plugged into my automatic dial."

Matt spewed off the numbers.

Dex seemed to swallow his tongue. Crider leapt into the silence. "You could have driven up here last night."

"That's true. I could have."

"What exactly were you doing 'here and there,' Guiliani?" Crider kept on.

"Scouting a sniper position?" Matt taunted.

"I knew it," Crider crowed.

"No." Matt shook his head. "You thought Fiona did it."

Crider gulped. "Well, you just admitted—"

"Yeah." Matt blinked. "That was an admission of guilt, Crider." He looked with pity at Dex, conveying his sympathies for having to work with this sorry slug of a deputy. He laid on the sarcasm. "I was going to kill the goose that keeps laying my golden eggs."

Crider looked a bit confused. Hanifen stared hard at Matt. "You've got a far piece to go before I'm gonna believe you switched sides, bub."

Matt spat an ice cube back into his Bloody Mary. "Believe it, Dex."

Dex pounded a fist into his other hand. "Far as I'm concerned, you're lying through your teeth. You've been after those damned vigilante TruthSayers far too long to suddenly—"

"Exactly," Matt cut in, in a way that brought even Dex up short. "Way too long."

Dex hitched a shoulder up and glared. "I don't have time for this right now—"

"I can see that," Matt interrupted yet again. "You've got your hands full with framing Fiona. Have you got a warrant for her arrest?"

"No, but—"

"I'll go with you now, Dex," Fiona interrupted, shooting Matt a look. "Or meet you there—"

"What Fiona means," Matt interrupted her, looking gently at her, "is that we'll both agree to talk to you when there's an attorney present. And before that,

she and I have to talk about what happened here last
night. Alone.''

She didn't want to be alone with him again. Not
for any reason.

''You think I'm leaving you two alone to get your
lies straight, you've got another think coming. The
clerk,'' Dex said, ''is typing up an arrest warrant as
we speak.''

''Then I suggest, Dex,'' Matt warned softly, ''that
you get hold of the clerk and tell her to take it real
slow.''

Hanifen reddened. ''We don't play these high-
falutin city games here, with one hand acting like it
doesn't know what the other's doing.'' Hanifen's lips
flattened. ''I swore out a warrant, the judge signed
off, and if I don't have the damned thing in my hand
when I arrest Fiona, there isn't a lot to say. Not here.''

''Dex, there's a lot to say!'' Fiona cried, wildly
frustrated. ''How can you have sworn out a warrant
against me when you don't know that it was my gun
that was used to kill Kyle? Or that someone else's
prints won't show up on it? Did you come out here
to ask me about my rifle or to arrest me?''

''Fiona.'' Dex's lips pressed together. ''Half-pint.''

Her throat seized up. For Dex to call her half-pint
was a deliberate bid to make her remember her long
history with him. The hours Dex Hanifen had spent
with her, as if he were her father and she were just
an ordinary girl, not the descendant of the neglected
younger sons of distant royalty. Hours, days, weeks
when Dex had been the one seeing to her needs because her parents went off jet-setting, spending
money as if it grew on trees.

He'd intended to make her think back to those

times, but that also made it impossible for her to understand how he could have come this morning having sworn out a warrant for her arrest.

He sat there looking uncomfortably at her. "Half-pint…"

"What, Dex?"

"Yeah. What, Dex?" Matt echoed. He put down the glass and stood leaning against the wet bar, one booted foot crossed over the other, his arms folded, cuff links winking. "What gives?"

She turned to him. "This really is between Dex and me."

Matt shook his head slowly. "That's what worries me, princess."

"Don't ever call me that!"

He shrugged idly, looking straight at the sheriff. "Heard it somewhere. Princess."

Where had he heard anyone calling her princess?

Hanifen's lips thinned to a blade. His eyes never shifted off Matt's. "Fiona," he said carefully, "you need to decide if you want this…this kind of help."

She shoved her hair away from her face in frustration. "Dex, please just tell me what this is about!"

"What I'm afraid of, half-pint, is this. I'm going to take your rifle and ship it off to the crime lab. When the ballistics and prints come back, if I haven't booked you, and you've taken it into your sweet little head to hightail it out of the country, I'm gonna have my tit in a ringer." He tilted his head minutely this way and that as if his collar was too tight. "See," he continued, "the D.A.—"

"Oh, yeah," Matt cut in. "You're going to assert accountability to your boss now that you've already sworn out a warrant? When did your D.A. have time to assess the investigation and pressure you to make the arrest, Dex?''

He bounced his glance from Matt to Fiona. ''I'm trying to be reasonable, here, Fiona. This guy is not making it easy.''

''Forget him,'' she answered. ''Explain it to me, Dex, because I don't get it, either. I didn't kill Kyle. Shouldn't you be out looking for whoever did?''

''I'm doing my job, half-pint. That's all. I'm sure you'll be cleared, given a little time, but we need…assurances. You'll post bail and—''

''With what, Dex? You know I don't have any money!''

''Look,'' Matt said, ''maybe Fiona's Remington is the murder weapon, maybe it's not. Say we concede the point for purposes of discussion. What does that prove? Not that she did it.

''I'll even give up the prints,'' he added. ''It would be suspicious if her prints weren't all over her own firearm. If you had an eyewitness, I'd say, okay, take her in, let's get this through to the bail hearing. But what worries me, Dex—'' his brows drew together in a clever parody of worry ''—is this. I haven't heard anything about a witness to the murder. Or, for that matter, any mention of a credible motive.''

She couldn't have put it better herself. ''That's the thing, Dex. I'm the last person on earth with a reason to want Kyle dead. You should know that better than anyone.''

It wasn't true. She hated Everly with every breath of Bar Naught air she drew. Hated him for the way he had lied to her, the way he had manipulated her, the way he had touched her as if he owned her as part and parcel of Bar Naught property. But most of all she despised him for using the ranch as a cover and a safe haven from which to conduct his gun-running business interests.

But every day she talked herself into maintaining the illusion that she had nothing but gratitude for Everly's many kindnesses to her. After all, he let her live and work on the Bar Naught. And it was important, vital to her now, that Dex realize that she knew she could only stay on the Bar Naught so long as Kyle owned it.

The sheriff drew a deep breath, pausing as if what he had to say would nail her coffin shut. But Crider jumped in again. "What?" He snorted. "Because Kyle let you come back? *Lets* you live here on the land your fancy-pants daddy lost in foreclosure?"

"Will you shut up?" Hanifen interrupted, as if Crider's remark went half a country mile beyond merely stupid. He turned back to Fiona. "Listen half-pint, there was one shot heard last night. Only one. All three of you here last night agreed on that much. And you failed to turn over your gun to me."

She wanted to interrupt to say she would surrender the gun now and when he examined it, he would know she hadn't tried to cover up the fact that it had been fired.

But he went on ticking off points. "Geary and his doxy alibi each other. You were the only other one around. Fiona, I want to believe you, and if it weren't for the shenanigans in the legal documents that return the Bar Naught to you in the event of Kyle's death, we might have a different scenario on our hands. But—"

"What?" He couldn't have meant what she

thought he said. "What documents? How would...why would—"

Matt interrupted. "He's saying there are documents on record that return the ranch in its entirety to you on the occasion of Kyle Everly's death." As if it were known fact.

"That's exactly what I'm saying," Dex agreed. "Which nails your motive, Fiona."

"Dex, that's impossible! The property went into foreclosure on notes Kyle owned. Why would he ever have agreed to return the property to me in the event of his death? He didn't have to cut any kind of deal. He had all the cards!"

Dex shrugged. "Maybe the SOB had a soft moment. How do I know?" He frowned. "Are you saying you didn't know?"

"If I knew, Dex, don't you think I'd have understood that no one stood to gain more from Kyle's death than me? Don't you think I'd have been smarter than to shoot him in the back, with no one to give me an alibi, using my own gun?"

"Let me guess," Matt offered, looking at the sheriff. "The D.A. has already embraced the tortured logic that says Fiona would be counting on the sheer illogic of all those factors to get her off. Hmm. Nobody trying to frame her would be that stupid."

"Twist it any which way you want, Guiliani." Dex sighed heavily. "The pointers are still all lined up in Fiona's direction. I'll hold off on the arrest—"

"Don't do us any favors, Dex," Matt offered. "I could have a lawyer buddy in here who'd have himself a grand old time suing on Fiona's behalf for false arrest."

She couldn't believe him throwing Dex's offer back in his face. "I'm not going to sue—"

"Fiona? Will you let me handle this?" Matt channeled all the considerable force of his will into warning her with his eyes not to contradict him.

She bit her lip and forced herself to break off their eye contact. "The rifle is racked to your right inside the stable door."

"And you're welcome to it, Dex," Matt offered. "But let's get back to Fiona's so-called motive. You were almost right about Kyle thinking the ranch should go back to Fiona, since he had no heirs. He tossed Harry and Marianne Halsey a bone at the foreclosure proceedings, but he never intended to honor the clause."

Dex flushed. "And you would know that how?"

Matt smirked. "I told you, Dex. Kyle and I had an understanding. His business became my business."

She watched Matt and knew he was shoveling complete bull. What was it to him, anyway, if she were to be arrested and forced to hit up her friends for the collateral to post bail?

But he was moving right along, acting as if he knew anything about Kyle's intentions. Unless she was very mistaken, Dex wasn't being taken in.

"Here's the bottom line," Matt concluded. "Kyle made Fiona sign—before a judge—papers saying that, in exchange for being allowed to return to the ranch, Fiona agreed to foreswear any and all interest in the Bar Naught."

"That's a lie!" she cried, jumping to her feet. She'd been played for a fool and she was going to lose big time, in no small part due to Matt Guiliani. "Dex, you can't believe..." but she trailed off, bitterly, suddenly aware that she was only damning herself for nothing. "Can't you see he's lying again? Doesn't it make sense that he killed Kyle? That—"

"Fiona." He cut her off with a look so fierce and still completely benign, so gentle that she felt wildly disoriented. Threatened to her core.

She lost her chance to speak up.

"The hell of it is, Dex," Matt said as he picked a piece of lint off his cashmere sport coat, "I'm sure Fiona wishes now, since we both know there's no way that she killed Kyle, that she hadn't signed the agreement. But she did sign. If you want, I'll have the judge's clerk courier the document here."

Dex Hanifen looked as if he might gnash his teeth to a fine dust. "Exactly what was your 'understanding' with Kyle?"

"I told you, Dex. We were partners."

"You and who else?"

Matt shrugged. "Kyle had a lot going on. I sat in the background. We didn't shoot skeet together," he said, separating himself from the kind of buddy-buddy relationship he must have known Kyle had with Dex. "We did business."

"And what are your intentions now?"

"My interests haven't changed. Except that since Kyle is no longer around to do his part, I'll have to take a more visible stance." He shot Dex a flinty look. "I'll be staying on awhile."

"I suppose you have documents that'll back up what you say? Some partnership agreement?"

"Not exactly. Ours weren't the kind of deals that generated a lot of paperwork."

Dex shook his head. "You're so full of it, your eyes are brown. He and I didn't only shoot skeet. If

Kyle had a secret partner, I'd have known about it. If he let you in on any damn thing at all, I'd have known about it.''

Matt smiled. ''D'you ever consider Kyle had lost faith in you, Dex?'' He let the easy, charming smile fade to something humorless. ''I don't like you very much, Dex. Well, even that might be a stretch,'' he amended. ''And it's a natural fact Kyle didn't trust you anymore. But I'll be real generous here. Give you the benefit of the doubt and not count this morning's goings-on against you.''

Dex turned toward Fiona, his hands clenched into fists, visibly shaking to be thwarted at every twist and turn in the road. ''I want your rifle, little girl. I'm going to ask you again to think about whether you want this cowboy talking for you. There's a lot of history between us, half-pint. A lot. You remember.''

''I do remember, Dex.''

''I trust you do. But you're in trouble, missy. You're in deeper than you ever want to be, and you've got a choice to make. You want me on your side, looking out for you in this murder investigation, or don't you?''

''Dex, please.'' She resented having to win back Dex's trust because of Matt Guiliani. ''There is no choice to make here. You know I didn't kill Kyle. You—''

''Fiona, the man's got a job to do,'' Matt interrupted her. ''That's all he's been trying to say, isn't that right, Sheriff? My question is, which job? The one the good people of Johnson County elected you to do, or the other one?''

Chapter Five

Dex's fingers tightened to fists again as he struggled to keep his temper. He stabbed a finger in the air at Matt. "I don't need you to interpret for Fiona what I mean, or the job I came here to do. She and I understand each other fine when there isn't some studly jackass butting in trying to play hero."

Matt let a grin shape his lips. "I've never heard myself described quite so succinctly, Dex."

Dex had had all he could stand. He spun around and unleashed his wrath on her. "Fiona Halsey, you are under suspicion of felony murder."

"Dex—"

"No. You shut it up and listen to me, now, missy. I've busted my butt for you all your sad little princess life—"

"That's not fair—"

"Fair, Fiona, is a freaking weather forecast, and this ain't one of 'em. I swear if I had the warrant for your arrest in my hands, I'd haul you in right now. You step one foot off this ranch and I will personally slap you in handcuffs so fast it will make your head spin. And if I find out that you're lying to me, you're going to find yourself with a whole lot of time to be figuring out what sorry means from the wrong side of a stinking five-by-seven cell.''

She felt numbed by the attack, not so much betrayed as completely baffled by Dex's blistering threats. He'd become unrecognizable to her, someone she didn't know. Someone she had no reason to trust.

The desperate flapping of wings that took over her heart in the night started up again. If he threw her in jail, even if the party of hunters who were really Kyle's partners in crime went ahead as expected, she could kiss goodbye her chances of regaining the Bar Naught.

Dex snatched up his coat, but before he could take his leave on the heels of his own tirade, Matt's words stopped him.

"We're not quite done, Dex."

Fiona had been around a great many influential men in her life. The unimaginably wealthy, the landowners, politicians, royalty, the very chic in whose circles her parents had traveled until the money ran out.

She'd dated a senator not quite twice her age, the son of the Secretary of State, the vice president of a billion-dollar multinational wireless communications business. And she'd nearly become engaged to Pascal Lariviere, an international playboy infamous for his ability to elude trouble snapping at his heels, a man the paparazzi referred to among themselves as the Sheik of Provence.

Somehow, posing as a rogue cop gone renegade to become Kyle Everly's partner, Matt surpassed the command and authority of all the men she had known. He elevated himself without seeming to at all, projecting membership in a more powerful elite than

Hanifen could even comprehend. He wore an elusive but compelling air of power, even entitlement, that intimidated and wore ordinary men raw. That most women fled, and the rest threw themselves toward with breathless abandon.

She wasn't the type to run. She'd already been struck by his lightning, and escaped mostly unscathed. Breathless abandon was not in her, either. She had too much at stake to let a man, even one such as Guiliani, interfere with what she wanted.

But it struck her that Matt had spent the last hour exercising bully-boy behavior for the purpose of giving the sheriff something more tangible than dim, slack-jawed resentment to lock horns over.

Men of Dex's ilk understood power only in its crudest form, like villains in old westerns, sixshooters blazing, bullets biting at the feet of the weak.

Guiliani almost certainly knew better. She didn't understand why he had come on with six-shooters when he clearly had the skills to charm a snake.

Dex turned around, still flying high, still believing he had finally gained the upper hand. He hadn't.

"I want to apologize to you, Dex. I haven't been aboveboard," Matt said. "You've asked a fair question and you deserve an answer. Kyle Everly was a ruthless man, but he had a wicked little insecurity. He needed someone to admire him, to appreciate his superior intellect. But he couldn't exactly walk into the local bar and toot his own horn, could he? You just don't do that when you're selling grenades that kill babies to madmen."

Fiona swallowed hard, unable to believe Matt would say those things to Dex. She watched the man who had ferried her to recitals and polo matches going rigid with fear.

Dex said, "I don't know what the hell you're talking about."

"Yeah, you do, Dex. You just don't want it to get out."

Dex managed a shrug. "Talk is cheap, Guiliani."

"Exactly. And you don't have to take me at my word. I had this same discussion with Kyle, just before we came to our little understanding. So I brought along a little something so you won't have to doubt that whatever went down on the Bar Naught, I knew about."

Dex had a trapped look in his eyes, but he couldn't help asking the question Fiona wanted to ask herself. "What would that be?"

Matt reached into his jeans pocket and withdrew something the size of small pocketknife. A tube in the shape of a lipstick.

He pulled off the cheap plastic cap and applied a thin layer of balm to his lips, then recapped the tube and stood thoughtfully, tossing the thing up and down, as if hefting to gauge its weight.

No more than a few seconds could have gone by, but the silence had an unbearable quality. Finally he looked up and tossed the thing to Dex.

"Seen anything like this before?"

Hanifen paled as if he'd been tossed a live grenade.

"Ever used one of those things, Dex?" Matt asked. "I've heard they can be put to an interesting variety of uses."

A nameless unease filled Fiona. Dex was a man of simple emotions, more comfortable reducing complex situations to a few pithy words, but the parade of emotions crossing his face was an oddly short one. The vacant look that had given way so quickly to suspicion and then horror morphed into something akin to loathing.

He started to speak, choked, then started over. "Where did you get this?"

"I forget."

A lip balm. She couldn't imagine what significance it had, why the tube had the power to strike Dex so nearly dumb. The tension in the library grew thick. Sticky. She felt smothered, sick, in danger of throwing up without even knowing why.

Dex could only stand there staring at the tube of lip balm in his unsteady hand. Matt made a sympathetic noise. "It really sucks, I know, when you've worked so hard, and you think you've got all your ducks in a row, and then something like this pops up to threaten everything you think you've achieved."

The arteries at Dex's neck and temple throbbed. He pulled a handkerchief from his back pocket to daub away the beads of sweat oozing out onto his forehead. He wiped the tube clean and launched it back at Matt. "Maybe I should warn you, Guiliani. I don't know how you got to Kyle, but I don't take well to threats."

Matt pocketed the tube of lip balm. "Then we've got something in common after all."

"What do you want?" he demanded.

"That's good. I like that. Direct, to the point, no room for future misunderstandings."

"You want me to lay off Fiona in this investigation? Is that it?"

Stunned by the hint that Dex would comply with whatever Matt asked, Fiona turned to him. Hope sprang up in her, but Matt only shrugged, as if he couldn't care less.

"Wouldn't it be great if it were that simple?" he agreed.

Dex rolled his shoulders, working it out, seeing an escape hatch. "Things can be handled...differently. Maybe it really is that simple."

Matt walked back around the bar and opened the lid from a canister of shelled pecans. "You do what you want about that, Dex. Trying to pin the murder on Fiona isn't a very productive use of your time, anyway, but that's your call entirely. What *I* need is some assurance from you, my friend, that nothing will come up to spoil next week's little soiree."

Dear God. Matt intended to go forward with the hunting party without Kyle. Had he foreseen this outcome from the beginning? Had he been the one to take her rifle and murder Everly, so that he could then walk in and seize control? For one instant the wild fluttering of her heart, desperate for all these hours with the certainty that Kyle's death would cause the party to be called off, was eased. She would have her chance after all if Guiliani pulled this off.

Just as quickly, despair circled around again because Matt had done everything in his power to force Dex Hanifen to the wall, where the sheriff would have no choice but to fulfill his threats and throw her in jail.

She couldn't do what had to be done to salvage the Bar Naught from a jail cell.

Dex seemed to strangle. Those minuscule motions of his head, stretching his neck this way and that when he'd been so ill at ease treating her like a common criminal, became nearly spastic. He couldn't force a word from his mouth to save his soul.

"Don't take it so hard, Dex," Matt advised in an overly sincere tone of voice. "A simple change in allegiance is all that's required." He grinned. "If I can do it, you can. What do you say?"

"DO YOU KNOW THAT MAN practically raised me?" Fiona waited until Dex and Crider had driven far enough away that the engine could no longer be heard. Matt could see that she was so angry she hardly knew where to begin with him.

"No. I didn't." He hadn't delved that far back into her life history. He hoped, for her sake, that she wasn't going to cling to nostalgic claptrap. Hanifen was much more than a pawn in Everly's empire, and she couldn't afford the trip down memory lane. "If you care at all about him, I'm sorry he's turned on you. But you'd better wake up and smell the roses, Fiona, because he has turned on you."

"Only because you bullied him so badly that he—"

"Slipped up and betrayed his true colors?"

She bit her lip. "You have no idea—"

"Cut it out, Fiona. I don't care if you want to pretend to yourself that I don't know what I'm doing here. I do, but it's not important to me whether you realize that. But don't kid yourself. If a critter walks like a duck and quacks like a duck, it's a duck. In this case, a very dangerous duck."

"My point is that I could have straightened everything out and none of this…this—" She broke off, her chin straining up, her teeth clenched, unable to find a word, he supposed, terrible enough to describe what had just gone down.

"Disaster?" he supplied, tossing a pecan into his mouth.

"This isn't funny! What were you trying to accomplish? Do you want Dex to slap me in jail? Is that it?"

He raised his brows. Too bad he hadn't thought of it. The solution took her out of a very nasty mix of variables and kept her safe. "Fiona, look at the facts. There was disaster brewing here long before I arrived on the scene."

"And nothing you did contributed to the enormity of it either, I suppose."

"I'll admit I shoved Dex around, but he was right about one thing. You are going to have to decide which side your bread is buttered on. Whom do you want on your team, him or me? He thinks you've chosen me. I'm not so sure. You tell me. What do you want?"

There were more important issues, but none closer to her heart. "Why did you tell Dex that I had signed something foreswearing any interest in the Bar Naught?"

"To spare your pretty little derriere the indignity of a stint behind bars. Simple quid pro quo. Tit for tat. One phony document deserves another. Did you hear Dex demanding that I produce the document?"

"No. You offered. Is that what you call being on my team?"

"I lied. But you could sign your life away and it wouldn't mean—"

"Never. I would never sign my name to something like that."

"I was going to say it would never hold up in court."

"Well, that's not a risk I would ever take. Dex *knows* that. And what if it's real? What if Kyle didn't care what happened to the ranch if he wasn't alive anymore and there is such a document?"

"Then your problem is deeper than ever."

"Because it gave me a motive to kill him? That's all very well and good, except that I didn't *know*."

"That won't matter, Fiona. The only thing that ever matters is appearances. You can swear on a stack of Bibles that you didn't know. Your parents can testify that they never told you. But twelve ordinary folks are going to find themselves nodding along when the prosecutor asks them, what's the likelihood? Is there anybody in the county who doesn't know everyone else's business? If you were a juror, would you believe you?"

He came around to the front of the wet bar and propped half his body on one of the plush leather bar stools. "Think about it, Fiona. With a motive as powerful as that, opportunity, the rifle you failed to turn over, your arrest was in the bag before I ever started with Hanifen."

Standing, pacing about, she gave a frustrated sigh. "I don't understand you. Was that all just posturing, then? That bit about what a waste of time it would be for Dex to try pinning Kyle's murder on me?"

"Partly." He watched her pacing, her slender figure seeming no more substantial than a paper doll, her mind spinning. Something didn't figure and she began to vie with Dex again for the wild-card designation.

"I can't go to jail."

"And I can't keep you out unless you help yourself." He took another stab in the dark. "Someone has decreed that you're the one that's going to go down for the murder, Fiona, and you'd better consider coughing up the reason why someone would want to do that."

She hesitated half a second too long. "I don't know what you're talking about. Why are you so convinced that anyone has decided I'm going to be the fall guy here?"

He bit off a curse. "Wise up, Fiona. You think things are going to change if you can just get Dex to believe you? Do you think, if only you could explain things well enough to him, he'd see how completely wrong he was?"

"You can mock me all you want, Guiliani—"

"I'm not mocking you, Fiona—"

"—but all you've managed to do here this morning is to fix it so that Dex digs in his heels to make the case against me stick. I *can't* go to jail."

"Save it, and get this through your head, princess." He was tired of the supercilious looks she cast off every time he called her that, but if she wanted to stamp her foot and act like she couldn't be touched, he was going to keep goading her.

He understood exactly where she was coming from. No one wanted to believe that the truth wouldn't hold its own. No one wanted to believe that the system could go so wrong as to haul a completely innocent defendant into court.

But if Matt hadn't been here, Hanifen would have conned her into riding into town with him to "do the right thing," and then he'd have served the warrant, busted her and had her clapped behind bars before noon.

"Listen up, because I'm telling you the truth. When I asked which job Dex had come to do, the one he'd been elected to perform or the other one, he knew I was suggesting he had orders to do whatever he had to do to frame you and make it stick.

"And if you don't think," he continued, cramming reality down her sexy little throat, "that he won't sacrifice the truth to get it done, you'd better think again. He's for sale, Fiona. For crying out loud, you heard him saying how the investigation might be handled 'differently.'"

He watched her trying to wrap her mind around that kind of betrayal, how Dex could turn on her, how he could fashion lies and fabricate evidence against her. And then, under a threat from Matt, with no more than a couple of seconds' thought, to flip the other way.

"What was that all about with the lip balm?"

He took the tube out of his pocket and tossed it to her. "Open it, and twist the plunger all the way." She pulled off the cap and rolled the dial as far as it would go. "Force it."

When she complied, the base broke loose and fell into her hand. "I don't get it."

"You remember hearing about the kid last winter who was on the run from the police in Montana for firebombing his parents' home?" She nodded. "The boy was framed. His mother's name is Ann Calder. She's married now to my partner, J. D. Thorne. They were here, in this house. Everly was supposedly offering them help finding Ann's son. But while they were here, Everly had Dex plant an electronic beacon in the base of Ann's lip balm.''

''Why would he do that?''

''So that his assassin buddies could track Ann and J.D. into the mountains.''

She swallowed hard. ''I don't understand.''

''J.D. was about to uncover the truth. Hanifen and Everly are supporters of the TruthSayers, Fiona. They're vigilantes. They're killers, and they get by with it because they're a secret society and they protect their own. They're the ones who firebombed the kid's house.'' He watched the color drain from her face. ''I think you'd have to agree. Dex's reaction wasn't what you'd expect of an innocent man.''

She had the look of a shell-shocked refugee. ''No. It wasn't.''

She turned around and stood with her back to him, her arms wrapped around her waist. He wanted to tell her to give up trying to make sense of all this, to see the kind of man she was dealing with. But he still had no idea what she was up to, what she was doing back on the Bar Naught. Or how she fit into the larger, far more dangerous game of cat and mouse going on here.

What intrigued him most was why, if whoever had killed Everly had wanted the frame-up to stick, they hadn't done a subtler job of it. An inelegant frame wasn't Matt's style, but if an inept setup did what it was supposed to do, if it knocked Fiona out of the game, then what else was there to say?

Her arrest would satisfy the D.A. and the citizenry that the murderer had been apprehended, but Hanifen's haste and determination convinced Matt that someone wanted Fiona out of the picture. She acted as if she hadn't a clue.

He didn't trust her. Too many questions surrounded her. She still hadn't acknowledged that she'd seen for herself how ready Dex was to abandon his case against her. He asked her again. "Who wants you off the Bar Naught, Fiona?"

She turned back toward him. "I don't know."

"But you do know what Everly was involved in here."

"Yes." She looked away, trying to make it seem as if she were searching for the right word. "A hunting club. Very exclusive, reserved to a small but extremely wealthy clientele."

She had the line down pat. He raised his brows, impressed. "Right off the brochure."

She didn't appreciate the humor. "There is no brochure."

"Doubtless. I just told you Dex and Everly sent professional killers after friends of mine—cops—and you want me to go with this hunting club craptrap?"

Her chin went up. "That's all I know."

He didn't believe her. "Were you supposed to play hostess?"

"Not exactly."

"What, then, exactly?"

"Just a wrangler, Guiliani. The flunky in charge of the horses."

"I find it hard to believe Everly would squander his assets that way."

She met his eyes with a brittle look. "What assets?"

"The pleasure of your company. The opportunity to decorate his arm with a beautiful woman."

"Do you think it's easy, taking care of a bunch of greenhorns with egos big enough to fill the entire outdoors?"

"No. But that's not what I'm talking about." He added insult to injury, feeling a cad, knowing he had to throw her off balance enough to admit what role she was playing here. The hunt-club flunky wasn't it. "I'm referring to the perks to Everly's elite clientele of hobnobbing with distant royalty. The quality of a geisha. The illusion of—"

"That's enough."

He was so close. "Is it, Fiona?" Unrelenting, he let his glance take in all that the ranch house had to offer, the luxury, everything around them. "What would you do to have the Bar Naught back?"

She clammed up. And he began to understand how fiercely she wanted back what Everly had.

Her home. The land. The entity known as the Bar Naught. She intended, some way, to regain the ranch her parents had frittered away on junkets to Sandringham and Monte Carlo and the Italian Riviera. And she wanted it so much that she had somehow left herself vulnerable.

He had to reconsider the possibility that Fiona might be involved up to her teeth in a different conspiracy than the one he'd been looking for.

He grimaced. He'd already cooked his own goose. He already cared what became of her. He'd already stuck out his own neck in her defense, and if he were to continue on in the vein of the heartless bastard of a realist he'd just crammed down her throat, he'd have to admit he'd already indulged heated fantasies.

It was possible that she had somehow sold her soul to the devil in exchange for some hope of getting the

Bar Naught back. He didn't want it to be true, didn't want her to be involved with Everly's crimes, and his thoughts wanted to go off on the crusade of making excuses for her.

She had no way of knowing whom she was dealing with.

She couldn't have foreseen how she could be used and manipulated and cheated out of the ranch again.

He wanted to believe that Fiona Halsey was an innocent bystander. Just a beautiful woman with a heart so tender that she would not give up on Soldier Boy, her soul intact and her body flinging off come-hither vibes because they were true and not because she needed to distract him from seeing what loomed right in front of his face.

He made his last stab. "Would you betray Everly to his enemies to get the ranch back? Is that what happened last night, Fiona? Or is that why it's so vital that you don't go to jail?"

The color heightened in her cheeks. A certain heat came off her, desperation he could almost feel. The tip of her tongue dampened her lips.

He looked at her and made himself look beyond the woman too soft to put Soldier down, past the mass of golden hair and sweet complexion, the classic cheekbones and hazel-blue eyes and her wetted, full, burgundy-shaded lips. He tried once more to convince her to wake up and save herself.

To let him help her out of whatever jam she'd gotten herself into.

"You've been framed, Fiona. Someone wanted Everly dead, and whoever it was wanted you to go down for the murder. You can't afford to cover your eyes and hope it all goes away."

"I'm not a child, Guiliani, and there is nothing I resent more than—"

Her eyes flared. She fell instantly silent, losing track of her scathing rebuke. He must have given something big away, betrayed himself, by an unwitting shake of his head. A child was not even in the realm of what he saw or thought of when he saw her. Somehow that insurmountable discrepancy communicated itself to her. She was a beautiful woman, no mistake about it. Awareness leaped between them, a current firing repeated, urgent signals.

She swallowed. "I'm not going there with you."

His own mouth watered and he watched her watching him swallow. "I hate to always be debating the point, Fiona, but you seem to be leading the way."

She scraped her fingers through her hair, dragging it back, baring her throat, and insisting with her words that she was doing nothing of the sort. "I'm not going there."

"I'm not exactly thrilled myself, princess, but again, I'm a realist. I'm not going to ignore the fact that there are sparks flying here."

"Well, you know, that's what adults do." She employed the heat inside her, packaged it up and sent it shooting out in her anger at him. "They choose whether to react or not." She stuck her hands in the back pockets of her jeans. "I'm not ignoring anything, I'm exercising my better judgment and choosing not to act on miscellaneous *sparks*.

"I don't need you to bring me up to speed on treacherous human nature in Dex's case," she continued, "or in idle sexual flirtation in yours. And I sure as *hell* do not need your protection. What you did was completely unnec—"

"I don't think 'miscellaneous' quite applies here, princess."

"I asked you not to call me that."

"I heard you."

Her chin went up, her hair fell farther back. There was not a chance in the world that she too naive to know her effect on him. "Then why do you do it?"

"Because, Fiona, you keep toying with me as if you were one." He eased his thigh off the bar stool and stood. "Because you keep daring me to take you up on your sideways invitations." Too late, he thought, to take it back. He moved toward her, betting with himself. Was she toying with him, or was she not? Would she stand, or run? He came toe-to-toe with her. "Lastly? Because I suspect you know exactly how to ask for what you want, but you're too... I don't know. Proud. Or is it scared?"

"Please."

He smiled. If she meant to infuse the word with derision, she missed her mark.

Chapter Six

By her posture, hands tucked away, her elbows poking out, he knew she'd meant it that way, knew disdain was her only weapon. She'd failed. "Please what, princess?"

Her throat caught, a hitch of meaningless sound. Her gaze fell to his lips, and hers parted. He moved in and put his hands on her biceps, let them stray down over long, lean, sexy and very unprincess muscles, along a length of silky mohair so common to her that she wore it to work in her stables.

His thighs came into contact with hers, her breasts brushed against him. Heat flooded his innards and he thought he would keel over with the full-throated moan coming from her lips. What had he been thinking? That he would teach her not to toy with him? No. To upset her. To tilt her world, make her give up the way she'd sold her soul. What she was prepared to do.

But he was tilting his own world as much.

"Ahh, Fiona." His hands slid along her forearms to her wrists, melded so close to her hands that his fingers threaded through hers deep inside her own back pockets.

She writhed against him, and he rocked toward her. He could not have held her closer and yet their lips had yet to meet, she had yet to answer.

He turned his head, inhaled her clean, crisp, powerfully seductive scent. He had never been with a woman who matched his height, and in her boots, Fiona Halsey had an inch on him, maybe more. He found himself turned on by it, the closer, intimate match of her body to his, the thought of a woman who was his equal in every way.

He touched his lips to the line of her jaw, and murmured, ''Please what, princess? What do you want?''

She turned her head and caught his lower lip in her teeth. Desire shot through his body, a bolt of lightning, branches shooting heaven to earth, to the root of him, to his connection with the floor, riveting him in place, unable to move, barely able to draw breath.

She released his lip from her teeth. Against her bottom, inside her pockets, her fingers tightened in his. She bowed her head, just a little, trying to get hold of herself, to make what was happening between them seem an aberration to be dismissed, a futile thing, a chrysalis trying to stuff itself back into the safety of the cocoon.

Her lashes kissed his cheek, and he thought, no, he knew, he had never felt anything so intensely sexual in the making of a butterfly kiss as he felt when it was her lashes languishing at his cheek.

Her voice was reduced to a whisper, a plea. ''I want you to stop.''

Cheek to cheek with her, the heat of their bodies indistinguishable, he breathed once, again. ''Don't lie to me, Fiona.'' Deep inside he ached as he had never ached before. Something about her, something rare he

couldn't define, a spirit that refused to be quashed or
seduced, made him want her more, even more than
he wanted to know what deal she had cut with what
devil. "Don't ever lie to me."

"As if..." She turned her lips to his ear and
touched her tongue to its lobe, and then she recovered
her voice, the gritty, sensual sound that plucked the
strings that connected his bones and made him weak-
kneed, wobbly as a newborn colt. "As if," she uttered, "you haven't lied to me."

He endured the touch of her dampened lip to the
shell of his ear. "That's different. It's my job."

"It's the same."

"You don't know—"

"No," she interrupted. "*You* don't know."

"Fiona—"

"No." She turned her head away from him till it
was her hair, flighty with static, caressing his face,
catching in the moisture left by her lips. "I—"

"You what?" He withdrew one hand from hers
and let his palm skim with a feather-light touch over
the mohair sleeve of her sweater, up her arm, to her
shoulder. "What is so important?" A shiver of pleasure escaped her. He knew she would rather have died
than let him know it.

He took her chin in his fingers and turned her face
to his. Their lips hovered so close he could feel the
moisture and excitement, the shallowness of her
breath.

Now or never.

He had pressed his advantage and he had to move
in for the kill—for the kiss as much as for the information he needed from her. He wanted the kiss over

and done with, the one that had been on both their minds since she had first breathed the word.

But as he guided her chin nearer he found the reluctant princess was more his match than he'd thought, more than his equal in height, surpassing him in character. Despite the trembling desire in her, from some well of restraint and discipline, Fiona Halsey summoned up the grit it took to break away from their embrace.

Her eyes were bright, her skin flushed, her mouth a little swollen on nothing more than anticipation, but she gave him her haughty princess look and cut him off at his wobbly knees. "Maybe later. Right now I have work to do."

WHEN SHE WALKED OUT on him, after the door had closed behind her, Matt went back to the wet bar, took out a bottled water and cracked it open. He guzzled down half, wiped his lips on the back of his hand and took his first half-decent breath in what seemed like hours.

The damned grandfather clock was all he heard, ticking away the seconds.

He could go on for days making the plays, acting whatever part, losing himself in the role du jour, and come out of every encounter energized, high on the adrenaline of pretense and subterfuge, the thrill of pulling it off. But for a few moments with Fiona Halsey, he wasn't engaged in any show or playing any role. He was engaged, instead, in something dangerously truthful, and he didn't like it at all. It sapped him. Undermined him. Cost him his precious facade. Made him see the real self, the hungry loner, lurking beneath a lifetime of undercover identities he used to stave off facing himself alone.

He longed for the truth, appreciated it in all kinds of art and sculpture, in films and in music, but life was definitely not art. Truth was the palaver of fools. Survival required masterful deception, and he couldn't afford to indulge lame fantasy.

Both Garrett and J.D. had fallen profoundly in love in the course of their undercover operations against the TruthSayers. And while it was easy enough to joke about it afterward—the standing joke around the water cooler being that it was high time that Matt tumbled—he knew how hideously vulnerable both his friends had been.

To put it in Fiona's own words, he didn't want to go there.

But she had exposed him to himself without even trying, and he had, more than anything, a sense of a disaster narrowly averted just now.

Involvement with Fiona Halsey was a train wreck waiting to happen.

He paced the exquisite Karastan carpet, admiring the O'Keeffe on the wall for the naked, blistering truth of a skull lodged in the sand, and gave himself a pep talk much like he'd given Garrett when it was his own little boy in the hands of the enemy. Matt was a veteran of many, many undercover operations. He knew what he was doing. He knew he could land on his feet. But he was also the one on which *this* operation depended. And narrowly or not, the disaster had been sidestepped this time.

He would have to take his own advice. Suck it up and do the thing that had to be done. That only he could do. Everly had been taken out, but that only meant evil men even more clever and dangerous were left standing. Matt wanted his entrée into The Fraternity, and he intended to have it.

He splayed a hand at his hip and sucked down the rest of the water, crushed the plastic container in his hand and skidded the crumpled mass over the green-veined marble countertop. It sailed over the edge into the sink and bounced around the polished granite bowl with a gratifying clatter.

He drew another deep breath, stared out the window as Fiona disappeared into the stables, then headed toward Everly's computer.

He needed to blow-torch his way past whatever firewalls had been installed to prevent tampering. Last night's upload had been a simple matter by comparison.

Over the months of planning this operation with Garrett and J.D., they learned that Everly had been in rare, abbreviated contact with his international cohorts through the Internet. One of the stickier problems of modern-era law enforcement—the badasses could not only find one another with ease, they could exchange information through nearly impenetrable lines of communication, and it could all happen in seconds.

He needed access to the user network of The Fraternity in order to pull off his sting.

He switched on the computer and sat down to work. He quickly got into the files that proved useless, and settled in to hack deeper, searching for the telltale file designations associated with private e-mail groups. He found a small gold mine of communiqués to do with local militiamen, but that was still not what he wanted. He copied the files and moved on.

He blew off the minor frustration, knowing he

would have to be suspicious of anything he could crash through too easily. At last, buried behind a video game, he struck pay dirt in the form of a private network unlike anything he had seen before.

Attached to brief messages steeped in veiled references to place and time, he gained access, be it only code names, to the hunt club clientele—the members of The Fraternity.

He identified himself, advised the brotherhood of Everly's crimes against them, and uploaded the bogus but finely crafted proof of his claims. He implied that he had personally exacted the price of Everly's cheating on behalf of the members. Live by the sword, die by the sword.

Lastly, he mentioned, he looked forward to the hunt.

As FIONA LET HERSELF OUT the door and headed down the steps of the wide, white-washed veranda, a gust of wind pelted her with dirt and grit. She raised an arm to protect her eyes and turned her body against the force of the wind so that she had to walk sideways. She headed to the paddock off the stable to work for a while with the polo ponies.

The riding was exacting. The discipline and concentration consumed her thoughts, relieved her of having to consider what Kyle's death had done to her plans, how much trouble she was in or how wispy her chances were of salvaging everything that mattered to her.

Or how close she had come to throwing herself under Guiliani's spell.

The sun shone brightly, though with the biting wind it was impossible to feel the warmth of its rays on her face, or to account for the heat in her face. Her body hummed, still quivered like a bell struck by the ringer from inside. She traded waves with Dennis Geary, who'd driven off the ranch near dawn.

She pulled on a pair of worn leather gloves and ducked through the snowy-white rails of the paddock fence, then whistled and called to the pony Everly had bought for forty grand, a tall, lanky Thoroughbred named Fincher. The gelding perked up his ears, swished his gorgeous black tail and broke into a trot toward her.

A part of her cringed that Soldier Boy would never respond to her like this again.

"Fincher," she crooned, turning away from him as he raised and then lowered his head onto her shoulder. She stroked his soft, elegant nose and reaching beneath his head, scratched the other side of his neck. When the big handsome loverboy nuzzled tight to her neck, she knew she'd unwittingly gone for Fincher because she knew he would do that.

She'd hoped Fincher would blot out the memory of standing in the otherwise silent library cheek to cheek with Guiliani, stuck with hearing her own muted, turned-on breathing. And his.

So much had been going on inside her. So much turmoil. She heard him rattling off his characterization of the document he claimed she signed forswearing any interest in the Bar Naught. *Quid pro quo. Tit for tat.* And she'd heard herself answering. But she was off in another world, too. Unadulterated fear shot through her to think of Guiliani producing such a document, but what she heard wasn't the essence of his answering gambit in the frame-up of Fiona Halsey, but the essence of old and familiar disillusion.

If love existed, if what she'd seen in her life was supposed to *be* love, then it was only a series of trade-offs and poor bargains. "Tit for tat" was her mother's own shorthand.

Men wanted convenient access to a woman's body and someone to carry on the name. Women wanted home and hearth and babies. *Look around, darling, you simply cannot miss the truth of it.*

Or in the more upper-crust case of the gentrified, a woman could demand, in addition to home and hearth and babies, pretty baubles and the illusion of control on holidays to the south of France.

Tit for tat, Fiona. Make no mistake. She could still hear her mother's British upper-crust intonation.

Faithfulness didn't enter into either bargain. Commitment was a sometimes charming notion, always a fairy tale, and anyone who claimed otherwise was deluding herself.

Her mother never had any patience for Fiona's romantic illusions to the contrary. The royal divorces polished off her illusions.

And it was no different for the women her mother referred to as commoners. Most of her local married friends were saying now that they knew, standing at the altar, that they shouldn't have gone through with their weddings.

But why these thoughts had sprung out at her in the middle of Guiliani's spiel, she didn't know, except that he attracted her, and she had never felt so threatened in all her life as by the man Soldier Boy had left standing.

Fincher followed her back to the stables. She reached into a bucket of treats and let him eat a handful, then reached inside the door for his halter and reins. She had looped the reins through a ring at the post, blanketed and saddled Fincher when the sound of a one-ton pickup, its gears shifting down, reached her.

She turned and saw the Bureau of Land Management logo on the truck towing an older, unadorned stock trailer.

Great. She had forgotten that the BLM mustangs she had contracted to gentle would be delivered to the Bar Naught this morning. She hadn't completed the necessary paperwork either. She walked up as Charlie dropped heavily out of the cab.

"Hey, Fiona." A large man, potbellied, with a tuft of wiry red hair that came near to filling the bowl of his baseball cap, Charlie was stuffing his shirttail back into his pants, shyly sprucing up for her. "What's going on? Sheriff's vehicle sittin' out there on the road at your turnoff, and that dumb-bunny deputy, Margaret, tried to tell me I couldn't come in here. What am I gonna do? Unload these mangy critters on the road, hope they decide to stick around?"

Fiona laughed. "That'd work, wouldn't it?"

"So, what's the deal with Margaret hanging around out there?"

Was it possible the news of Kyle's death was not out yet? "I don't think I should say anything, Charlie, if Dex has sent someone out here to keep a lid on things."

Charlie sucked the inside of his lower lip, hard, in the manner of a guy who'd given up his chewing tobacco and missed it dearly. His brows pulled together, telegraphing suspicion. He'd never been invited to hang around in the same circles as Kyle Everly and Dex Hanifen, who were tight with both the local politicos and the ranchers. He was, after all, only a lowly government employee. "Well, what the hey." He had to shout to be heard over the howling wind. "Save it if saying anything's going to get you into trouble."

Shivering violently, she pulled up her collar. The wind was more than she could take today. "Frankly," she shouted, "I don't think I could be in any more trouble, Charlie. Kyle was murdered last night."

Charlie's face seemed to unfold into a blank. He gave a low, unholy whistle. "What happened? Dex know who did it?"

"At the moment, I'm the prime suspect."

"Come on…" Disbelief swept all too fast to doubt. "*Did* you kill him?" He backpedaled pretty fast at her look. "I mean, of course you couldn't have—"

She clenched her teeth shut. "If Dex believes it, then it must be true, is that it, Charlie?"

"Fiona—"

"Save it." Stung, she just wanted relief. To be alone. She turned and shaded her eyes from the sun, pointing out the pasture where she wanted to unload the feral mustangs she'd won in the BLM contract to gentle and ready for adoption.

"D'you think maybe I…shouldn't leave the…you know." He wouldn't meet her eyes.

He didn't know what to say to her at all, but she got his drift. She might not be here to do the work she'd contracted to do. She was not going to go on that assumption. "Unload them, Charlie."

"Fiona, it's just that—hell's bells." He got a look on his face that reminded her of Dex's unwillingness to say hurtful things to her. He gave up trying to keep the wind from snatching the cap off his head. He lifted it off himself and stood there clutching the thing in his rough hands. ''If I have to come back and get these animals, I'm going to have to charge a couple hundred dollars back to the ranch. And there's a penalty, you know, if you don't complete the work on time, so maybe—''

''Maybe,'' Guiliani interrupted, appearing out of nowhere at her elbow, dressed now in jeans and sweater and sheepskin vest, ''you should go ahead with what the lady wants and unload the stock.'' He'd exchanged his black cashmere sport coat for one of Everly's sheepskins. He reached into his jeans and pulled out a money clip, counted out five hundred-dollar bills and put the still-thick wad away. ''This should cover you.''

Charlie darted a glance behind Matt as if he could figure out where he'd come from, then looked at the money and Fiona. ''That's not— I can't take cash.''

Matt smiled easily, somehow eliminating the risk, the possible infractions with a look. ''No big deal.''

''Yes, it is a big deal, Matt.'' A bubble of hysteria lodged in her throat. She wanted to stamp her foot at the universe and demand that he be made to go away. ''It's illegal to bribe a public official.''

''Name's Matt Guiliani,'' he said blithely, offering his hand to Charlie. ''Consider the money a deposit, good faith. Give me a receipt. That ought to do it.''

''Charlie Norville.'' Outmaneuvered, not as reluctant as he should have been, he reached for the money. ''I s'pose I could do that, seein' as Fiona's maybe gonna have her hands too full—''

''That she may,'' Matt purred, turning Norville's meaning on its head as he put a possessive arm around her shoulders. Locked in, she had no way to move but toward him, into him. Cheating a look at Norville, Matt took her hand and angled his head and brought his lips to her neck.

"Play it, princess," he murmured.

His words infuriated her, but the barest touch of his lips, the warmth of his breath on her skin, left her still-tuned body hungering and her tongue stunningly mute. A snarl died in her throat. She couldn't think what move to make next.

Naked envy lit Charlie Norville's eyes.

Embarrassment flooded her, and that, in turn, alarmed her even more deeply. Embarrassment, her mother made clear, was for the sweaty masses, the hopeless commoners, the tacky lower classes. With the royal blood flowing in Fiona's veins, she must on such occasions adopt a certain presence that even an untimely interruption could not upset.

Or envy in another man's eyes.

Her upbringing was all about such issues. The lessons had begun early and continued on into her late teens. She'd been coached into a shameless flirt by the age of two. She knew to pat her daddy's cheek, or any man into whose arms her daddy placed her. She knew how to curtsy by three, how to say no prettily by four, how and when and at whom to flutter her lashes by five.

In her past, it would simply never have occurred to her to feel embarrassment over such a dalliance as Matt's behavior now implied. One embraced such a moment, never apologized. But she felt the heat of it in her face now, flaring up from her breasts to the top of her head. For an instant there, dalliance felt like a promise.

One dangerous instant. One vastly vacant promise.

She shed his embrace as an indifferent princess might, understanding at some level that she wouldn't have gotten away with it if he hadn't let her, and gave Norville's arm a gentle touch. "Charlie, drive on down to the pasture. I'll just go get the paperwork and meet you down there."

She cut Matt a dismissive glance. In return he patted her butt. "I'll ride down with Charlie and give you a hand."

"I don't need a hand." She nearly did stamp her foot.

He winked at Charlie, male-bonding, indulgent of a temperamental woman asserting herself.

"Stop it," she hissed, glaring at Matt, turning to Charlie. "I started once to tell you where the pasture is—"

"I know where it is. I've been by there before."

"You have? Why would you—"

"This and that. Brought in some winter wheat a time or two."

She didn't know when Charlie would have done that. She shrugged. "I'll see you at the pasture." She left both men standing there and walked back across the yard to retrieve the BLM contracts from her desk.

Inside her rooms she pulled off her gloves and shed her coat, leaving them on an overstuffed chair her mother had once had in the master bedroom of the main house. Alone for these few moments, given a little time to be alone, out of Matt Guiliani's orbit, she would get a grip on herself.

Her tabby cat, Clarissa, darted out of the bedroom to wind herself in and out of Fiona's legs, meowing piteously for her breakfast. Fiona picked up the cat and held her close, crooning sweet nothings, and let herself absorb the familiarity of her furnishings and small treasures to dispel the confusion rattling around inside her. She went to the kitchenette to put out a fancy feast for Clarissa, then to her desk, to sit down and give the papers a brief read-through.

She found them lying more or less where she remembered putting the contracts, except that one entire corner of the sheaf stuck out over the edge of her blotter. Was there the smudge of a dirty finger?

She picked up the contract, angling the papers in the ambient light to have a closer look. There was a definite smudge, which hadn't come from her hands, and certainly hadn't been on the paper in the supply bin of her printer.

Unease moved through her like a ghost. She put the papers down. Her skin crawled. She turned slowly, forcing calm on herself, searching for evidence that anything else had been touched.

Nothing seemed even so marginally out of place as the BLM papers had, but if she had the time to look closely, would she find other faint smudges? She sat down, her pen gripped tightly in her hand, and reminded herself that nothing was as it seemed, that everything that could go wrong had either done so, or was unfolding moment by moment. She could not afford to let down her guard, or leave her quarters unlocked, or—

Stopped midthought by the blinking light of her computer alerting her to e-mail, she went quickly through the motions of retrieving the message. The return e-mail address was her father's.

The message was terse. *Do not give it up. Keep the faith. Remember the old saying, "Three can keep a*

secret if two are dead.'' No good deed goes unpunished, Fiona. Regards, Dad.

Of course, the message was not from her father,
just made to seem so. The adage was a threat, meant
to keep her quiet and compliant, and it made her spit-
ting mad. She exited her online connection, turned
back to Charlie's papers and scrawled her signature
on the bottom line of the contract and receipt.

She had her orders, and she knew she was meant
to keep Guiliani in the dark. Keeping the faith was
becoming more and more impossible, because Matt
was onto far more than anyone thought.

And he was knocking over her barriers left and
right.

Chapter Seven

Matt rode with Norville in his pickup down to the pasture. The drive took less than ten minutes. He wanted to follow up on Fiona's evident confusion as to when and why Norville had been that far back onto the property. Though weeds had overgrown the tire tracks, he could see ruts continuing on east. He jumped down out of the pickup cab and made a comment in passing.

"Looks like there must have been heavy equipment on this so-called road at one time." He knew the hunting lodge lay to the east and somewhat south, and suspected that the tracks were ones he'd seen on satellite photos that led to the lodge.

Norville slammed his door shut. "I wouldn't know anything about that, saving a stock trailer as big as this one will cut some pretty good ruts in the road after a while."

"You wouldn't be driving a trailer back here much, would you?" He followed Norville around to the back of the stock trailer. "Couple times a year, maybe, when you've got to load up cattle to take to the sale barns."

"I s'pose," Norville agreed.

"Ever been up to the hunting lodge?"

"A time or two."

"You drive, or ride up?"

"Ride." But Norville wouldn't look Matt in the eye, instead talking as he climbed up to check on the mustangs in the back of the trailer. There was a lot of stamping and snorting going on. He was bad-mouthing the critters inside the trailer when he climbed back down. "Fiona's got her hands full with this bunch, all right."

"She do this often?"

"Couple of times. But people all over the country-side have been bringing her their hard cases to break for riding since she was…oh, I don't know. Musta been since we were in high school. She's good, I'll hand her that. Danged good." He looked sharply at Matt. "You know anything about what happened to Kyle?"

"Just what the sheriff tells me. Fiona is who he's looking at, apparently. I think it's a crock, myself. Fiona wouldn't hurt a fly. Who should know that better than Dex?"

Norville gave him a flinty, sideways look. "Dex knows what he's doing."

"Is that right? He's never been wrong?"

"I don't go debatin' the ins and outs of things with Dex," Norville snapped. "I watch my own p's and q's and we get along fine."

Matt shrugged. "Guess he's probably smart enough to orchestrate a frame, huh?" Charlie's jaw hung slack. Matt opened the gate into the fenced pasture and offered to guide Norville as he backed the massive trailer up to the gate.

"Yeah, sure," Norville answered, still bristling on

Hanifen's behalf. "Just let me know when we've got five feet to spare. Leave room for the gangplank and rails to funnel these critters into the pasture."

The trailer was in place and the rails dragged even with the gate when Fiona rode up on a steel-gray with black mane and tail. She dropped easily off the left side of the horse and looped the reins around a permanent rail. Norville lowered the gangplank and the mustangs bolted through the temporary chute and into the pasture, racing like the wind to the far end where the six bunched together.

Fiona handed Norville the signed contracts and a handwritten receipt for him to acknowledge the five hundred in cash Matt had put up. He signed off on the receipt with a pen she took from behind her ear. The paper snapped in the wind. She handed the receipt to Matt.

"Thanks, Charlie. I appreciate the help."

He grunted something unintelligible, put in a sour mood, Matt thought, by questions he'd raised as to just how smart Dex Hanifen was. As Norville slammed home the ramp, Matt turned to Fiona. "Do you need help?"

She shook her head. "I'll just be running them through the pen and chutes for a while." She checked her watch. "A boy from town is coming out in a while."

"Do you mind if I watch?"

"Don't you have someone else to irritate?"

Half grinning, he stuck a cedar pick in his mouth. "Not at the moment."

"Suit yourself, then. But you'll either have to walk back or be stuck out here all afternoon unless you go with Charlie."

He hitched a ride back up to the house. Norville kept his lips zipped. As Matt watched the BLM man drive off the Bar Naught, he suspected Charlie Norville's name would come up on a list of TruthSayers sympathizers.

Another of Sheriff Hanifen's true believers.

WITHIN THE CONFINES of the pasture was a circular training pen made of red-lacquered round pipe, and within the pen itself was a chute, an alleyway of sorts with fencing on both sides. Using her own mount, her gelding named Fincher, she gently crowded each mustang in turn to the fence where they could run in circles, but each time around, in order to keep running, the horse had to pass through the metal pipes of the chute.

At the far end of the chute was a solid wood gate that could be closed. The gate hung from the same pipes used to build the pen, only these stood on end, extending six feet in the air. Hinged on those vertical pipes was a flat wooden device that reminded Matt of a pillory with the space carved out of the wood to accommodate some wrongdoing Pilgrim's neck.

The space cut out of this panel was deep as a horse's neck and heavily padded. It was clear to Matt that at some point Fiona would close off the chute to which the mustangs had been gently acclimated, and lower the top of the pillory.

He had saddled one of the horses from the stable, Pilsner, and ridden back down to watch Fiona after Norville departed. He stood outside the reinforced pasture gate watching her for a couple of hours.

A little after two o'clock, a teenaged boy rode up on one of the Bar Naught working horses. He leaned down and opened the gate, urging his mount into the training pen. He gave Matt a leery, insolent look, then called out a bored greeting to Fiona.

"I'm here."

She'd been cantering in easy circles around the training pen, but the mustang she was working with chose that moment to challenge her and break out. He was a huge animal, a paint, and the unmistakable ringleader of the bunch Norville had trucked in. The mustang drew up short, planted his feet, attempting to cut behind her when she rode by, to make a break for it across the pen.

She wheeled around on Finch and before the mustang could bolt, she confronted him with Finch head to head. Fincher danced side to side, matching the mustang's feints, cutting off escape each time. Without missing a beat or looking at the boy, she gave him the business. "You're late, Robbie."

"Ah, c'mon, Fiona—"

"I don't want to hear any excuses. You get your butt out of the training pen, and wait till *I'm* ready now." Finch finally maneuvered so that the mustang fell back into the circle. "Outside the paddock, Robbie," she scolded softly when the boy failed to move. "Go on."

Matt planted his arms along the top railing, chin resting on his hands as the kid rode back out of the pen and slammed the gate, muttering curses and empty threats under his breath.

When the kid finally looked at Matt, who was standing there with a smirk on his own face, he laughed nervously. "She ticks me off." He got off his horse and flopped the reins over the railing.

"Stickler for rules, huh?" Matt wouldn't have predicted it, but he saw a certain hard-core discipline in her.

"Worse," Robbie groused.

"Really."

"Yeah," the kid said. "She might as well be running the jail."

"So why do you come?"

"Gotta."

Matt laughed softly. He watched Fiona dismount and lead Finch out to the pasture. She was in the ring alone now with the brute that wanted nothing to do with civilization. "Nobody's gotta do anything, Robbie. Unless the alternative is worse. What'd you do?"

"B and E, if it's any of your business. Got away with it three times."

"Is that right?" The kid sounded more and more like Matt had at his age, all attitude, zero respect, less hope of steering clear of much, much bigger trouble unless things turned around soon. "Where I grew up they'd have had you cleaning out toilets in Grand Central Station, and that's just for starters."

"Yeah, what makes you such an expert?" The boy tried to come off disinterested, but his eyes were riveted on Fiona working alone, on foot, doing much the same thing with the mustang as Finch had done, crowding the horse every time he turned his hind end to her, giving him space when he faced her.

"I pulled a few community service sentences in my time." He'd done much worse than B and E's, in fact, but he didn't think this kid needed to hear about it. "You're getting off easy."

Robbie rolled his eyes in disgust. "I'd like to see you get in there with her."

But what Matt heard beneath the heavy scorn was

an admiration for Fiona that no one else in the boy's life came close to earning. And it struck Matt then that the princess was more in her element here than cruising the Mediterranean on Pascal Lariviere's yacht or sipping tea with her distant cousin the queen.

The ranch wasn't just a place to her, or a piece of prime real estate or a symbol of the propertied elite. The Bar Naught was the place of her heart. Something almost spiritual in the way she interacted with the big, angry, mangy paint revealed itself to Matt, in her voice and the sweet, disciplined language of her body. Something profoundly respectful of what was wild and true. That horse, he knew, would fall for her, hard.

She took his breath away.

He watched the kid watching her and saw all the signs of a very secret crush.

"Robbie," Fiona called softly. "You're on. You do this. Come on."

The kid's hard expression vanished. Most of the color drained out of his face.

The mustang stood now with his front feet planted and his ears laid back.

"Tough guy like you?" Matt scoffed softly. "You can handle it."

"Yeah," Robbie gulped. "But I don't see you doin' it."

"C'mon, Robbie," Fiona called. "Show time."

Robbie gulped again, his Adam's apple poking against his skin, then hopped up on the fence and dropped lightly to the other side.

Fiona took him in hand with her voice alone. "You don't want him to know you're scared—"

"I'm not scared."

"—so just keep coming toward me. Remember how much he hates this. Think about what it's like for him to be caught and confronted by all this stuff he's never asked for. He really doesn't want to be here any more than you, but you're the one, Robbie. You're the one who can show him the way. Make him see it's not so bad. Show him respect, show him you know what kind of hell he's going through." She took a step back as Robbie drew even with her. "You're the man."

"I don't know," Robbie croaked, seeming to freeze.

"You do, Robbie. You know. Give him a name, show him that much regard."

"Ball-Buster," Robbie said, his voice cracking.

She touched Robbie's shoulder with a little restraint. "Let's say Buster." She guided him with as much respect and gentleness as she had the mustangs in their circles, toward and away to teach the horse how he should behave around a man. And even when the stallion wheeled and laid back his ears, she was still talking. "You know what Buster's feeling, Robbie. Let him know you know how pissed he is, how much better it can be for him."

Matt stuck around long enough to watch her coach Robbie through half an hour of establishing himself as the dominant one in the relationship with the mustang. He watched, chewing his cedar stick to splinters as Robbie herded the horse into the chute that Fiona had blocked.

As soon as Buster moved forward enough, spooked by the rear gate, Robbie climbed quick and agile as a monkey up the slick pipes and lowered the pillory over the mustang's head. Buster gave a shrill cry and struggled a moment or two, trying to rear up and escape the hold around his neck. But Fiona was right there to guide Robbie through calming the horse by his voice.

Matt stayed until Buster was set free and Robbie let out a war whoop to go with the high-five Fiona gave him. And though he remembered what Norville had said, *She gentles that sucker and she's got more'n half the battle won,* what choked him was the change she had wrought with the boy.

He turned away, then mounted Pilsner and rode away, noting for the record that there was a sob breaking loose somewhere inside his chest.

HE RODE AS FAR as the creek that meandered along the northernmost border of the Bar Naught, five or six miles out from the ranch house. The property extended several miles to the east of the highway, and it was there, in the high mountain valleys, that the lodge used as a base camp for hunting was set. It would take a full day to explore the surroundings, familiarizing himself with the landscape.

He had studied countless satellite photos and topographical maps, but until he could get in and see the lay of the land for himself, he wouldn't feel comfortable heading into the backcountry with anyone else.

Not Fiona.

Not Everly's cohorts.

From what he knew to be the lowest point in elevation on the ranch, at the creek bed, he dismounted and left the horse drinking from the shallow running water. He took Everly's more elaborate binoculars and stood searching the distant hills for ten, maybe fifteen minutes. The meadow where Fiona had had Charlie Norville unload the BLM mustangs from the stock trailer lay due south. He could just see the top of the chute where Robbie's transformation had happened.

The meadow gave way swiftly to foothills south and east of the paddock, one of which reached, fingerlike, down to separate the ranch house from the clearing where she worked. The way the chill wind blew at gale force, he saw how the land had taken shape over eons of time.

The last time he'd set foot in the state, going after Ann's runaway son, Jaz, he hadn't the time or inclination to admire his surroundings. Out of his element, he'd been too busy sweating the fact that from any of a thousand angles, he and Jaz could have been picked off like toy duck silhouettes in a carnival shooting gallery.

But this was postcard Wyoming, formidable mountains under vast skies, sweeps of barren land, forests more sparse by far than existed in the East, completely foreign to the pinched alleys and narrow streets and patches of dingy sky where he'd grown up.

He turned away, satisfied for the moment with his reconnaissance. He let the binoculars hang from the leather strap around his neck and sank to his haunches by the stream, shaping his hands into a bowl to treat himself to a swallow of the fast-running water.

He wasn't prepared for the iciness, for the way his flesh numbed in the two or three seconds he'd dipped his hands into the stream. He slurped up a couple of mouthfuls of water, shivered violently, then shook his hands hard and tried to wipe them dry on his jeans.

He sat down by the stream for a while and let what he'd seen in that training pen back into his head. One of those things you had to see to believe, and even then, even now he wanted to discount the possibility that anything lasting had really changed in Robbie. But he knew something fundamental *had* changed. The kid had stepped up and taken responsibility for dealing with feelings he shared with a majestic wild mustang.

Something elemental had moved in Matt.

He pulled his small wireless out of his coat pocket and sent Christo a secret agent message on Garrett's handheld receiver. *CW 006,* it read, referencing the little boy's initials and age. *Recon in progress. Saw a mustang tamed. Awaiting instructions. MG 036.*

He stood and dusted off his behind along with the melancholy mood. As he turned, he glimpsed something out of place high in the foothills south and east of his position.

He raised the binoculars to his eyes and tightened the focus to keep the visual field intact. He didn't breathe, didn't move. The trees, thick stands of pine, were just dense enough to make him think he was wrong.

He couldn't have detected motion that far away, in that kind of background, with the naked eye. Hell, he was the last one driving down the road to spot wildlife in plain view in the middle of the bald prairie. When you grew up in the city, you weren't exactly looking out for pheasant darting out along the roadside or antelope streaming down the hillside. It was unlikely he had seen any movement at all that far away.

Impossible.

But instinct held out over reason. He'd seen what

he'd seen. It might have been an elk or a smaller animal of some sort.

He rolled his shoulders, knocking back the tension to a manageable level, and watched a moment longer. After several more moments, he was rewarded at the extreme right of his field by the impression of another darting, downward motion. He looked to the right, but the tops of the trees blocked his view as effectively as a stockade.

But then, toward the bottom of his visual field, he caught the unmistakable glint of metal and for an instant, the barest impression of mottled, muted colors that made him think instantly of combat fatigues. And when he calculated the trajectory of movement, he leapt to the unlikely conclusion that a killer was closing in on a position from which to pick off Fiona Halsey from afar.

His heart thudded nastily in his chest. He spun around, took up the reins of his mount, pulled Pilsner about, away from the creek, planted his foot in the stirrup and shouted the horse into a dead run as he flung his right leg over the horse's back.

He had to fight Pilsner's inclination to head west, toward the stables, instead pulling constantly to his left to keep the animal headed toward the paddock. He had no idea how soon the shooter would be in range to fire on her, but it would be desperately close.

He sat low and bent forward to keep his seat, nearly lost it when he reined Pilsner into a sudden right turn to take advantage of the concealment a slight elevation in the landscape offered him. The decision was a toss-up. If the shooter saw him coming, he might abandon the attempt. But it was equally likely that sighting Matt would spur the shooter on to greater efforts or afford him two targets.

Pilsner's hooves pounded the earth, and Matt knew the cloud of dust rising up behind him might tip the shooter to his approach. The ridge he rode behind kept Fiona out of his own view for three or four minutes. Gauging the distance Pilsner's wild run had covered, he crested the hill and scoured the tree-covered mountainside for any indication of the shooter's position. He took precious seconds to rein the horse to a stop and look through the binoculars, then cursed the waste of time.

He'd seen no movement, and the inference that the shooter had already taken up a position made his blood chill.

He spurred Pilsner to an all-out run again. He had a quarter to a half mile before he reached Fiona. The wind would keep her from hearing the frantic beat of Pilsner's hooves. If she happened to glance in his direction, she might realize something was terribly wrong, but he had no doubt that she would run in a beeline toward him, giving the shooter a clear shot at her head and back.

Riding full bore, he watched her walking alongside one of the mustangs inside the training pen. Every trip around the circular pen took her into the shooter's line of fire and then out again as the mustang blocked a clear shot.

He screamed at her against the wind to get out of the pen, knowing it was useless. But inside that pen there was no way he could get to her, and that was her only chance.

Otherwise, the sniper had her like fish in a bowl.

She was dog tired, he could see that when he had

less than five hundred yards to go. Then she looked up and saw him coming, and he let his senses go wild with hope that she would somehow know that if he was riding at her this hard from one direction, there was a terrible danger lurking from its opposite.

All she had to do was keep the mustang's body between her and the sniper. Instead she walked away from him and opened the gate to turn the mustang out into the larger paddock. And she was left standing there with no more protection than the steel pipes shaping the training pen, put together like tinker toys.

Two hundred yards out…

She was halfway across the pen in Matt's direction when the first bullet rang by her ear and ripped into the ground six feet in front of her. The shooter had aimed for her head and missed, but in that split second, she must have put it all together—the danger, the bullet, Matt coming at her hell-bent. She dove to the ground. The second bullet bit the dirt no more than six inches to the left of her head.

She screamed and scrambled, crawling, hurling her body forward to get under the lowest steel pipe of the training pen. The third shot slammed into the pipe as she scrabbled beneath it.

With forty yards to go he screamed at her again to get up. She had no chance at all unless he could scoop her up onto Pilsner with him, cut and turn and ride out of range of the sniper's rifle, but she had to be terrified to rise up and make a bigger target of herself.

She crawled away from the fence, toward Pilsner, her attention splintered in ninety different directions. Who? Why? She was going to die. How many shots would it take? She could feel through the earth the pounding of hooves now but they seemed out of

synch with the reality of Pilsner bearing down on her.
She heard Matt screaming at her again and again to
get up. At the last second she understood what he
wanted her to do, how he was going to save her life.
She gathered together what wits and strength remained in her, crouched into a position to spring up
toward him, and when he was upon her, she leapt up
and reached for his arm as a fourth bullet bit into the
ground where she had just been.

He slid halfway off Pilsner's back, leaning down
to scoop her up without tearing her arm from its
socket, and for one terrifying moment as Pilsner leapt
forward and bolted on, she thought she would drag
them both down.

Matt threw his body hard back up into the saddle,
lowered the horse's reins in his left hand and with his
right arm and centrifugal force, swung her high
enough that she could throw her left leg over Pilsner's
head. Her leg cleared but her foot tangled in the reins.
Nearly on top of the saddle horn, she could not lean
forward to free her foot, for if she jerked her tangled
foot and yanked back on the reins, Pilsner would
come slamming to a stop.

At Pilsner's dead run, jolting like a rag doll, Matt
rose up in the stirrups and reached around her with
his right arm to untangle her foot from the reins. She
collapsed back against Matt, her body forced tight to
his by the steep angle of the pommel, but she was
alive.

She seated herself tighter still to his body as his
arm closed around her waist, giving Matt the space
he needed to guide Pilsner's wild run. Her head spun,
her thoughts came disconnected. Cradled against the
solid, comforting mass of his chest and his arms

around her, all she could think was that it took stunt-men weeks of practice to do what he had just done. How had he been able to do that?

How had he known she would come under attack at all? It seemed suspicious to her, but nothing was as it should be anymore.

The terrain grew steeper, and then they came into the trees, and still he spurred Pilsner on. The horse was laboring hard now, sweating, frothing, his breath almost gone. She took handfuls of Matt's shirt and reached down to touch his thigh and get his attention. "Matt, you're going to kill this horse if you don't stop now."

"Another hundred yards," he grated, "into the trees."

But through her rattled brain and aching body she knew that after another hundred yards had come and gone, he wasn't going to stop. Pilsner would go until he dropped dead; he had that kind of heart. He was a polo pony, bred and cultivated for sprint and en-durance, but he ran in the open on grassy fields, not a steeply pitched and treacherous forest floor. He had never been tested like this. He wouldn't know when to stop.

She had to do it for him. Before Matt could react, she had grabbed hold of Pilsner's reins and pulled sharply. The horse reared midstride and she threw all her weight backward against Matt, hard enough that though he fought for balance, he lost it and they both fell off onto the carpet of pine needles inches deep.

Pilsner shook his tremendous head about, stamping and snorting. Matt was on his feet, coming at her, looking to throttle her. She scrambled to her own feet and they stood there like a pair of wrestlers.

Nearly doubled over, Matt fought for the air that had been knocked out of him. "If you ever do anything that damned dumb again—"

"You'll what, you—you idiot!" She threw her arm in Pilsner's direction. "Look at him, Matt! His sides are heaving so hard he's—" She bit off her tirade. "Look, I'm not ungrateful, it's just that—"

"Oh, yes, you are." His hands were planted on his thighs and he couldn't help stooping, he hurt so bad.

"It's just that he's exhausted. And don't tell me I'm ungrateful. You know squat about my feelings!"

Dragging in the thin mountain air, he glared up at her sideways. "Oh, I think I know squat enough, princess. You're a pampered, spoiled little *brat* who has to have everything her way."

"Are you done yet?" Tears flooded into her eyes. He had saved her life.

"I haven't even covered ungrateful yet." He forced himself to stand up straight and tall, despite the pain. "And cut the waterworks display, princess. It ticks me off."

"Oh, well, we can't have that! What about any of this suggests I'm having my way?"

"The fact that you're standing here screaming at me when you should be kissing my feet?"

"How about the fact that in another hundred yards, carrying both of us, poor Pilsner would have collapsed and died?"

He spun away from her and snatched up his half-smashed hat, knocking it back into shape. "Start walking, then, if you're so worried."

She got to Pilsner's reins and started to turn him back down the mountain.

"Wrong." Matt eased his fingers into Pilsner's halter and began pull gently the other way. The horse started up with him. "We're going uphill."

She double-timed several paces to catch up to him, nearly tripping over a tree root half buried in the thick layer of pine needles. "Matt, it's almost dark! What is wrong with you? Did you hit your head? Where uphill?"

"The hunting lodge."

"The lodge is at least another couple of miles from here!"

He stopped midstride, let go of Pilsner's halter and turned on her. Toe-to-toe with him, he stood uphill from her, towering over her. "Fiona, I know where the lodge is, okay? The ranch is just as far."

"But at least it's downhill that way!"

"Yeah, and there's a sniper waiting that way."

"Oh." She scraped her hand through her hair and the tears came flooding back. She couldn't stop them this time. She didn't know what to do, what to say, why it hadn't occurred to her muddled brain that the sniper might be lying in wait.

Matt reached out and yanked her into his arms, took a handful of her hair in his hand and pulled back till her lips were a whisper away from his. "So help me God, princess, I am going to keep you alive." Still angry with her, he crushed his lips down on hers. Still half in shock, she returned his kiss with a fierceness, a depth of anger and passion she had never known.

Chapter Eight

When his mouth opened, she bit his lip, not too hard, but hard enough. As she eased the pressure he bit hers, just as hard. They were wild and angry nips, deadly silent, separated by heated thrusts of their tongues dueling, tasting, staking possession, claiming shelter and abandon.

Frantic to get closer, to feel safer, to create between their bodies the punishment they both dished out in that fierce and hungry kiss, she thrust her arms beneath his and took hold of his shoulders with her hands. She uttered a growl of her own and curled a long leg around the back of his and pulled herself up, climbing him until she could lock her legs around his waist.

He took a step back to rebalance, but misgauged and they fell to the forest floor together, not a far distance for the steep angle. Pilsner stamped and snuffled and the wind howled in the trees above them. She lay straddling Matt, closer and safer in his arms but in another realm of danger altogether, and still their lips never parted, save for ragged gaping breaths.

He brought his hands up to frame her face. Cold and roughened and scraped, his gentle touch simply took her breath away. And the angry kisses, the biting and tearing at each other, grew into something less frenzied, far deeper, a kiss to end all kisses.

Emotions of every stripe clawed at her. Fear and sheer terror. Anger, gratitude, shame. She lifted her mouth from his and looked into his beautiful dark eyes. "I'm sorry."

He cupped her neck with his fingers, stroked her chin with his thumb. "I'm not."

She swallowed back tears. "Will we ever agree on anything?"

"Not so long as the kissing and making up is this swell." He gave a pained grin. "Makes me hurt."

She blushed. One of those acquired skills to be dispensed with care and feminine cunning, perhaps Year Seven in the sequence of flirting and curtsying, patting masculine cheeks, and saying no prettily. This blush arose without the first thought of any artifice at all. "We should go."

"Yeah. We should go."

THEY REACHED THE LODGE an hour after dark, exhausted and hungry. Fiona took Pilsner into the stable, unsaddled, brushed and fed him while Matt scouted the perimeter of the building.

Unprepared to pick any locks, he hunted around for a rock to break the window of the door.

He crashed it through to make it look as if common vandals had done the deed, then reached in and opened the door. "After you," He said to Fiona, who'd joined him.

She stepped in, crunched over glass and reached to flip on the light switch. He stopped her. "We can't afford to take any chances. Are there any flashlights around?''

"Of course. In the service pantry. Or paraffin lanterns, whichever.'' He came into the pantry with her and chose the lanterns and lit two with a wooden match, turning the flames low. "Can we at least turn up the heat? It won't warm the place up much before morning, but—''

"Do it. I want to take a look around for a while. Can you open a few of these cans, make us something to eat?''

"You want dog food or artichoke hearts?'' She turned around but he had already slipped away. She dashed off to the bathroom, then turned up the thermostat. They would need some hot water to wash up, so she lit the pilot to heat a pot of water.

She found a canned ham and green beans and put them both into an iron kettle to heat. Matt still hadn't returned by the time she'd washed her face and hands. Or by the time the ham and beans began to boil. She turned the flame low and went to look for him.

Carrying the lantern, she went through all the main-floor rooms, calling softly without finding him, but then noticed the door leading to the cellar stood slightly ajar.

She'd never been to the basement.

She scolded herself for a ninny and descended to the cellar, ignoring the chill and eeriness of her shadow against the wall. "Matt? Are you down here?''

He didn't answer. After a moment she heard a distant thump and followed the noise through an unexpected door in what should have been a foundation wall. The moment she opened it and saw the long cinder-block hallway, fifty or more feet of it, her pulse began to knock about.

She wouldn't have gone on without the certainty that this was what was keeping Matt. She followed the hallway to the end where she dragged in a breath to steady herself and opened yet another door onto yet another hallway of cinder-blocks. There were four heavy metal doors off this hall.

She shoved the handle down on the first door, and from behind it, saw the soft glow of Matt's lantern. She shoved open the door and entered a dark, echoing cavernous space, which on all sides was stocked with large wooden crates stamped with discreet black letters. Matt sat on the concrete floor with his back to the cinder blocks.

A crowbar lay on the floor beside him, and an opened crate. In his hands was the kind of automatic weapon she had only seen in movies.

There were stacks and stacks of those crates.

Nothing she had seen prepared her for this. The stench of virgin metal and gun oil. The eerie silence of this cavern filled with death-dealing tools.

Matt spared her a glance, but whatever he saw couldn't begin to describe how defiled she felt. Kyle Everly had built a virtual armory, carving it into the side of the mountain beneath the hunting lodge her father had built thirty years ago.

She turned and fled through the door, back the way she'd come, flying up the stairs to the bathroom because her stomach was heaving and she knew it wouldn't stop.

MATT REPLACED the assault weapon in the crate he'd pulled from a shelf. Hunger finally won out over the need to further explore the chamber of horrors he'd discovered beneath the hunting lodge. He came upon a wine cellar on his return through the bunker and quickly selected a white wine from among the most expensive bottles.

He found Fiona sitting at the table in the dark kitchen, her lantern extinguished, her fingers fisted and tight against her lips. She'd just gotten one hell of a reality check. And though the bunker had sent shock waves coursing even through him, he knew she must be grieving for what Everly had done to the ranch.

The scent of ham and green beans made his stomach growl. He put his lantern down on the countertop beside the stove, dug around in the drawers until he came up with a corkscrew, opened the wine and poured glasses for them both.

He wouldn't coddle her, wouldn't try to soften the blow or minimize the horror. She had to come to terms with the facts. There wasn't just the odd notion now that she was in danger. She had been shot at. Someone had tried to kill her, probably the same sniper that had taken Everly out. And now she'd seen with her own eyes how high the stakes were.

Despite his intentions, he found himself taking the serving utensils out of her hands, drawing her into his arms. She came without a fight, without a whimper. She rested her forehead against his, her breath mingled with his, her body softened against him. Her tears fell into the hollow beneath his throat.

He supposed he had meant to give her some comfort, but stirrings of desire, of heat, rose up in him and for a few unguarded moments he wanted nothing more than to make love to her. To chase away the pain of her memories and the fresh insult of seeing how Everly had defiled everything she cared about.

Embracing her head in his hand, her scent filling his senses, he nearly gave in to the temptation. So nearly. She dragged in a deep breath and pulled out of his arms.

"Are you going to be okay?"

She took back the utensils he'd taken out of her hands. "I just didn't think it was possible to hate Kyle Everly any more than I already did."

"You want to tell me what happened with Soldier?"

She stirred the pot one last time, and began to talk about coming back to the ranch. About her decision to bring Soldier Boy with her. What a mistake that had been from the start. Everly behaved from the first as if he owned them both.

"A time came when entries had to be sent in for the National Western stock show in Denver. Kyle wanted to me to show Soldier Boy. I told him I wouldn't do it. Soldier Boy was head and shoulders above the competition there. I'd competed with him in the Olympic trials, Matt."

She interrupted herself to direct Matt to the cabinet where the plates were kept. "It just wouldn't have been fair, but Kyle had it in his head that he wanted a big win at the National Western and he didn't care what it would look like, how it would offend people. He was a lot like my mother."

She ladled beans and ham into oversize soup bowls. "How much of this do you want?"

He inhaled the aromatic steam rising off the pot. "I'll be having seconds." She filled his bowl and handed it to him. He sat down and dug in. "Go on. I'm listening. About your mother."

She sat down with her own bowl. "Growing up with Marianne Halsey was a little like having Morticia Addams for a mother."

Matt grinned, though she wasn't smiling.

"It's true. Do you remember how it thrilled Morticia when her bratty offspring exhibited some evil behavior?" He nodded. "Well, my mother was just like her, though maybe a little more subtle. To give a second thought to the feelings and opinions of commoners was simply a dreadful waste of time. Of course, it would never have occurred to her to enter a horse of Soldier Boy's caliber into such a gauche and common exercise as a rodeo venue, anyway."

"But Everly would."

"Yes. He had the same attitude. The world was his personal oyster."

Kyle Everly was a profiteer without conscience, Matt thought, and the attitude didn't stop at money. "He usually got what he wanted, didn't he?"

Fiona nodded and took a drink of her wine. "I wasn't going to give in. There was no point in entering the National Western. I still retained title to Soldier Boy, but all his training, all those hours of practice, all the feed, the board, all of it was on the Bar Naught's nickel. The way Kyle saw it, I owed him. Just a month before I'd refused to go to a Winter Ball in Sheridan with him."

Matt swallowed and cleared his throat. "Was he hitting on you?"

"A lot of the time, yes. Mostly waiting, I think, for me to accept, so he could put me right back in my place." She paused and took a few bites of her dinner. The light flickering from the lantern cast threatening shadows on the wall that transformed her memories of Kyle to something even more sinister. "Anyway. The National Western. I refused to go. The weather was bad, the roads were guaranteed to get slick and dangerous. He got very angry at me, but I thought the discussion was over."

Matt could predict what had happened next. Everly had loaded up the horse and taken off down the road himself, knowing it was a pointless exercise without Fiona to ride Soldier in the show. He let her go on at her own pace.

"I went into town for an errand. It took me longer to get home than it should have because the roads were already iced over. By the time I got back, he was gone with Soldier Boy." Even now she couldn't think of those events without tears glazing her eyes. Her throat felt hot. "I went inside to call the highway patrol, and then I heard a truck pulling into the yard. Until I heard the second door slam shut, I thought he had given up and come back."

"He'd had an accident," Matt guessed.

Fiona nodded. "A couple of guys from the highway patrol came to get me. Kyle had crashed the truck in such a way that Soldier's trailer broke the hitch and rolled over and over down a ravine. These guys told me the trailer was crumpled and in flames when they got there. They managed to put out the fire. Soldier wasn't dead, but they figured there wasn't any sense trying to get him out. They'd have to bring in someone with an acetylene torch to cut through the metal."

"So why didn't they put him down?"

"Kyle wouldn't hear of it. He insisted they come

get me. He told them he thought I would want to put Soldier Boy down myself.''

Matt clamped a hand over his face, a thumb gripping one side of his jaw, his fingers on the other. His fingers seemed to waver in her vision. She knew it couldn't be hard for him to believe Everly could be so emotionally brutal as to bring her out to destroy her beloved Soldier Boy.

All these months. Still, she hated Kyle Everly till it wore her raw in her heart. Every hour she spent with Soldier was another hour she spent hating Kyle Everly. Maybe Matt could see now why she *would* have kissed the man who killed the son of a bitch.

Maybe he would even understand why she had to be there when the members of The Fraternity gathered on the Bar Naught for the big game-hunting trip.

She straightened, stiffening her spine. Her instructions via the e-mail from her father were clear. She had to keep her trap shut.

She brushed away the tears and went on. ''I took my rifle in case I had to do it. There were already a couple of guys there trying to cut Soldier out. He screamed for hours, until I could get a clear shot with a tranquilizer gun. He was lame for a while. His flesh had burned against the metal, that's why he's scarred, but he didn't have even one broken bone.''

Matt put down his fork. ''Fiona, I'm so sorry.''

What else was there to say? Her heart was broken, and Everly had done the breaking.

She looked at Matt for the first time since she began. ''I should never have returned to the Bar Naught with Soldier. Don't you see? He trusted me. Soldier trusted me completely, and I left the ranch and gave that bastard the opportunity to drive off with him.''

''Fiona, you couldn't have known what would happen.''

Her lips pressed together but their trembling didn't stop. Her focus went soft, as if she were seeing Soldier Boy in her mind's eye, refusing to stand still for her, bent on driving her away forever. ''I wouldn't trust me again, either. But God help me—'' she broke off, her voice thick with tears she would not let go ''—it hurts.''

Most of all, Matt thought, because of that first night when Soldier had tolerated Matt's touch, and she didn't know why.

He wished he understood it himself. And that he hadn't rubbed her nose in it when she'd caught him in Soldier's stall.

CHRISTO FINALLY FELL ASLEEP, an achievement unparalleled in the annals of childhood. Matt had sent him another secret agent message with word of taming mustangs. Garrett carried his son up to bed and wandered into their bedroom. Kirsten was propped up in bed, as uncomfortable as she thought it was possible to be. She refused to turn cranky, but after eight days, her mood was on a downhill skid.

''You're worried about him, aren't you?'' she asked.

He shrugged and sat down beside her. ''Matt can take care of himself.''

''I know he can. That's not the point.''

Garrett cleared his throat and announced abruptly, ''J.D. and Ann are coming over.''

''Now?''

''Just for a beer.'' He tried to make it seem casual, for no particular reason, but as usual, Kirsten saw through him. They needed to talk away from the operations headquarters.

"Hand me my robe and brush."

"Nope. I'm not bringing them up here. We won't bother you."

She gave him a look. "I want to know what's going on, Garrett."

"I'm not giving on this, Kirsten. The answer is no."

"I didn't ask you."

"You know what I mean. You're not well. You shouldn't be worried about anything right now. You've got enough going on as it is."

She dug in. "We've been through this, Garrett. I'll be more upset if I don't know than if I do." The doorbell rang. "Can I have my robe now, at least? Please?"

He sighed heavily. He was sure he must have refused her other things, other wishes, but at the moment he couldn't remember one. It was about to turn him into a sorehead, which he didn't have time to indulge. He indulged her instead, gave in and helped her sit forward to spread the robe over her shoulders and breasts, then gave her the brush. "One sign that you're tiring, Kirsten, and—"

"Answer the door, Weisz." She relented a little, too. "If I'm too tired, okay. But I'm not now."

He returned with J.D. and Ann, beers in hand for the three of them and a bottle of juice for Kirsten. J.D. looked so pained just looking at her mountainous belly beneath the covers that Kirsten groaned aloud. "That bad?"

Ann laughed. "Don't mind him. He's in shock."

She gave Kirsten a sweet, glorious smile. "We just tested this morning. We're pregnant."

Garrett busted out all over, crowing. J.D. had been accusing him of being crabbier than Kirsten ever since the no-sex dictate had come down. "I told you, Thorne. He who laughs last laughs best."

Ann and J.D. sat together on Garrett's side of the bed. Kirsten asked about Ann's son, Jaz. The couple exchanged anxious glances, then Ann gave a bittersweet smile. "He seems all right at home, but he was caught shoplifting yesterday."

"Oh, Ann, I'm sorry," Kirsten murmured, holding out a hand to the one friend who knew what it was to be unnaturally separated from her little boy. "I'm sure it's just a phase."

"I wanted to call in a few favors," J.D. said. "Give the kid a break. Ann thought he ought to have to face the music now, before it gets any more serious." The strain between them, especially on what should have been a joyful day with Ann's pregnancy, was hard to watch. "He's in juvie hall for the weekend. We'll see him on Monday."

Garrett offered whatever help he could, but J.D. was clearly anxious to get on with the problem at hand. The conversation turned quickly to e-mail that had been intercepted coming out of and into the Bar Naught. Fiona Halsey's e-mail.

Garrett told Kirsten now what the issue was. "She e-mailed her father in Florida that Everly had been shot."

"No mention of Matt at all," J.D. put in.

"And her father returned a message within a couple of hours." Garrett recited from memory. "It said, Do not give it up. Keep the faith. Remember the old saying, 'Three can keep a secret if two are dead.' No good deed goes unpunished, Fiona. Regards, Dad.''

"What a swell dad," Kirsten murmured. "What does it mean?"

Ann answered. "It makes you wonder if Everly is now dead so some secret doesn't get out."

"We've also thought the 'no good deed ever goes unpunished' remark might have been a warning to Fiona to keep playing along with whatever brought her back in the first place," J.D. suggested.

"Something happened today to clarify it all?" Kirsten asked.

"That's why we're here." J.D. gave her an apologetic glance, then spoke to Garrett. "I wanted there to be no chance we were overheard by anyone when I showed you this." He rose up off the bed and pulled a couple of folded sheets of paper from his back pocket.

J.D. handed the papers to Garrett, who unfolded the sheets where Kirsten could see them as well. They were hard copies of the messages from Fiona Halsey to her father, and back. Exactly the same, Garrett thought, as he had already seen. "What am I looking for?"

J.D. grimaced. "I didn't know, either. This is where we usually punt to Guiliani. He'd figure it out in maybe five minutes. Me? Forget it." He sank back down beside Ann. "Long story short, Fiona's messages to and from her dad passed through a network we've never heard of. *No* one's ever heard of."

"The tech, Skip Tsumagari, is alarmed," Ann added, "because e-mail is so vulnerable that even novice computer hackers do it for kicks. But this is different. This is what Tsumagari called a 'node' in the networks that even he can't trace.''

Garrett finally understood the reason J.D. needed to talk outside the office.

Matt had been compromised, and the threat to him lay concealed at the heart of this operation.

Chapter Nine

"When I was a kid in New York, we lived in a walk-up. The kind you see on television with fire escape stairs that swing down the side of the building. I was five or six before I got heavy enough to make them go down. I didn't really have an escape hatch from my old man till then. Once I could get away from the son of a bitch, he walked out on my mom. No sport anymore."

Still at the kitchen table in the hunting lodge, sitting with a second bottle of wine, he'd racked his brain for a way to put her finally at ease enough to tell him the truth. Maybe if she knew him, knew where he'd come from, he thought. Women were like that. He knew it to be true. The more he talked, the more they talked. The more vulnerable he appeared to make himself, the more they opened up. He hadn't made a study of the subject, but he knew. He wasn't above exploiting what he knew, but the truth was, he loved women. He was crazy about Kirsten and Ann, and in some ways he was closer to them than either Garrett or J.D.

He turned on the charmer inside himself and started to tell Fiona what a loner he had always been. What a freaky little kid, who'd been knocked down enough that he should have figured out early on that it was safer if you didn't pop back up like some empty-headed jack-in-the-box. "Never quite got the hang of playing possum. When I did…" he shrugged. "Guess I never looked back."

He'd figured out that he wanted no part of another SOB destined to beat the crap out of him. When his mom let another one just like his father move in, and Matt's attitude failed to adjust, his mother had shipped him across town. A place where being a loner punk made him a target of the pups who ran together. He started running his own scams.

If only he could have seen his way out. He thought again of Robbie, how lucky the kid was.

Matt polished off the dregs of his third serving of ham and beans. His hunger pangs had worn off. He used a paper towel for a napkin, poured more wine and went on.

"One day a cop on a horse chased me down and whacked me alongside the head with a billy club. Dragged me up by my raggedy collar and hauled me off to a cell next to men the cop said would soon be my peers."

The night he'd spent in the hoosegow got through to him. He changed his mind on the fly about the direction his life was going to take. He decided he wanted the power to knock a few heads together.

"There I was, minding my own business." He had her listening now, reveling at twists and turns his evolution to undercover cop had taken. "I was getting paid to be a snitch for the cops and looking to get into the police academy so I could thump heads together with impunity. I was doing my thing, horning in on the business of low-life drug runners, when a call came down from One Police Plaza. Turned out I was a dead ringer for the son and heir of Alex Karamedes.''

"The Greek antiquities dealer?'' she asked, drawn into his story now.

Matt nodded. "Seventh-richest man in the world and a crook of the highest water. He didn't speak a word of Greek, by the way.''

"Really?''

"Really.''

"I remember when he went to prison,'' she mused. "I was in high school. The story was all over the news.''

Matt nodded. "Sixteen years ago. The son, my double, even had the same name as me. Mateos. The New York City police commissioner and his staff were working with international authorities to put an undercover agent into Karamedes's inner circle. Their plan was to snatch young Mateos and return me when Karamedes paid the ransom.''

"How could they know Karamedes would pay it?''

"They couldn't be sure, but the timing was critical. They knew Alex doted on his son, and that he had begun bringing Mateos into all his deals, teaching him the ropes. You couldn't ask for a better undercover setup, since Matty-boy was being tutored and groomed to take over one day.'' He shoved his bowl aside and laid his arms on the table. "The dicey part was making me over to be able to pull off the switch. I didn't have to learn Greek, but we're talking the Musketeers elevating a country bumpkin DiCaprio to the throne of France to get rid of a tyrant monarch— and about as traumatic all around, too.''

"You actually pulled it off?"

He nodded. "I spent five months learning the bit, and another eighteen playing Mateos Karamedes. Alex never doubted I was his son. I was changed, no question, but a stint in the hands of brutal kidnappers will do that to a young man."

"How did they keep the real Mateos hidden away that long?"

He grinned. He had her nearly smiling now. "That was the easy part. It didn't take the real Mateos long to see the handwriting on the wall. His old man was going to go down, and when he did, Mateos would come into his father's fortune." He gave her a self-mocking grin. "And that, princess, is how I became so suave and debonair."

She smiled, teasing. "An unqualified success."

"Thanks." He mimed a bow. "But it wasn't unqualified."

"What do you mean?"

"We never got close to identifying the man Karamedes called his 'guardian angel.'"

"Are you saying Alex Karamedes was the victim of a protection racket?"

"Not exactly. Alex would call it insurance, if he talked about it at all, which he didn't." Matt sat back, took a cedar stick from his pocket and stuck it between his teeth. "Over a year's time, I personally wired more than twenty million dollars to one account in the Cayman Islands."

"Twenty million? A year?"

Matt laughed. "Pocket change for a man like Karamedes, Fiona. To him, it was just the cost of doing business." He looked at her puzzled expression. "What?"

"I was just wondering why Alex wouldn't have told you who this guardian angel was."

"He told me I would know when the time came. But Alex wouldn't give up a name even when he went to prison."

"What about all the little people this guardian angel would have had to pay off?"

Matt grimaced. "Nothing ever panned out. Underlings are notoriously cheap. He could have made a small army of dirty cops and customs agents, harbormasters, even tax collectors exceedingly happy with even one million in payola. That's billions of drachmas, you know." He shoved his empty bowl away and drummed his fingers on the table.

"It really bothers you, that this guardian angel got away?"

He thought a moment, not because he couldn't answer her in a word, but because he'd seen both sides. "I've known cops on the take, Fiona. Most of them were basically good men. I remember one who tithed his ten cents on every dollar of payola he took. The money sent their kids to college, or paid for the mother-in-law's cancer operation. And sometimes, it seems like Robin Hood, you know? But you just can't get past the fact it's wrong. It's evil. It's... I don't know. Dehumanizing. Cops shouldn't be dirty. So the short answer to your question is, I would rather have lost Karamedes and nailed his guardian angel."

He sighed heavily. "And here we are again. We started out to get Everly, and he's dead, hit by a professional we will never get. My guess is that his own man pulled the trigger—"

"Geary? You think Geary did it?"

"Yeah, I do. I could be wrong, but the way Dex

is handling this, no one will ever be prosecuted. We might eventually nail Dex with obstruction of justice, but other than that we might as well dismantle the bunker, close up shop and call it a day. Everly's dead, and the rest of these bastards in The Fraternity aren't in U.S. jurisdiction, anyway.''

She sipped her wine, considering. ''Matt, if Everly was your target, why are you going through with all of this?''

He moved the cedar stick from one corner of his mouth to the other, regarding her more closely than she could have imagined. There was no point any longer in not telling her what he was doing, why he was here. He'd been angling the conversation toward giving her reason to trust him. To finally give up what her own purposes were.

He knew she was in some kind of trouble. His best guess was that she had made some kind of deal with Everly's enemies. He knew desperate times led to desperate measures. He wouldn't blame her if she had tried, but he couldn't afford to be blindsided. Not going up against the kind of men who stockpiled an armory in the middle of Wyoming and doled it out for mind-bending profit.

So he laid it out for her. ''Because Interpol wants Everly's cohorts. All of them.''

She put down her wineglass very carefully. ''Interpol?''

''Yeah.'' His heartbeat slowed. He'd been in the game too long to miss her studied indifference. ''What about Interpol, Fiona?''

''You tell me.''

''I just did.''

She stood up with her studied indifference and started to take away their plates.

"Sit down, Fiona."

She set down the bowls. "I'm tired, Matt."

"Look on the bright side. You could be dead." He watched her expression go slack, but the time for dealing gently with her had come and gone. Whatever else he had accomplished with telling her his past, a confession from her wasn't one of them. And if seeing the bunker hadn't put the fear of God into her, he didn't know what would.

"What do you want from me, Matt? What do you want me to say? That I'm scared? Okay. I'm scared. But that doesn't change anything."

He cut through all her evasions. If she was dealing with Everly's enemies for the ranch, she might see herself as a target of Interpol. But she had bigger worries than that. "Has it occurred to you, princess, that you may not survive the week? That whoever wanted Everly dead has no use for you, either?"

She started to say something and then choked. She made a joke of it. "Maybe no one would have tried to kill me if you had let Dex take me off to jail." She gave a wavering sigh. "Is there any way out of this, because I really don't like either alternative?"

"Not if you stay on the Bar Naught."

"I'm not leaving, Matt."

"I'll put the gravedigger on notice then." He reached for the wine bottle off the countertop and sloshed the remains in his glass. "Where do you want to be buried?"

She swallowed. Her fingers fell slack at the base of her own empty glass. The faint hiss of oil burning in the lantern filled the silence. "Do you have to work at being so callous?"

"Nope." He shook his head. "It comes naturally now."

She could only stare at his rigid expression. "How do you do that? How do you act as if you don't care?"

"Just like that. I act as if." He shrugged. "It's my personal gold standard." He was angry at her blithe little assertion that she was staying on the Bar Naught—and that after seeing what she'd seen in that bunker, and after coming a couple of measly inches of death in the training pen. More angry than he had been at anyone in a very long time.

He didn't care if she understood him. In fact, he'd prefer it if she didn't. He'd been wild-eyed scared in his heart, watching her with Robbie and that mustang, that she'd turn her wickedly smart intuition on him.

If there was a gene for "callous," he'd been born without it, like some albino without protective pigment. He'd spent his entire life compensating, pretending he had a double dose of it instead. It had taken him too damn many years learning to fake disregard for people's feelings—his own for that matter. Too many years to give it up to her now.

"I've been undercover most of my life, Fiona. You don't get to have feelings."

"What an inspired choice of a career for you!"

"Yeah," he snarled. "I prefer it that way. Feelings get you nothing but trouble. Feelings make you vulnerable. Feelings are the leading cause of stupid decisions."

"Like staying on the Bar Naught?"

"Like staying on the Bar Naught. Damn straight."

"Which accounts for you staying."

"It's my job."

"It's my *life*," she cried, standing up. "Don't you get that?" She banged the heel of her hand against her head. "What am I thinking? Of course you don't get that. You are Mr. Secret Agent Man! You don't *have* a life!" But she was mocking him. She already knew him too well. "Would you be this damned mad at me if you didn't have feelings? If you weren't worried about me? If we weren't—"

He jerked her down into his lap and clamped his mouth tight against her, to shut her up, to keep her from saying aloud what he couldn't imagine hearing. If she wouldn't tell him the truth, he would just have to find a way to take her out of the picture himself. But he *was* half in love with her, and apparently, he hadn't hidden it very well at all.

Not even from himself.

THEY RODE BACK DOWN to the ranch from the hunting lodge under cover of lengthening shadows. Matt had spent most of the morning going through the armory and scouting out the landscape surrounding the lodge and the bunker beneath it.

He used up most of an hour just familiarizing himself with the security system and the locks to all exterior doors, including the two entrances to the bunker itself. He wanted to know how to get out, and fast, if…when the time came. It mattered just as much that he be able to get in.

At one o'clock they began the long, arduous ride back down to the ranch house, made more difficult by the zigzag path they cut to foil the sniper, should he still be waiting. Matt had also taken from the bunker bulletproof gear, which they wore over their clothes and draped over Pilsner's head and neck.

In all, the ride took over five hours. A half mile from the house, Matt left her in the cover of a thick stand of pine with Pilsner, and set off downhill to make sure the sniper hadn't put himself in a position to pick them off as they approached the house. She waited nearly two hours for Matt's whistle, the signal they arranged indicating all clear, then rode down, still fearful that a marksman could pick her off from a greater range than Matt could possibly have vetted.

The waning, brilliant orange sun had long since dropped beneath the tree-studded horizon. For the last half mile, headed for the stable, Pilsner barreled along at a faster and faster clip. Fiona rose up in her seat as the horse approached the stable door, then swung her leg up and over, dropping to the ground, dead tired. The saddle creaked as she dismounted.

Matt took Pilsner's reins from her. "I'll put him away. You go to your rooms, pick out a pretty dress and—"

"For what?"

"For me."

"Forget it." She shook her head now, emphatically. "I'm going to feed the horses and then go straight to a hot shower and my bed. I want to be alone, I want—"

"I'm not talking about playing dress-up, Fiona. We're going out to dinner at the country club." He walked off, leading Pilsner inside the stables. "Shower in the main house. Take some extra clothes. You'll be staying with me from now on."

Frustration nipped at her exhaustion. What was she

going to say? *No, I'll take my chances alone and iso-lated.*

Alone.

That was what got to her. Not that in refusing to go with Matt she'd be taking her chances with a killer on the loose. It was that alone, she realized suddenly, was the last place she wanted to be. She'd had time to figure that out lying in the same room with him, pretending she was asleep, listening to the sounds of his breathing.

She followed Matt and Pilsner into the stable, and checked in Fincher's stall. The horse she'd taken down to the training pen last afternoon had found his way back, but he was still saddled, and his reins hung to the ground. Dennis Geary had clearly gone AWOL. Fincher looked reproachfully at Fiona, tossing his head, stomping his displeasure. She quickly unburdened Fincher, fed him and the others while Matt took care of Pilsner.

"You're not serious about going out, are you?"

"I've never been more serious in my life, princess." He glanced up, and she realized that no matter how tired he was, indulging weariness was a thing he didn't know how to do. "The Johnson County upper crust has a pressing need to meet Everly's replacement."

"Well, you don't need me for that."

He kept currying Pilsner's coat. "I thought we'd reached an understanding, Fiona." In the lantern light, she saw anger skid across his face. A sudden unguarded emotion. "I thought we were done with the bickering. Now can I have a little faith?"

She ducked her head, clasped her hands and came foolishly close to wringing them, but the word alone seemed to paralyze her for an instant. What faith had she left in anyone?

She knew he had meant to win her over last night, to give her reason to have faith in him. He'd laid all his cards on the table, been frank and even unflattering about himself with the odd, stark pieces of his history and his undercover life as Mateos Karamedes.

She was no one's fool. She had watched him spin elaborate lies off the top of his head. His personal stories could be complete fabrications offered up with cold calculation in a callous bid to fake her out and win her over. But the flash of anger was true.

He was disappointed in her.

Her chin went up. She blinked to make the dampness in her eyes go away. "Seating is always at eight. Even if I could be ready in time—"

"Listen up, princess, because I am dog tired of debating every move with you." He planted his feet in space she considered hers. "Your life has been threatened. If I hadn't been there to snatch you out of harm's way, they'd be gussying up your coffin as we speak. So here's the deal. Unless you want to go into hiding or take yourself off to a nunnery, where good girls aren't even safe in the movies, you're looking at twenty-four-seven in my company."

"I know that, but that doesn't mean I'm going to play out your fantasies."

"No danger of that."

She took a step back. The look he sent her made it clear his fantasies didn't involve a mixer with the country club social stratum. She swallowed.

"Look." He jammed his hands into his pockets. "Fiona, did I take advantage of you last night?"

The question was not a fair one. If by "taking advantage'' he meant had he laid a hand on her, then the answer was no.

"Answer me, Fiona.'' It was her crack about indulging his fantasies that had him still bristling.

"No. You didn't take advantage of me. So what?''

"So, I don't intend to do that tonight, either. Or any other night.'' He gave her a stern look, which might have persuaded her but for the smoldering. "I'm not asking you to do this for my own gratification. I'm telling you because, as you will recall, someone was firing honest-to-God bullets at you, and—''

"And going out in public together is going to stop bullets? My God, Matt, I'm under suspicion of murder myself!''

"It will send a message, Fiona, that has to be sent.''

"What message?''

"That you're mine. And that messing with what is mine is not a life-enhancing proposition.''

Mine. She shivered. "Send a telegraph.''

"Fiona...''

She ignored the warning. "Send it Pony Express. Beam it off some satellite. I don't care. I wouldn't play Kyle Everly's plaything. I'm not going to do it for you, either.''

He closed in and took hold of her upper arm and pulled her close into his body, so angry with her she could feel the scalding heat of his wrath. "Then imagine, princess, that I am your Latin-lover boy-toy. It will not compromise the message. Pretend, if that's what it takes, that I am head over heels in love with you. Imagine I would go to the ends of the earth to avenge the loss of a hair on your pretty little head.''

He pulled her closer still. "Imagine," he whispered into her ear, "that I would track down and kill the offender with my bare hands because you were my one true love. My soul mate. My inamorata. Either way you want to play it, no one will dare lay a hand on you, and that, princess, not my gratification, is the point."

She opened her mouth to apologize, but the words would not come. Her heart stuck in her throat. He meant none of those words. He didn't love her. She wasn't his one true love or his soul mate or his inamorata. He'd taken care to cast them all in terms of pretending whatever she must, but for an instant that would be forever indelible in her mind, a thrill rocketed through her. The angry passion felt real. The words a declaration of feelings he had already gone out of his way to deny.

"I'm sorry," she whispered at last, more so for what passion, what devotion she would never have. "I'm sorry."

"Don't waste your time. Just decide, Fiona, because we don't have all night."

She backed away, spun on her heel, as much to conceal the tears pricking at her lids as to do his bidding. He was back to his heartless self, and she would do well to follow his example. She would have to trust him, no matter that when it was done, that indelible moment would haunt her the rest of her life.

She didn't want to die, tonight or any other. She must put her life in his protection. She turned back. She still needed answers.

"What were you really doing at the ranch that night?"

He went on currying Pilsner. "You mean, did I kill Everly?"

She waited him out.

He shook his head and exchanged the currycomb for a brush. "I didn't kill him, princess. No."

"Then why did you leave open the possibility that you had?"

"Because that's what I do, how I work." He started to explain, and she was sure he could spin her many more stories that would blow her away as to what you had to do, become and say if you lived the chameleon life he must lead. He shrugged. "You can't exploit an opportunity you've already closed off."

"Were you the one on the phone with Kyle when he was shot?"

"No."

"How did that lie keep your options open?"

He took long, firm strokes over Pilsner's glistening coat with the brush. "First of all, I didn't lie. I let it be assumed. But I wasn't just busting Hanifen's chops, Fiona. I was goading him to find out if he was the one on the phone with Everly."

"Dex? Why?"

"Because it's not out of the realm that whoever had Everly on the phone was the one setting him up for the kill."

"Dex?"

"Yes, Dex." He put the brush aside, turned Pilsner by the reins, slipped the halter off of his head and whacked the horse's flank. Pilsner headed for his stall. "We don't have all night, Fiona. What else do you want to know?"

He waited a moment, then said, "Go get whatever

you need from your apartment. And don't pull punches, Fiona. I expect something drop-dead gorgeous.''

She walked through the barn to her quarters, going straight to her closet and packing her things.

He was waiting for her outside the stable door. Apparently twenty-four-seven had not been an exaggeration. He walked along with her toward the house, allowing her her silence. At the top of the stairs she headed for her girlhood room. He took her elbow.

She understood his intent, but here she drew the line. "I'll need a couple of hours—"

"You've got *one*, princess."

He would have it all his way.

She would do exactly as she had been told. She would make him the envy of every man present. And a vengeful, foolish part of her hoped she would also make Matt Guiliani the envy of himself.

Chapter Ten

He took a long, hot pounding shower to ease his various aches and pains. The insides of his thighs were tender as boils, the bruise on his torso had spread down as far as his hip, and if he'd had his druthers, he'd have fallen onto the fluffy white duvet on the king-size bed in the guest suite and died.

But all that was required to get him going, he already had—the promise of the constant adrenaline drip he would get playing the role of himself gone over to the wrong side.

He wrapped the overlarge towel around his waist and shaved for the first time since he'd had only Miss Aimee's tired little looking glass to use for a mirror, then dried his hair and took down the suit he'd left hanging in the shower to steam out the wrinkles. It wasn't a tux; he owned three, but not having foreseen this night, packed none of them. The suit would have to do, but it would probably do fine.

He loved his clothes, had acquired the taste in his stint as the missing son of the world's seventh-wealthiest man, and he tended toward Italian designers. He drew on the trousers, satisfied that the crease remained sharp, then sat on the white duvet and put on silk-blend socks followed by his ankle holster, his shirt, a pair of ruby-studded cuff links, his suit coat and finally, dress boots.

He went outside and turned the engine on in the Bronco to warm the vehicle, then returned inside to the library. He was pouring himself a shot of Scotch when he heard Fiona begin to descend the carpeted stairs.

From his vantage point, her feet appeared first, clad in crystalline-looking Cinderella slippers with to-die-over heels. She would have him by three inches. He swallowed the exquisite single-malt brew, grateful that it wasn't his tongue. He was not so certain, when her shapely calves came into view, muscles lean and long enough to evoke tears from Michelangelo, that his tongue wouldn't be next.

The dress started well above her knees, a classic black slip of satin coaxed by design into clinging most faithfully to her hips and breasts. He swallowed again. Not a lot of fabric there, barely there.

Her hair was caught up by a diamond-studded comb in an artfully random tumble of curls. He knew the look, the innuendo, the suggestion. He turned away, doused the early outbreak of fire in his belly with the Scotch, poured more and turned back with a cooler version of appreciation.

He gave her the slow smile she deserved. "You clean up well, princess."

She returned the haughty look he expected. "I suppose you know you're no slouch."

Her eyes sparkled, a smokier blue than he'd seen up to now, a fusion of conflicting qualities of light he couldn't reconcile. Lord. He was going to have to keep the lid slammed shut. "Thanks. You want a drink?"

"No." She handed him her stole. He applied the length of luxurious wool with expertise and flair to her shoulders, then drew it upward to cover her nape before he could act on other impulses. He moved off toward the front door and when he opened it, she swept out.

He ripped off and stuck one of his eternal cedar slivers into his mouth after he'd helped her into the Bronco and closed the door.

She looked out her window all the while he drove. The road settled him, helped him tamp down the fire in his loins to the soft glow of coals. He wondered why it hadn't occurred to him that if he asked her to pull out all the stops, she would comply.

Or maybe he had. Maybe he'd counted on it for sexual energy he could channel into his evening's performance. He settled himself lower in the driver's seat, easing the ache, and laughed softly to himself, at himself. He'd catch his breath any moment now.

He pulled into the circular drive of the country club, and despite the obvious fact that everyone else had parked off the drive, he stopped directly in front of the clubhouse and killed the engine.

Fiona gave him a look. He gave her a wink. She was beginning to learn what to expect from him. Arrogance more comfortable with itself than diamonds set deep in platinum.

THE DINING ROOM, of a size to accommodate wedding parties, was not nearly filled, but the people on whom Matt wished to impress his message were there. Notably Dex Hanifen, whose dinner companions included his wife, Marilu, the federal district court judge, Henry Bell, and his decades-younger trophy wife, Jocelyn, and the owner of the Bar Naught's neighboring ranch, Gary Bright.

As she hesitated at the partially drawn mahogany pocket doors, memories sharp as shards assaulted her. In her mind, she slammed the door shut on them and focused carefully on the present. Dinner had been served promptly. They were half an hour late, but with the inducement of one of those seemingly unending hundred dollar bills, Matt and Fiona were shown to a table for two.

Tables for two were the exception, and clearly the result of the tip Matt had doled out.

The low hum of noise ceased, the clink of silver, the rustling of napkins. Fiona waved in the direction of people she had known all her life. People who hadn't much for her but pity after her parents left town in disgrace. Servers lit the candle tapers as Matt held her chair and nodded in Hanifen's direction.

Matt sat across the table from Fiona, ordered a bottle of the finest wine available and, extending his hand to hers, drew her fingers to his lips.

He gave her a wink. "Melt, princess."

But he didn't have to tell her what to do. She lowered her eyes, then raised them in adoration. "I know how to do this, Matt."

"Tell me." He threaded his fingers through hers and drew her hand up, her palm to his so that their elbows rested on the table and their forearms came together like lovers. His thumb stroked hers.

She felt dizzy, felt adored. The wine hadn't even arrived yet. "Tell you what?"

"That little stutter-step as we came in. What was that about?"

She angled her head, flirting, playing the game. "Nothing I want to share with you. Can we just do this without—"

The waiter arrived with the wine as another delivered their salad plates. Trying desperately to be unobtrusive, sensing, as must everyone else in the room, that a moment was unlikely to develop in which it was possible to discreetly interrupt them, he lost his grip on Matt's plate so that it clanged against the brass charger. "My apologies, sir. I can't imagine—"

"Don't give it another thought." Matt let go of her hand, though in increments, shaking his head. He gave the waiter a glance, rueful enough to suggest the faux pas was entirely his fault for having been fathoms deep in the woman opposite him, arrogant enough to chastise at the same instant.

He accepted the splash of wine, rolled it around in the glass, inhaled briefly. "Give it a moment." The waiter backed away.

He attacked the salad. He must be starving. She was starving, but she picked at hers. At his nod, when his plate was polished off, the waiter poured the wine then left. After he'd sipped the white, he touched his fingertips to his lips, then splayed his fingers, releasing the kiss. "Taste it, *cara*."

She took hers up a little too fast, sipped and sipped again. "You are utterly shameless," she scolded. "Every matron in the room has taken up a napkin and begun discreetly fanning herself."

His brows raised. "Mock me, will you?"

Her throat quivered. "Do you think I'm kidding you?"

"You're not?"

"You know I'm not."

"Then the script would seem to call for you to be fanning yourself."

"I prefer the heat. I've a tolerance."

He smiled. "And the men in the room?"

"Gobbling down water. Trying not to notice. You should give them a break."

Their meal came, and salad plates were whisked away. Fiona tasted more of the stroganoff than she did her salad. Matt devoured the meal in a hurry without seeming to rush. She thought at this point, since desserts had come and gone for the rest, that it was becoming awkward for people not to get up and move around. Matt's pace through the meal reflected a wish to get on with it himself.

They refused dessert, and the tension seemed to spring events loose. Several of the women overcame their attitudes toward Fiona and approached their table, touching cheeks, blowing kisses. But it was clear to her that the women were stealing as many glances at Matt as their less enthusiastic husbands.

Matt rose, and Fiona joined him, slipping an arm through his, billing and cooing as she introduced him to the women.

He doted on each woman in turn, then returned his attentions to Fiona, touching the nape of her neck with an intimate, possessive gesture that made the women stare in envy.

Gooseflesh erupted along her bare arms. He bent near to whisper in her ear. "Almost done." He nipped at her ear. Her eyelids fluttered. Her breasts throbbed. "Swoon, princess."

She complied. He excused himself with an air of

terrible reluctance to be separated from her. He approached the group of men having a smoke in the corner of the dining room where an antique spittoon absorbed the refuse.

HANIFEN WAS GNASHING his teeth again. He dragged on his cigar and sent up a plume of smoke while he tossed his head in Fiona's direction. "Kyle would have fed you your family jewels."

"Kyle isn't here."

He shook his head, chewing on the inside of his lip, darting looks at Fiona as if he were the one she was screwing around on. "Little tram—"

"Keep a civil tongue, Dex," he warned softly. "Kyle knew what was going on between Fiona and me. He knew exactly. What else do you think kept him stuck on ground zero with her?"

Hanifen could only stare in disbelief. Eventually he cleared his throat, but by that time, one of the other men, no one Matt recognized, stifled a furtive smile and offered Matt a cigar.

Must have made for interesting fare, seeing their sheriff flummoxed, he thought, accepting the smoke. He bit off the end of the cigar and expertly blew it off his tongue at the spittoon. Accepting a light from the same sly dog, he took a few seconds to appreciate the subtle cherry-scented tobacco and then introduced himself all around.

None of the faces surrounding him looked happy to meet him, more wary, which suited Matt fine, but Hanifen had had it up to his gills already. He stepped outside the circle of men, unlocked and flung open a sliding glass door. "I need a word with you. A private word."

Matt shrugged vague apologies at the other men
and stepped out the door, sliding it home behind him.
The wind was blowing like hell. Hanifen ducked
around the corner for some protection and sucked
deeply on the cigar before the wind could overwhelm
the fire at its tip.

He coughed.

Matt preempted him. "Interesting times we live in,
huh, Dex?" He knew the sheriff understood very well
what he meant. Dex had accepted that Matt had
switched sides, turned coat, that they were in league
together now with The Fraternity.

And it was either Dex Hanifen or Dennis Geary
who'd pulled the trigger and laid Kyle Everly to his
uneasy rest. Probably on the orders of one of the other
brothers. Matt would stake his own life on the truth
of it. Fiona's rifle could only have been put back into
place so quickly by one of them. But the sheriff,
backed into this corner of buying into Matt usurping
Everly's throne, had to pretend he hadn't done the
deed because Matt was claiming to have killed Everly
himself. And the only way Fiona figured in was that
framing her got her out of the faces of the bad guys.
"How's the frame-up going?"

"An arrest is imminent, in case you haven't gotten
yourself aligned with a mouthpiece licensed to practice in Wyoming."

"How imminent?"

He dragged on his cigar. "I should have the foren-
sics in by tomorrow afternoon."

Matt said nothing. Dex seemed to dance around a
bit trying to sneak up on other topics.

Finally he asked. "Where did you get that lip gloss
thing?"

"A gas station, just up the road." He feigned a bit of a double take. "But you're probably interested in the original. The electronic beacon. The one with the chip in it with your thumbprint, which is…missing, shall we say, from the evidence lockers up in Seattle."

Dex plucked a bit of stray tobacco off his tongue. "The most that's on that thing is a partial."

"A clear partial, Dex." Matt savored another drag off his cigar. "Points all match."

Dex shivered, but tried to conceal it beneath a careless shrug. "If it's missing, the chain of possession is screwed."

"That would be true if anyone knew it was missing, Dex." He flicked the cigar butt onto the bare earth and ground it out. "There's the rub. All I have to do is call in a favor. Have one of my old friends on the Anti-TruthSayers task force put it back?"

Hanifen's face contorted slowly into pure loathing. He could only guess why he hadn't been charged with anything, but before he could discipline himself enough to launch into anything else, Matt went on. "I don't give a rat's ass about nailing your carcass to the wall, Dex, with one exception."

Dex all but snarled. "Let me guess. No one touches a hair on fair Fiona's head."

"See? You're a quick study, Dex. Something else we have in common."

Hanifen snorted. "Everly—"

"Was careless. Frankly stupid, bringing those undercover cops on the ranch, planting the beacon on Thorne's woman."

The sheriff tilted his head. "Sending a National Guard chopper after the two of them?" He nodded.

"That was over the top. Kyle lost all sense of proportion, I admit, but then it was his old friend J.D. looking to do him in that got Kyle's nose outta joint."

Matt rolled a shoulder. His ribs ached more every hour. "As long as you know where your limits are, Dex, and you don't get your nose so far out of joint that you do something careless, you're going to be okay. As long as Fiona Halsey stays healthy, you're ducky."

Hanifen smirked and cut Matt a look. "Is she good?"

"You don't want to start off down that path, Dex."

"You're right. Totally inappropriate. But humor me one second. All I want to understand is if she's in this thing with you."

Despite the ferocious wind, Matt began to sense the stir of subtler, more dangerous currents, felt the hair rise on the back of his neck. "What thing?"

"The 'soiree,' as you called it. When that goes down, do you intend for her to be there?"

He had no idea where Hanifen was going with his bit of fun. "I haven't ruled it out."

"That's what I thought. And that makes you a bigger fool than even I imagined."

"Why don't we cut to the chase here, Dex? The Fraternity is meeting as planned, no matter what else happens. If you've got something to say—"

Hanifen swore. "The girl's trouble, Guiliani. I don't know what's got into her. Used to be a sweet thing, but she's changed. She'd lay down with—"

"Watch your mouth, now, Dex. You do not want to tick me off."

Hanifen shook his head. "It's always a skirt, have you noticed? It was a skirt got ahold of that hero running the TruthSayers operations—what's his name—Weisz? It was a skirt that got J. D. Thorne crosswise of Kyle, and now, sure as the sun's coming up tomorrow, it's our own little Fiona that's got you wrapped around her little finger.''

"Quite a recital, Dex." If he had needed to hear from the horse's mouth how thick the sheriff was with the TruthSayers, Dex was playing Mr. Ed. "I keep waiting for the punch line."

"You're a cluck, Guiliani," he muttered beneath the wind. "Poor dumb bastard that you are, you're so enamored with our little princess that if you was drowning and the bubbles were makin' an arrow pointing the way up, you still wouldn't get it."

Foreboding sliced through Matt with a chill deeper than the wind could muster. "Spit it out, Dex."

The sheriff gave Matt a contemptuous look. "I'll spit it out. The facts, my friend, are these. I fixed up a reservation for the princess in the jailhouse, which you bollixed up completely. Then I figured, what the hell, I know a couple of sharpshooters in the neighborhood. I'll just send one of 'em out to wing the miss, and she'll either wind up spending time in the local hospital or she'll hightail it out of here. But then, here you come, bustin' butt playing hero again." He spat on the ground. "You take your jollies where you see fit, Guiliani. I got a lot of concerns for her, you know, but I sure as hell am not extending myself for the girl again."

Matt had a sincere feeling that he did not want to hear what Hanifen had been pussyfooting around with. He broke out another of his ubiquitous cedar sticks and stuck one in his mouth, shoving it to the side. "I'm still waiting for the punch line, Dex."

Hanifen clacked his tongue. "Pay attention, hero, 'cuz it's comin' at you like the Titanic hell-bent on an iceberg. Fiona Halsey is Interpol. Ain't no Fraternity brothers going to be attending any soiree with that kinda nuisance around."

LATE SUNDAY NIGHT, the pager on the nightstand in Garrett and Kirsten's bedroom began to beep.

He tried to silence the thing before it woke Kirsten, without success. Propped on one elbow, he punched the backlight button to read the digital display.

"What is it?"

"Matt wants me to call him. Now." He flung back the covers and got out of bed, pulled on a pair of jeans, tried to keep the concern out of his voice. "Probably just lonely."

"Probably not," she uttered, worried.

He braced himself and leaned back over the bed to kiss her forehead. "Try to rest. I'll go call him. If there's anything, Kirs, I'll tell you. I promise."

He ducked out of the room and took the stairs down two at a time, picked up the secure cell phone designated for a call like this and went outside onto the porch. He only had to key in a preset code to reach Matt directly.

"Are you in trouble?" Garrett asked without preamble.

"Some." He paused. The silence, coming from a motormouth like Guiliani, was unnerving. "There's a bunker concealed beneath the hunting lodge. An armory of assault weapons, a firing range, an operations room like you've never seen outside the freaking Pentagon. All of this completely out of view of any satellite surveillance."

Garrett's tired mind plodded along, trying to imagine how a facility like that could be built and stocked without anyone in law enforcement ever the wiser. He and Matt knew each other's thinking so well, Matt answered the question before Garrett needed to ask. "No one was keeping an eye on this guy. If it hadn't been J.D. out there with Ann last winter, if the two of them hadn't grown up together, if Everly hadn't gotten cocky and interfered with that whole thing, we still wouldn't know he was even here."

Garrett knew it was true. Everly would have skated right on by with no more notice than the occasional glance of bored U.S. customs officials. But their intelligence had developed to the point where moving against Everly had become crucial. They knew about the gathering of international badasses on the Bar Naught, or Matt wouldn't have gone in yet.

But however much worse the reality was than their intelligence had revealed, Garrett knew Matt would not have wasted his time calling unless there was something immediate pressing. "What is it, *paisan?*"

"Hanifen informed me a couple of hours ago that Fiona Halsey is an Interpol snitch."

Garrett swore softly. The so-called "node" mystery could be put to rest. It had to be Interpol on the other side. The bastards had agreed to join this operation and then done what they damn well pleased, anyway, putting Fiona Halsey back on the ranch themselves, and sending Elliott Braden to keep tabs for Interpol on what went on in Matt's operation.

But it certainly explained a lot. Like why Fiona Halsey was on the Bar Naught at all. And why someone had tried to kill her.

And if Halsey was blown, then the possibility that

Matt was equally well known to the enemy was, for all practical purposes, a given. "Does she confirm or deny?"

"I haven't asked. Yet."

Garrett hesitated, knew Matt so well. "What's that about?"

Another heavy sigh. "It's complicated."

Complicated. "Okay. Want to—"

"No."

Way complicated, Garrett thought. He wanted the details, wanted to know what it was about Fiona Halsey that had his friend so tongue-tied, but this wasn't the time.

"Can you contain her?" he asked at last, then bounced the heel of his hand off his sleep-deprived head. "Forget that. Obviously nothing's going down if The Fraternity knows she's bearding for Interpol."

"There's the problem."

"What did you say to Hanifen when he dropped that little bombshell?"

"I said I wouldn't stand in the way of her arrest."

"Which will happen when?"

"He volunteered to take her off my hands tonight."

"What a guy." Garrett hesitated, waiting for a clue as to what had happened, sensing he was skating on thin ice now. "So is that why you haven't talked to her about her Interpol connection?"

"No." Matt sighed heavily. "We were out to dinner. The local country club. He'd have clapped cuffs on her in front of—" He broke off. "I don't want her humiliated."

"I hear you, *paisan*. What do you need from me?"

"I want you to go crack a few skulls open and find out what rot pours out. Find out what the hell Elliott

Braden is up to. What Interpol thought it was doing.'' He bit off a curse. ''Am I missing something, or did Braden get on board with us?''

''Yeah, but I'll go out on a limb here and predict that Braden will say they already had Fiona Halsey in place. What difference did it make? Might even give you an added layer of protection with her reporting directly to them.'' He could spout Braden's justifications without thinking about it, but that didn't mean he wasn't going to ream the Interpol flunkie a new air passage.

''While you're at it, *paisan,* find out from Braden what other tricks they have up their sleeve. I'm really not interested in hanging around here to provide target practice.''

Garrett joked because joking was their refuge and routine when all hope was lost and there was nothing left to say. ''You're toast whether you're there or not.''

''Thanks.''

''Welcome.'' Frustration gnawed at Garrett like a slow-acting, corrosive acid.

''Christo get my secret agent messages okay?''

Tears sprang into Garrett's eyes, and his throat clogged up. Matt Guiliani was a marked man, but the last thing he wanted to know, what he worried about most, was that he hadn't disappointed Christo. ''Every one.''

Chapter Eleven

Matt closed the cell phone and started back into the house when there came the noise of a commotion from the stables. He saw by a narrow strip of faint light, where the door at the east end of the stable stood slightly ajar.

Tucking the cell phone into his coat pocket, he crossed the dark yard in a quick, no-nonsense stride. Reason would tell him it could only be Fiona, but he'd told her to go into the main house and stay there until he was ready to talk to her.

Reason might have told him she would lie to St. Peter at the pearly gates, that she had lied to him by her silence after he laid out everything to her. Either way he was in no mood to be defied. He knelt only as long as it took him to grab his gun from the ankle holster, then stood and slipped inside the door, pulling it closed without springing the latch.

He stood a moment without moving or breathing, and he knew in his heart there was no threat, no reason not to put away his piece. There was no intruder, only Fiona trying again to make up with Soldier Boy. But he didn't put it away, thought about firing off a round just to mollify his mood, and moved swiftly down the rows of stalls on the balls of his feet.

He had serious issues to take up with her. How and why and for how long she'd been flipped into an Interpol snitch, not to mention the truth of her intentions when The Fraternity convened. He was so angry with her, so thoroughly pissed at himself for having been taken in by her lies. Was any of it true?

He came within view of Soldier's stall. Stil he couldn't see her but saw instead that Soldier had wheeled around, a hock raised threateningly at the half door into the main hall, ready to lash out with a double-barreled kick. A deeper, far more deadly and aggressive stance than Soldier had leveled even after Matt had crashed into his stall.

Then he saw Fiona coming out of the shadows, taking a step toward Soldier, murmuring gently, smooth as silk, but Soldier shrieked and lashed out with a vicious kick. Fiona ducked away and fell backward, stifling a scream as Soldier prepared to let fly again with hooves big and powerful enough to land a killing blow.

Matt reacted without thinking. Dropping his gun then slamming up the latch on the half door, he threw it wide open, wide enough that Soldier's kick struck the boards, splintering the wood.

Soldier screamed and wheeled around, stunned and enraged by the jolt of having struck the door, but Matt gave no quarter. Crouching low, he launched his body, leading with his shoulder as he had the first time, straight at Soldier's head. He connected, felt the jarring of his teeth, the rattling of his bones, pain shooting through his shoulder all the way down his back.

Soldier backed off, tossing his own dazed head, eyes darting wildly for space in which to escape, but Matt wasn't done. He'd forced Soldier to abandon the attack on Fiona. Now he had to know who was boss.

Compared to what he had seen Fiona accomplish with the mustang Robbie called Buster, Matt knew nothing. He'd watched her dealing with those feral mustangs, seen her behaving toward them with respect and understanding for the nasty plight of captivity they hadn't asked for. But she'd lost her connection to Soldier and her grief had knocked her off balance with him.

He tried to put himself in the mind of the ruined stallion, to understand what would finally break through Soldier's fanatical mistrust of the two-legged creatures that had failed him so badly.

Without looking away he told Fiona to get to her feet as he sidled within reach of Soldier's head. The horse was cornered, with nowhere to bolt, and Matt slipped an arm over Soldier's neck, intending to have her try again, together with him, to break through to Soldier. The huge beast sidestepped in anxiety. Matt told her softly, "Now."

She moved forward, her arm and wrist extended, her fingers curled under to emulate the nose of another horse as he had seen her do over and over again with the mustangs, but Soldier shied and reared back.

Fiona backed away again. Matt tried to go near her but she warded him off with the set of her jaw. "Don't." She mopped her face with the edge of her woolen stole and let herself out of Soldier's stall and walked away, the heels of her shoes tapping in the semidark.

He jerked down the knot on his tie and followed

her into the house. His chest hurt, ached in the vicinity of his heart, and it had nothing to do with the physical punishment he'd absorbed in three short days.

GARRETT HUNG UP THE PHONE and went looking for the number of Kirsten's friends in Wyoming, the couple from whose home Christo had been kidnapped over a year ago. Things were heating up, boiling over, and he had to have someone Kirsten could be easy with come to stay with her and Christo. Her friend agreed to come before Garrett had half explained.

A pang of gratitude for friends like these hit him sideways. He rang off and then sent a terse page to every member of the operation planning team, calling a mandatory immediate meeting. He had to look up a number for Skip Tsumagari, and then, for good measure, the U.S. attorney himself.

Kirsten was asleep. He left her a note. Hopefully, he'd be back before she woke in the morning.

As he'd predicted, Elliott Braden tried to skate all around the issue of having compromised the life of an agent in the field. Fiona Halsey had been on the Bar Naught for months. Big deal.

"You should have told us." Garrett smashed a fist into his other hand. "You've been parsing out bits and pieces all this time regarding Fiona Halsey. Yes or no?"

"Parsing is one way of putting it," the Interpol liaison answered coolly. "Adhering to the doctrine of need-to-know is another."

Garrett flew off the handle, launching himself nearly across the conference table at the smug, narrow-eyed Canadian. He'd been lied to, manipulated, stalled, and it was Guiliani's life on the damn line out there. Garrett got only close enough to get hold of the jerkwad's tie, and he dragged Braden back across the table before J.D. walked in, took Garrett by the collar of his shirt and pulled him away.

Garrett shrugged off J.D.'s hold, jerked on his shirt to straighten it and gave Braden a look to establish the fact that their discussion wasn't nearly over, then stalked off to the corner for a cup of coffee. The glaring fluorescent lights buzzed in the silence hanging over the room.

J.D. poured coffee and handed Garrett the insulated cup. The situation he'd walked into didn't really require any explanation.

Garrett slugged back a swallow. "You look like hell."

J.D. shrugged. His eyes were bloodshot and he hadn't shaved or slept in more hours than he could remember. "Came straight from juvie hall. Jaz picked a fight with a little thug who tried to kill him."

Garrett bowed his head. When things started going to hell, they went in a big way. "You want to take off?"

J.D. refused. "I dropped Ann at home. She needs some space. I need some space." He looked at Garrett through his reddened, bleary eyes. "You gotta knock it off with Braden. Don't get me wrong. When this is all over—" He broke off, shook his head. He would strangle Braden with his bare hands if Guiliani didn't get out with his life.

They went back to the table, but the fight was gone out of Garrett. And the truth was, it didn't matter that he'd been put in charge of all operational details, that the decisions to be made about Fiona Halsey on the ranch should have been his. He'd been preempted and blindsided by Interpol, and all he could do now was find a way to salvage Matt's life.

After the others had gone back home to catch a few hours of sleep, Garrett and J.D. sat with Skip Tsumagari and told him what they needed. Braden wasn't going to suddenly pop forth with the information they needed to spring Matt from this trap. They needed to know what Interpol had. Garrett wanted him to chase down the node and hack his way into the computers.

And do it in twenty-four hours.

FIONA HAD IT IN MIND to fly up the stairs and lock herself away in her childhood bedroom, but there was small comfort there. Even if anything meaningful to her had been left in the room—and it hadn't—she would only be facing little-girl dreams.

She left the front door standing open, knowing Matt was not far behind, and went to the library. She took an unopened bottle of premium brandy off the shelf, then made a fire.

She kicked off her shoes and shoved one of the leather chairs on its casters near the fireplace, then sat down with her legs stretched out on the thick Persian carpet. She leaned against the chair, aware that Matt had followed her in, that he stood only a few feet away observing her. That he didn't know what to do with her.

The only light in the room issued from the fireplace. Standing there in his beautiful dark suit, his powerful physique silhouetted, he seemed to her to have walked out of an edgy dream. His white shirt reflected the light, as it might under ultraviolet, casting an otherworldly glow upward on his face.

His eyes were dark, fathoms deep. His jaw made her feel silly, feminine. His aquiline nose cast a shadow on his clean-shaven cheek. Staring up at him, she cracked open the brandy, and took a very unprincesslike slug of the liquor, not so much for courage as to bludgeon her feelings out of existence. Then she said, "So, enough about me. What's with you?"

He unfastened the buttons at his collar, and then another two, and dragged the matching leather chair to a position facing her. He bent wearily to strip off an ankle holster and remove his boots.

He lay the gun in its holster aside. She took another sip, two before he was quite done. "That's not going to help, princess."

"I think it might." She cradled the bottle at her nearly naked breasts. "Come on, tough guy. Give it up. What's got your shorts in a knot?"

He exhaled sharply. "You're blown, Fiona."

She chose to misunderstand him, examining the level of brandy in the bottle against the firelight. "Not yet, I'm not."

"I'm talking about your secret life as an Interpol snitch."

Her eyes flew to him, then darted low. She held the pretty bottle against her again.

Watching her—she could feel the intensity of his eyes on her—he stripped off one sock, then the other.

She was blown. How did he know? But she could guess, it was what had put him into his mood. Dex. It must be Dex who knew and told Matt in their chat outside the country club. If it was Dex, that explained a great deal of the sheriff's rudeness toward her, his mistrust, the speed with which he'd acted to pin Kyle's murder on her, the shots fired at her yesterday.

"Dex."

Matt spoke softly. "He's in up to his eyeballs, Fiona."

"Well." She heaved a sigh. Those damnable tears pricked at her lids, but really, what did it matter anymore? What mattered to her was unreachable, and Soldier Boy was a symbol of all her flawed hopes. "There you go."

"We have to talk about this, Fiona."

"Why?"

"Because I need to know the truth."

"Well, Matt, the truth is, the bad guys have won, and it has finally sunk into my pitiful brain that I am not in for a happily ever after. I am in for—" She broke off. She hurt. But what was it to him that she hurt? What was it to anyone?

She could hope that Interpol would see that she had done her part right up until Kyle was murdered. She could hope that they would honor their deal to return the Bar Naught to her after The Fraternity was busted up and Everly's arsenal was dismantled and liquidated.

Realistically, the Bar Naught was lost to her. Her family, her life, Soldier Boy was lost to her. She had only one thing left to want—what it was about Matt Guiliani's touch that Soldier Boy tolerated, that soothed the savage—no, *savaged* beast.

Could Guiliani take away her pain, too?

She pulled the pins from her hair, careful to keep her bottle upright, and fixed her gaze on his bare feet. "You're not stopping there, are you?"

He scowled. ''Fiona, are you listening to me? You—''

''I heard you, secret agent man.'' She blinked. ''Will you seduce the truth from me now?''

''Fiona, for crying out loud—''

''James Bond would do that. No? Well, let me just take off my stockings, too, and we'll see.'' She drew one foot up to her bottom. Her skirt slid along the length of her thigh, whisper of silk against silk, and fell into her lap.

Her courage nearly failed her, but she had to know what magic it was in his hands that even Soldier Boy would accept. She hadn't drunk so much brandy to not know that whatever it was might not translate well, only enough to believe it might.

She'd been led to believe it in all those long, difficult hours in the saddle with him. Grueling hours that she wished would never end. And by the long, difficult kiss, heady and aching and sweet and fierce and overpowering and gentle.

She still didn't know what it was about him. She had to understand it, and to understand it, she had to experience it one more time.

She fisted the skirt pooled in her lap and, lifting the brandy once more to her lips, watched his eyes track her silk stocking up her bent leg to the garter holding it tight, and the bare naked tops of her thighs and a certain glimpse of her panties.

Funny, she thought, how powerful she felt in the moment she gave it all up.

His Adam's apple dipped. He clamped his teeth shut and he dropped slowly back into the chair, his arms draped over the sides. His thighs fell naturally apart. Proof of his certainty that he would not be affected by her?

Watching him, she slid her hand up her thigh and caught the garter in her fingers. She pushed the rubber knob down the trolley until the silk sprang loose. She began to ease the sheer black silk down her leg.

When she touched the back of her other thigh, searching for the garter, he shot bolt upright. "Fiona, stop it." But it was desire she saw in his posture.

"Why?" A fierceness in his features sent a panic scurrying through her. Had she misjudged so badly?

Would he think her desperate enough now, with her cover blown, that she would trade in alliances, appeal to him to save her, that she was offering up her body, a sexual favor, and not herself? Not Fiona, not the woman with the wild creature inside her, clawing furiously, flapping its wings like a trapped moth. Not the pretend princess who only needed to know if his touch would heal her, too?

She shivered and plunged ahead. "Would you rather do it yourself?"

He bowed his head. Seconds passed.

"Please."

The heavy pendulum in the grandfather clock swung back and forth, ticking away the time of her life beneath the crackling and licking sounds of the fire. She thought she had lost, that he would look back up at her and shake his head. Or that when he looked at her again, it would be rejection steeped in pity she saw. But he stood and shed his elegant suit coat and stripped the knot from his tie, leaving its ends hanging loose, and the look in his dark eyes when they met hers was the same as a caress.

"Please what, princess?"

Her heart thundered. "Please do it yourself."

"It won't stop there, Fiona."

God help her, let it be. She could no longer hear the pendulum ticking for the surge of her blood in her ears. Every part of her craved his touch, his hands, his mouth. Her voice was breathy, little more than a whisper. "Is that a warning or a promise?"

"A promise." His gaze fell to her breasts and then her skirt, pooled in her lap, at last to her bare thigh. He sank to the floor beside her, on his knees, cushioned by the plush Persian silk. He took her face in his hands and drew it up and his lips crushed down on hers. His eyes fell shut, but she was too frightened to find it all a part of that edgy dream to close her own.

But in another heartbeat, other sensations—the feel of his tongue dipping into her, the hunger of his groan, the scent of his male heat—drove the fear of rejection from her mind.

He buried his hands in her hair and tilted her head back even more, and his lips strayed to trace the line of her jaw, hinting at straying lower to her neck and lower still to her breasts, teasing hints that made her cry out with wanting.

It was her cry that sent him over the top, that made his flesh go painfully, fully erect in an instant. He broke off the straying kisses and rested his forehead against hers, his breathing ragged. Though he was ready to take her in her party dress, ready to answer her cry and give her reason to cry out again, he made himself slow it down.

He wanted to trifle with her garter.

He wanted to release that slip of sultry silk from its mooring, as they slipped from tethered wanting to a sea of fulfillment. To follow her stocking down to her toes with his tongue, and all the way back up. All the way.

To bring them both toward a single hovering prolonged moment in the history of time that would make it simply stop for them.

"Please, don't—" She started to speak, to beg him not to stop, but his thumb darted to her lips, silencing her plea.

"Shh, Fiona. Ask for what you want, but don't think you have to ask me not to stop. We haven't even begun. Don't you know that?"

Her throat simply closed, and she made a hiccuping sound. His thumb traced a path from her lip to her neck, over her throat. Still flattened, his hand skimmed the tops of her breasts, skimming over the surface of both, slipping inside the loose bodice to finger her tightened and aching nipple. At the touch she bucked upward with a flush of heat, a riptide of desire.

"Fiona. Fiona." He praised her with murmurs of approval, uncontainable groans of power and pleasure of his own. Her hips drew upward as he continued the long, seamless stroke of her body, gliding from her breasts to her midriff to her belly to linger at the juncture of her legs and body.

She felt racked with fever, with desire. She hadn't moved, save that single buck of exquisite pleasure and pain all mixed up together. She understood he wanted to give her this, but knew as well he wanted her to talk to him, to tell him. She looked into his eyes, and said the words. *Touch me there. Take me there.*

He exhaled sharply and moved his palm to cup her

in the in-between place where all her senses converged and moistened. Nothing she had ever felt verged on the love he made to her with only his palm in that place. "Yes…there."

"In a bit, Fiona. A little while yet." He continued on, curling his hand from between her legs to the underside of her thigh and the garter that would be the beginning of the end of his mooring.

He took the silken elastic strap into his hand and with his thumb drew back the smooth rubbery knob until it sprang free of the cool metal pin. A powerful shudder took him and he slipped from that place where he had always before held tight, where he had always, always held a little of himself back, a part of him ever alert, watching himself, always in perfect control.

He had never gone so astray, so missing in action from the role-playing that had consumed his life, so absent from the menagerie of false personas he adopted to do his work. With Fiona Halsey he forgot not to be himself.

In the quiet licking of the flames, held tight in his arms as they came together again and again, Fiona still didn't know what it was about him. Beneath the physical, the thrill, the mastery of his touch and his lips and the ultimate joy of his penetration into her, she felt as safe as she was cherished. She thought it must be something akin to the way her mustangs gentled, to be held and confined, prevented from bolting, stayed and reassured and set free to roam in safe pastures in far greater safety than they ever had before.

That must be what Soldier Boy sensed in Matt Guiliani, someone to meet his rages and safeguard his being. He was a man she could trust beyond question, a man to whom tit-for-tat was meaningless, a man who had sacrificed his own well-being for her over and over again. A man to whom she had lied and whom she had put at risk.

Chapter Twelve

He sat in the chair at Fiona's computer, staring at manna from heaven, solid proof against the estimated eight-member conspiracy of death-dealers known as The Fraternity. Fiona had spilled onto her desk blotter a stack of digital-camera memory cards from a flimsy box that once held bags of Earl Grey tea. The cards were no larger than a matchbook, but flatter.

Nearly three dozen cards in all, containing digital photos of documents detailing agreements, invoices, payments to accounts in Geneva and Grand Cayman, delivery of arms and mercenaries and assassins. Enough to secure the arrest and convictions of every member but one. Kyle Everly.

"How did you get these?"

She wore jeans now, and a bulky sweater, no socks. She sat perched on the back of an overstuffed chair, her legs drawn up, her arms wrapped around them. Her skin still glowed from their lovemaking. "I stole them."

She had his attention. "Want to start at the beginning?"

"If you want."

"Oh, I definitely want." He let the remark reveal all his wants.

Her glance flew to his. A shiver went through her. "Me, too." She paused, and looked away and then back at him. She cleared her throat and cast him a look. If he wanted to hear this, he'd have to keep a lid on the intimate innuendoes. "One day almost a year ago, I was on board a yacht owned by Pascal Lariviere."

Reining himself in, Matt nodded, recognizing the name of the playboy she had broken off with, a man with suspected connections to the arms consortium. The Fraternity. He really didn't want to hear about her relationships before him, but this was key. "Go on."

"We had been at sea for nearly two weeks. That morning he was angry with me. I'd never seen him like that. To others, he could be a very unpleasant man—even when he felt good. But he had always treated me very well. I thought I was in love with him. But he'd been diagnosed with Parkinson's disease the day we set sail, and it didn't matter how small the tremors were, now he knew what they meant, and each time he became furious. He couldn't stop them, and they were happening every day, even in the morning. We moored at Mykonos, in the Aegean—"

"I know the place." The Greek isle was a favorite of international jet-setters.

She nodded. "Pascal had decided that I would not be allowed to join him on the island. He'd grown totally irrational over those couple of weeks. I had decided that when I got off the yacht, I wasn't going to get back on. I still thought I loved him, but I was afraid of him. There was nothing left of the relation-ship that I wanted to salvage. I think he knew that. He has that kind of prescience, a predator instinct. Now it was directed at me, and I knew the idea of keeping me isolated and captive made him feel pow-erful, especially in his terrible mood.

"Anyway, after he and his buddies went ashore, I went down into his office. I'd been forbidden ever to even go down to that level of the yacht, but I had to use his computer and find help getting out of his clutches."

"There were no phones?"

"Of course there were. A dozen at least, but he'd seen to it that they were all locked away."

Matt listened to her telling the story almost as if it had happened to someone else. He saw that stiff upper lip of her British heritage at play, her refusal to play a victim of any stripe. But Matt could see it all as it had happened to her, a rich and ruthless man growing sick and desperate, snapping his fingers, getting off on his power trip over Fiona in those weeks.

"After just a few moments I heard some men ap-proaching in the hallway, speaking French, and one of them sounded very much like Pascal when he spoke his native language. I was trapped, there was nowhere to run because I would have had to open the door into the same hallway they were using. But there was a louvered door and I hid in the space behind it.

"There was no room to move. The space was filled with all sorts of cords and wiring on an electrical panel. I don't think I even had the door quite shut when they came in, it was that close."

Matt had seen similar setups, including a louvered door that kept heat from collecting and the air circulating freely to protect the integrity of the electronics. "He didn't see you?"

She shook her head. "It wasn't him. It was a couple of agents from Interpol."

It had taken her a long time, standing utterly still, hardly breathing behind that door, listening to the pair talking, to comprehend that these were Interpol agents who had somehow simply walked onto Pascal Lariviere's yacht.

Matt felt as uncomprehending as she must have been. Given what Garrett had told him about the Interpol liaison to this undercover operation, it was now crystal clear that Interpol had been hoarding significant evidence to themselves, that their pledge of cooperation was meaningless. But Lariviere would never have left his yacht unguarded, especially with the added necessity of assuring Fiona did not disembark. "How in the hell did they even get on board?"

"I have no idea." She shook her head. "All I could ever figure out is that they must have bribed Pascal's security men. Or maybe his thugs were double agents or something, and Pascal didn't know it."

She sighed deeply. "Matt, the thing is, they knew *exactly* what they were going for. They went right into a safe concealed in the floor and drew out a locked box, picked the lock and took out files of papers maybe four inches thick. I watched them photograph every document with a digital camera. They went through all these memory cards, and one by one, stored them in a fanny pack one of them wore around his waist."

"Did you understand what they were saying? Why didn't they just confiscate the files?"

"I could understand a lot of what they said, but they weren't exactly explaining themselves as they went." She paused and unlocked her arms from around her legs, letting them stretch out. "The impression I got was that they had not come onboard with a proper search warrant.

"You have to understand, Matt, that I had no idea what they were looking at, what Pascal was into, anything like what we saw in that bunker last night. Then I heard them muttering about floating certain copies of the papers to Pascal's associates, laughing because it would trigger an all-out war between them, and in the fray, they'd somehow all be apprehended. Or wind up dead. That's when I heard my name."

A violent shiver went through her, much, Matt imagined, as it must have when she stood concealed behind that door.

Her chin went up, her voice wavered. "You see, it was not by coincidence that Pascal and I met. His romancing me was a deliberate campaign to bag me. I was the perfect choice. I was distantly related to British royalty. I knew all the right people, or my parents had. Best of all, I was penniless for all practical purposes. Pascal wanted to do business with Kyle Everly, and he must have decided that I would come in handy as a courier for them."

Matt clenched his teeth against a vile epithet, for the words she used, "to bag me," were unsparing and unflinching as the calculated behavior of the men who had used her. But her story dredged up much more in him that wasn't pleasant.

The quick raid of Lariviere's yacht in a marina off Mykonos had to have been the result and culmination of investigations in far greater depth and detail than

Interpol had ever revealed to the DOJ in Seattle. There was evidence enough on the digital memory cards to cripple, if not destroy, The Fraternity. Photos of illegal arms dealers in the act of conveying and receiving, insurgent mercenary operations against struggling legitimate governments in Third World countries, even assassinations of key figures made to look like accidental or natural deaths.

He knew why Lariviere would have collected the evidence rather than destroying it. A line from a song echoed in his mind—''vultures and thieves at your back.'' Men like Lariviere and Everly would always need leverage to hold back the vultures and thieves, to control the black market trafficking. The two, it would appear, had been preparing to make a preemptive move on all the others. Fiona was to be their courier, though the need had never arisen in her months on the Bar Naught.

But with this evidence, Interpol had known enough to make its own strike against Lariviere. Against the entire brotherhood of The Fraternity. They'd clearly been thwarted, since Fiona had the memory cards.

''What happened then?''

''I opened the door and walked out and threw myself on their mercy.'' For the first time, she cracked a smile. ''They were thrilled.''

''They put everything back as it was. They decided to exploit the opportunity to throw Pascal off their real purpose, so that when or if he learned that they had been aboard, I would seem to have been the reason.

''They made a huge stink with the harbormaster about taking me into custody. I really couldn't tell whether they were claiming to be rescuing me from being held on the yacht against my will, or if they were playing it as if Pascal had been harboring a fugitive.'' She shrugged.

They flew her off Mykonos in an Interpol jet, back to Paris. She was taken to a tacky hotel by the pair of agents who, it seemed to her, wanted to keep both her and their booty secret until they had time to go through the memory cards themselves.

Within forty-eight hours, locked away in the hotel with the two men, she began to understand the nature of Lariviere's international business concerns, the scope of what these Interpol agents now had, how Everly was involved. How he was the one they couldn't get, the one stopping them from a clean sweep.

And she saw how she might turn the tables to her own advantage. But to do that she had to get away from the two men, and she had to take the memory cards with her.

Matt was completely intrigued. He had seen her under the worst of conditions conducting herself with a certain grace he had never seen before. He had watched her transform a feral mustang and a defiant delinquent kid with insight and perception that he feared her ever turning on him.

He had seen her in tears for the damage done to Soldier Boy, and in her juices telling Charlie Norville where to get off. Telling Matt himself where to get off, for that matter.

And he had lost himself in making love to her not an hour ago.

Now he was seeing yet another side to her. A woman with the strength and smarts and guts to snatch crucial evidence, get away from career cops and blackmail Interpol. "How did you escape?"

"One of them went out for cigarettes. I knocked the other one out with a lamp while he sat working at a laptop. I walked out with the memory cards. They had my passport, which the harbormaster on Mykonos had demanded from Pascal's ship captain. I stole that back and what money there was, which turned out to be the equivalent of several thousand dollars. Then I mailed the cards to the States, got on a train for Geneva and made my deal with Interpol. They would give me a reward in exchange for the memory cards. Enough to buy back the Bar Naught."

Matt frowned. "I must be missing something. Why wouldn't Interpol go back and confiscate the originals from Lariviere's yacht?"

"They would have, I'm sure. But Pascal was not a fool. He went underground within hours of learning what had happened from the harbormaster. He stripped the yacht clean of every personal possession, including all the evidence, and abandoned the yacht that day."

Matt whistled softly. For Lariviere to abandon his own ship and forfeit its value told the tale. The evidence against his conspirator brothers in The Fraternity was more valuable to Lariviere than anything.

"There's something else I don't get," Matt said. "Why would Everly sell the ranch back to you at any price?"

Fiona shrugged. "That was the flaw in my plan, of course. Interpol had the perfect solution. I would beg Kyle for a job—which was a no-brainer because it would stroke his ego no end to have me back, literally on his whim, at his beck and call. Once I got back on the Bar Naught, I was to do anything Interpol wanted me to do to get what they needed to build their case against Kyle. They would have a complete triumph. And when Everly was caught up in it, I could have the ranch back.''

Matt saw now what had led Interpol to take a subordinate position in the undercover operation. The U.S. attorney's office was not going to back off Everly's case, so a compromise was essential. Fiona was already in place, and could report to them on Matt's actions and progress.

And he saw as clearly why she had not shared the evidence with him before this, or even told him of its existence, even after he had laid his own cards out on the table. If he succeeded here, independent of the evidence on those memory cards, Interpol could renege on their deal with her. And in the worst-case scenario, if he failed, they could still deal with her to acquire the memory cards and whatever testimony she could give to fold Everly into their massive conspiracy charges.

Especially after she learned that first morning with Hanifen that Matt intended to replace Everly and proceed with the summit meeting of The Fraternity on the Bar Naught, she could still hope that her cause wasn't yet lost.

Two concerns gripped Matt.

Elliott Braden had been in on all the details of Matt's undercover extortion of Everly. If all Interpol wanted was to nab Everly in their sweep of The Fraternity members, why hadn't Braden put an end to the charade when Everly was killed?

And as important to him, because he was so nearly

in love with her, why had she handed over the evidence to him now?

Instead he asked, "Were you able to give Interpol anything useful?"

"No." She shook her head. "What they wanted was for me to be back on the ranch long enough that Kyle would feel he could trust me, or trust that he had me under his own thumb and comfortable using me as the wrangler when the hunting party convened." She hesitated, drew an unhappy breath. "Your geisha remark probably wasn't all that far off. I was absolutely supposed to manage to stay close to their discussions, whatever that required."

She got up and led him into her bedroom. Rummaging deep in her closet, she came out with a velvet-lined box within a shoebox, full of miniaturized, state-of-the-art equipment to capture the deals as they were made. Recording devices, a video feed concealed in a small medallion she would wear around her neck, dozens more to be hidden wherever she could.

Matt had variations on all the surveillance toys himself.

"Over the months, I've done dry runs with all of this to make sure that it would work. Everything was ready. I was ready. Now…" She shrugged, caught her lip in her teeth. Tears of frustration shone in her eyes. "Now none of it matters at all."

Matt took her into his arms and held her close. She'd returned to the Bar Naught and endured every indignity Everly could dream up, most of all, what he had done to her beloved Soldier Boy. Even if her secret alliance with Interpol was blown, she wouldn't have had to hand him her leverage, her only hope of getting the Bar Naught back.

The enormity of her sacrifice came home to him. Blew him away.

As usual, it took her only a few moments to get beyond her emotions. She pulled out of his embrace and put away the box of spy gizmos.

He picked up the spilled memory cards and began to fit them back into the empty tea box. The lighting was low in her bedroom. He couldn't see her well, or imagine that she could easily read his own expression. "Fiona, why now? Why after all this time, after keeping these from me this long, why give them up now?"

Her chin went up, her gaze met his. Tears welled again in her beautiful hazel-blue eyes. "I don't want you to have to go through with this."

She put on her coat and walked out the door of her humble-pie quarters.

MATT USED EVERLY'S vastly superior computer to encrypt the digital photos before he uploaded them to Garrett and J.D.

They watched as the photos of conspirators in The Fraternity came up on the screen. Fiona could put names to faces of several of the men because of their connections to Pascal Lariviere. Though she studied each one carefully, there were a couple of men she didn't know or couldn't place.

He began the upload to Garrett's personal computer to avoid any chance of it being intercepted, then sat back in Everly's chair and invited Fiona into his lap. The scent of him on her was not gone, and though his flesh hardened again, he contented himself with holding her.

The magnitude of her sacrifice to spare Matt had him stumbling inside. Reeling.

Still, he didn't know, and couldn't assume because his heart was so nearly won over, whether she had yet told him everything.

He felt like a heel, with her sitting so trusting in his lap, so sweetly, powerfully seductive, but there was one last test he must conduct. He asked her, "What did you do about making it up with Lariviere?"

She shifted her weight in his lap and put her arm behind him, let her fingers play in his hair. Her lips sucked gently at his ear. "I don't want to talk about him anymore. Ever again."

He gulped. He wanted her desperately. But he had to have the answer to that question. "Humor me until this upload—" he broke off as she rubbed her bottom against him "—is done. And then…" He flattened his hand against her torso and dragged it up over her breasts. "Then."

"I'll talk," she whispered, "so long as you keep that up."

His heart was simply swamped. Fiona was a woman who knew not only what she wanted and how to ask for it, but how to make sure she got it. He ached down low so fiercely that he gave up trying to stave it off and let his hand repeat its motion beneath her bulky sweater. She knew how to get more than her way in making love. "Talk, princess. Did you reconnect with Lariviere?"

She arched her back at his touch of her breasts and answered him. "Not for a while. I didn't know where to find him. Yes," she moaned, as he licked his fingers and applied them to her nipples. "There. Right there." She broke off, writhing in pleasure.

He hugged her fiercely. *Tell me,* he thought.

He didn't say it. Instead he took off her sweater and looked at her breasts in the glow of the light from the computer until he couldn't only look anymore. Between strokes of his tongue, he urged her on. "You were saying?"

She turned to straddle him, and as he gently suckled her, she told him how Lariviere had contacted her from an Internet café in Milan.

His heart began to thud even more deeply. "What did you do?" He knew the answer. Her lone e-mail to Lariviere was what had alerted them months ago that she was worth watching.

"I e-mailed him back." Again she hesitated, absorbing the keen, intensely sensual pleasure of his sex rising hard against her and his lips and his teeth and his clever, clever tongue making love to her breasts. "I gave him the only explanation I thought he would believe. I wrote that after I was taken from his yacht, certain…police had tried to convince me that he had been holding me against my will. I told him I had never believed them. I never heard from him again."

She sat lower in his lap and took Matt's head into her hands. He felt drugged on her now, as she looked consumed by him. "Are you listening to any of this?"

"Yes. And making love to you at the same time." His heart was at peace and beating a hundred miles an hour at once. She had told him the truth. And now he wanted any memories she had of Lariviere banished from her, heart and mind and soul. "But I don't want to talk of him ever again, either."

She cradled his face in her hands and looked deep

into his eyes. "There is no one but you for me, Matt. No one."

He nodded. He felt it, too. "I know."

GARRETT CALLED ON their secure cell phones an hour after the upload of Fiona's evidence. Matt scrambled out of Fiona's canopied childhood bed and streaked downstairs to retrieve the phone. She followed, wearing only his shirt, bringing with her his pants. He was pulling them on as Garrett invoked the conference call capability and brought J.D. on the line. They sat in the dark, cross-legged, facing each other, on the carpeting in Everly's office.

"First of all, Matt, you need to know I've got Tsumagari tracking backward to find the phantom computer beyond our so-called node. No doubt we'll find Interpol on the other side, but until we do, we're hamstrung."

Matt scowled. "Why doesn't that surprise me?" At Fiona's curious look, he leaned toward her so that she could hear what was going on.

"Secondly," Garrett added, "the files you uploaded to my computer are staggering." He cleared his throat. "Is this Fiona's work?"

"In a manner of speaking." Smiling, Matt reached over and stroked her hair. "You can thank her yourself later." He gave Garrett and J.D. a quick recap of how she'd come into possession of the memory cards. "So is it enough?"

"To bring indictments, you mean?" J.D. asked to confirm. "There's a problem, Matt."

"You should know J.D. and I don't agree about what he's going to say here," Garrett warned.

"Yeah, but you're sleep-deprived," J.D. complained.

Matt closed his fist around the cell phone. "What is it?"

Garrett deferred to J.D. "The thing is, we ran this all by Elliott Braden on a hypothetical basis—*if* we had photos and documents like you uploaded to us, would that be enough?"

Matt made a noncommittal noise. A part of him wanted to fly off the handle at his friends for running anything past Braden. If Interpol was on the other side of the node and his undercover role had been blown like Fiona's... He forced himself to give Garrett and J.D. the benefit of the doubt. He had his own question as to why Braden hadn't called off Matt's sting against The Fraternity after Everly was killed. Matt had a feeling he was about to hear the answer.

And that he wasn't much going to like it.

He laced the fingers of his free hand with Fiona's and said into the phone, "I'll bite. What did Braden say?"

J.D. swore. "He laughed. If he'd been in the room instead of on the phone, I'd have taken him apart with my bare hands. He said he knew all about Fiona Halsey's evidence, so we could skip any assertions that our question was hypothetical. He said the documents might eventually prove useful, but until that time, there was still a vital link we must uncover."

"Let me guess." But for Fiona, who had sacrificed so much sitting with him here in the dark, who had been repeatedly used, lied to and betrayed, he'd have come seriously unglued. "The Fraternity has someone inside Interpol."

"You've got it," Garrett said. "They wanted Everly, which is why they jumped on our bandwagon, but not nearly so much as they need to find out which one of their own is The Fraternity collaborator sabotaging every damn thing they do.''

Even in the dark, Matt saw Fiona's color drain away. She scraped a hand through her tousled hair. "Who's to say they haven't sabotaged *you?*"

"What was that?" Garrett asked.

"Fiona wants to know who's to say they haven't sabotaged me?"

Garrett cleared his throat. "No one, *paisan.*"

Matt grimaced. "But Braden wants me to go through with the meeting of badasses on the Bar Naught.''

"He makes the case," J.D. put in, "that you're in the perfect position. Everly is dead. You've taken credit for solving a very big problem they didn't even know they had.'' Which was the evidence they had fabricated that Everly had stolen millions from the death-dealing Fraternity. "If they want you in, no one will ever be in a better position to learn who the Interpol collaborator is.''

Matt nodded. Braden's reasoning held up on the surface. "Garrett?"

"I don't like it, *paisan.* I think we should pull out now. Let Interpol do its own dirty work. DOJ is leaving it up to you. This is not what you signed on for.''

But it was what he had signed on for, in a larger sense, Matt thought. All the way back to his stint as Mateos Karamedes. Nailing the shipping magnate was an international coup, but they'd fallen short of the coup de grâce. Alex Karamedes's guardian angel, whoever he was, had eluded capture and thumbed his nose at justice.

Déjà vu all over again. Matt was looking at another

law enforcement insider, collaborating, as Garrett had put it, with the big-time crime.

Nothing made Matt's blood boil more. Having so nearly lost his life—and Ann's—taking out dirty cops in league with the TruthSayers, J.D. understood best where Matt stood on the issue. He wouldn't be done with the job until the Interpol collaborator was nailed. "Let's play this thing out and see if we can't end it."

A brief silence. Garrett asked at last, "What about Fiona?"

Sensing tensions riding up in her, Matt tightened his grip on her long, slender fingers. "She'll be safe."

"Yeah, I suppose," Garrett mused. "But I'm not even convinced The Fraternity brothers are going to show up."

"I'll make them an offer they can't refuse," Matt replied. "I'll let them know, as the new kid on the block and the pretender to the throne, that there is all this evidence about to fall into the wrong hands. Maybe send them a few telling photos. And then, in a show of good faith, I'll suggest a bonfire once we've all gathered here on the Bar Naught. For solidarity, you know?"

Garrett whistled softly, poking fun because he really would rather Matt walk away from the summit meeting. "So this is why they pay you the big bucks."

"Or else, we might conclude," J.D. added, "that this is what happens when the boy gets a little action."

As it always did, J.D.'s occasional blunt, uncanny perceptions gave Matt the willies. Looking at Fiona's shadowed eyes, he felt heat crawling up his neck. "You'd know, pea brain."

"Just operational protocol."

"Yeah. SOP," Garrett joked. "Did you have to use your Latin lover routine, or—"

Matt cleared his throat. "You two want to move it along?"

"You bet. But unless you have some compelling reason against it, I think pea brain here ought to come in and cover your backside. Say, Wednesday morning?"

Caressing Fiona's hand, Matt smiled. Sweet, he thought, to be appreciated. Sweeter still to be so appreciated in so many ways in so short a time. "All right. So how are you going to get J.D. in?"

Chapter Thirteen

Fiona sat there in the dark listening to Matt's side of the conversation. He simply took her breath away, the way his mind worked, the way he had with her, the way he touched her, the things he revealed. And she was stunned again, on every level, by the depth of intimacy that had gone on between them in the past few hours.

He understood what she had given up for him. To keep him safe. To keep him from having to meet those cold-blooded killers to salvage his operation. He valued what she had done in handing over the evidence. He hardly knew how to be himself. Life was so much less messy undercover. He didn't have to acknowledge his own feelings. But with her, making love to her, he became himself, sacrificing his various roles, the hundred ways he had to escape his own feelings. For her. With her.

But her heart began to sink, to grow chilled from the start of this conversation with his closest friends. Most of all, the Latin-lover routine remark.

Imagine, cara, he had whispered into her ear. Was it less than eight hours ago? *Imagine that I would track down and kill the offender with my bare hands because you were my one true love. My soul mate. My inamorata.*

Cross-legged, she rose swiftly, pulling her hand from his, walking, almost numb, half sick to her stomach, out of the library. At the stairs she heard him coming after her.

"Fiona?"

She darted up the risers. "Leave me alone, Matt." At the second-story landing she ducked into the bathroom for toothpaste and a fresh brush and turned back to take them to her room. Bare-chested, backlit by the chandelier hanging almost directly behind him, he blocked her way.

"I'll have to get back to you later," he snapped into the phone, then shut it down and tossed it onto the carpeted floor. "Fiona, what's the matter?"

"Let me by."

"When you tell me what's wrong."

"Go to hell." Her throat tightened. She wrapped his shirt tighter around herself and clasped her arms around her sickened middle. She would not cry. Of all the ways he was prepared to betray her, this should hurt the least. Hadn't she known, her whole life long, that sex was just a commodity, nothing at all to shed tears over?

Hell no. She would not take that line with him. There was enough else to attack, like the fact that it wasn't the ranch hanging in the balance anymore, it was her life. He was going to let Dex put her in jail. "You know how hard I've worked for this, how much I've—"

"Fiona—"

"I thought it all meant something to you, Matt."

"It means everything—"

"Really? I gave you the only leverage I have so you wouldn't have to risk your stupid neck." She broke off and wiped a tear away with the back of her hand. "I can't believe you're going ahead with this."

He rubbed the back of his neck with his hand, staring at his bare feet, frowning as if he didn't understand her. "Fiona, I don't know what you want." He started to touch her arm.

She jerked away.

Irritation flashed over his features, and he grabbed her by her wrist and steered her forcibly down the hall and into her room, and didn't stop until she was sitting on her bed amid the tangle of sheets and the scent and memories of their lovemaking. "Now, what's this really about? I told you hours ago that you were burned. I'm sorry as all get-out, princess, but you knew—"

"Stop it," she cried. "Don't you dare say you're sorry when you're not. I gave you a way out, for *us,* a way for *us* to get out of this and be together, and all the while you're planning to go right on ahead...and worse, to let Dex throw me in jail." She cut him off before he could protest that it was for her safety. "I told you days ago, Matt. I cannot go to jail."

"Fiona, there was never any other way. You know that!" He shoved his hand through his hair. "The meeting will not take place if those guys didn't have it from Dex's lips that you are in jail, that you're going down for the murder of Kyle Everly, and that you are not going to be a factor now or ever again. You can't just leave, you can't—"

"To keep *your* options open," she snapped. "Your precious operation."

He looked hard at her. "Do you get that this is important? Thousands of lives are at stake, tens of thousands. You saw that bunker. You know how many people those kind of armaments can kill and maim apiece?" He paced her carpet, bit the bullet and finally owned up. "It's what I do, Fiona."

"I know. I've been warned." She bit her lip and dashed away a tear before it could fall. "No matter who or what gets sacrificed."

He drew a deep, shuddering breath and tried, she thought, with a false but brilliant display of empathy, to apologize. "I'm sorry Interpol is going to screw you over. I'm sorry you're probably not going to end up with the Bar Naught. I'm sorry—"

"You know what?" she cried. "I don't care anymore!" She stared at her hand, at the toothpaste and brush still clutched in her fist, and pitched them onto her vanity. "My cousin has a ranch in California where I can go and work with kids and horses till I die. But that's only if I don't go to prison for Everly's murder!"

"That's not going to happen." He stabbed the air with a pointed finger. "I won't let that happen."

She swallowed hard, daring him to straighten her out. "Tell me one thing, Matt, one thing that's happened here in the last three days that you could predict or control! So for the convenience of your operation, I go off to jail with a posyful of meaningless assurances? What happens if you die, Matt? What then?"

He crouched down before her, but she pulled away, scooted back on the bed. He flared up. "I can't believe we're fighting about this. You don't have to worry about it, Fiona. I work for the DOJ, for crying out loud. That's Department of *Justice—*"

"Yes, and there's so much justice happening here."

"I promise you that they know in the U.S. attorney's office that you've been framed. No matter what happens to me, they'll take care of you." Balanced forward on his toes, he hung his head a few seconds and then looked back up at her. "Fiona, I can't believe that after…that you still don't trust me."

She stared up at the ceiling to staunch her tears. He was either the most principled man on the planet or the least, the most discriminating liar, picking and choosing his moments of truth, or everything out of his mouth was a lie. "What was tonight about, Matt?"

His eyes narrowed. "What is that supposed to mean?"

"Don't pretend you don't know, Matt!" she uttered, low, guttural, her voice so thick with disappointment she could hardly hear herself. "You told me yourself Dex is in all this up to his ears. If he had had his way, he'd have slapped me in cuffs and taken me into custody in front of everyone. Instead you had yours."

His jaw tightened. His dark eyes bored into her. "What are you saying, Fiona?"

"You're smart. Figure it out. No, skip that. You know what I'm talking about."

"It had better not be what I'm thinking it is."

"Why not? It's the truth, isn't it? Reality, that's what we're after here. Isn't that what you've been telling me?" Her chin quavered, tears filled her eyes.

She was a skeptical creature, a woman trained in the finer points of tit-for-tat arrangements.

The part that was already in love with him wanted to walk away from her skeptical self and be real. It had seemed to her a real possibility with him. She was wrong. She gritted her teeth.

"Was I good, Matt? Was it good for you? Was I worth pissing Dex off again so that you could make jokes with your friends?"

He flushed. "If you knew Garrett and J.D., Fiona…" He hung his head. Frustration came off him like a scent all its own. "If you knew them, you'd know the joke was on them, on us. Not on you." He cleared his throat, tight with emotion she didn't want to be so gullible as to believe. "Would you rather I had let Dex take you away in front of everyone?"

"I don't care about that!" she cried.

"Do you really believe I foiled Dex again just so I could get in your panties? Who was seducing whom Fiona?" he demanded, his voice low and strained. "Or are you saying I somehow tricked you into seducing me?" He shook his head slowly, as if to say he was good, but not that good. His gaze never wavered from her eyes. "I'm falling in love with you, Fiona. There's your check on reality."

She stared at him and felt herself go still as a doe cornered by her mate, not trusting herself or what she had heard or what it meant. Her throat seemed not to work. She couldn't swallow, or drag her gaze off his face, or even breathe. "What did you say?"

"I said…" His jaw tightened. Tension strung him out like a hangman's noose. "I said, Fiona, that I'm falling in love with you."

She stared up at him, at the wealth of his nearly

feral masculine features, his muscled and hair-strewn chest, his deep, dark menacing eyes. And somewhere inside her she knew. Matt Guiliani had never said those words before. Or never meant by them what he meant now. That he had existed too long in the skin of some undercover persona, making his flesh and sinew conform to knowing better, showing higher judgment, exercising finer discipline than to permit himself to feel those feelings. Or open himself up to the sliver of a chance of heartache.

Matt Guiliani, secret agent man, had never before known what it was to be so vulnerable.

And he stood there doing it for her. She rose up from the bed of tangled sheets and threw herself into his arms. "Don't go. Don't do this. Don't ask me to do this. Whatever else—"

"Don't," he croaked, clamping one hand to her bare bottom, one to her nape as he drew her into a kiss like a death spiral, to silence her pleas, kill off her worries.

His mouth fitted to hers, her bare breasts to his, as if their two bodies were created for each other. She clung to him, and he lifted her and lay her gently back on the bed and broke away for the three seconds it took to strip out of his jeans. And then he was beside her, kissing her again to be sure that she wouldn't renew her pleas to him to back out of what he had to do.

He was an honorable man, bent on justice, and he would do what he had to do, and ask her to do the same, because they were only their own just desserts to each other if they gave what they were called upon to give in this world.

He rolled on top of her, holding his weight up,

stroking her till she parted her legs and he brought his sex home to her, deep within her, as he cried out her name.

He was everything to her she had ever longed to know, ever hoped to have to herself, more than all that. But her heart refused to follow him over the precipice. Or at least, her heart pretended not to be caught up.

She believed in him utterly. He was not only good enough to trick her into seducing him, but good enough to take on any five killers and live to tell the story. But there would be eight, or ten. Conscience-less men.

She would go off to jail to keep herself safe for him, but she didn't really believe, despite all the sweet and savage love he made to her, that he would return to her alive.

ON TUESDAY NIGHT, at lights-out, which was a just a bad joke since she was the only one in a cell, Fiona lay down on the hard cot in her jail cell and tried to sleep. She dozed uneasily, jerking awake a couple of times to be confronted again with the stark reality that she was behind bars. The silence unnerved her. She was used to the quiet of the ranch, but this was a humming, institutional silence. She couldn't hear the wind. And when she broke down, all she could hear was the echo of her own quiet sobs.

Sometimes she just couldn't remember Matt's voice in this place, his reassurances or his promises or the raggedness of his breathing amid the scorching kiss he had given her as Dex drove up the country lane with her arrest warrant clutched in his fist.

At the worst of times, she doubted him. She knew he would not make it out alive.

She woke briefly and turned onto her side, curling into a ball to avoid seeing the bars in the near total darkness, and clamped her teeth together to give herself the illusion that she would not start screaming soon. She clasped her hands and tucked them between her knees and sent her mind into vast empty spaces where no one could intrude.

She might have slept an hour when she heard keys rattling in the door leading out of the cell block followed by a brief pneumatic blast of an electronically controlled door. She heard low voices murmuring and the lights came on, so bright she had to shade her eyes. By the time the footsteps reached her cell, the voices had fallen silent.

Dex Hanifen unlocked her cell as another man, tall, athletically lean and wearing a black cashmere topcoat, looked on.

She sat up and asked, "What's going on?"

Hanifen shoved open the door. "This gentleman has come to take you out of here, into his custody, and—"

"Allow me," he interrupted, offering her his hand. He had a full head of steel-gray hair, an unlikely tan and a mustache, and he reeked of an expectation that his will would be done. "Elliott Braden, at your service."

"Fiona Halsey." She shook his hand. His flesh was cool and dry. He turned her hand in his, bent from the waist and brought her fingers to his lips in a continental manner she had only seen in European men. She felt put off, vaguely uneasy. "Am I confused, Mr. Braden, or is it the middle of the night?"

He gave her a smile. "You must call me Elliott, and I shall call you Fiona. It is midnight, but I could not allow the travesty of your imprisonment to go on another hour."

Her uneasiness edged higher. He seemed vaguely familiar to her, but as desperately as she wanted to be out of her jail cell, this shouldn't be happening. Dex knew that. The meeting at the hunting lodge of The Fraternity would be scuttled if she were to be released. "Did Matt send you?"

Dex cleared his throat. "The judge isn't going to be happy to be kept out of his bed any longer than necessary."

Braden ignored Dex. "Friends sent me, Fiona. You may trust in that. Don't worry."

"Have we met?" she asked.

"Come along, now. Sheriff Hanifen will give you your clothes and then we'll make an appearance before the weary magistrate." He ushered her out of the cell she was suddenly reluctant to leave. "We will secure your release into my custody, and then we'll make you comfortable for the night."

"Wait." She stopped at the door out of the cell block. "Who are you?" Had things changed so quickly that it no longer mattered for her to be jailed? Did he need her? Was it possible Matt wouldn't have come himself? "What friends?"

"There, there, my dear," he said, brushing her questions aside and forcing her through the door. "Make yourself presentable, now." He gave her a look that suggested she would know what she needed to know outside the sheriff's earshot. "We have much to accomplish and not a great deal of time."

She took her clothes and purse from Dex. She went

to the dressing room, which was by design no more than a windowless closet with a skimpy, inadequate privacy curtain. She stripped off her prisoner garb and changed quickly into her own jeans and sweater. She grabbed a hairbrush from her purse and ran it through her hair, then applied a touch of lipstick.

Braden waited with her pea coat and woolen scarf over his arm. They walked across the darkened street in the first real snow of the season. Dex punched a code into the electronic lock at one of the side doors to the courthouse and led the way through echoing halls to Judge Bell's chambers.

Dressed in a plaid shirt and blue jeans, not even bothering to don his robe, Henry Bell was no more gracious to her than at the country club on Sunday night, but he bowed and scraped for Braden.

"Your Honor," Braden said, sliding smoothly onto his agenda. "I appreciate your willingness to hear this motion to release into my custody an important witness, even in the face of charges pending against her."

Bell lifted his thick white brows and eyed a court reporter seated at her machine in the corner of the room. "My clerk is on overtime."

Braden assured him his costs would be reimbursed.

"By whom?" Fiona asked. "You mean the U.S. attorney—"

"You, Ms. Halsey," Bell interrupted sternly, "will speak when and if you are spoken to. Am I clear enough on that?"

"Yes, but I have a right to know—"

"My apologies, Your Honor," Braden interrupted, gripping her upper arm. "Ms. Halsey is understandably distraught—a situation I will remedy after you have ruled—''

"Now," she demanded. "Henry, I need to know *now* exactly into whose custody I'm supposed to go."

Bell stonewalled her. "I am told—and this is the last time you and I are going to address each other, missy—that it is essential for your own safety that you be taken from this jurisdiction immediately. And that the government prefers you *not* be forewarned of exactly what is expected of you."

"That is ridiculous!"

"Once more, Fiona. Once!"

"Or what, Henry?" she cried. "You'll toss me back in jail?"

Fuming, Bell poked a finger in the air at her. "I can and will have you physically gagged." He gave her a dismissive look and addressed Braden. "Your motion is in order, and granted, Mr. Braden." He addressed his clerk. "Custody of Fiona Halsey is given over to Mr. Elliott Braden under provisions of—''

"Wait," Fiona tried once more. "Henry, for God's sake, I have a right—''

"Oh, for pity's sake," Bell snapped. He sighed and scrubbed his drooping face with his hand. "Mr. Braden here is an agent of Interpol."

"Interpol?"

"That's what I said. I've seen his credentials myself, and he has the complete cooperation of the Department of Justice, Fiona, so just try to relax, huh?" He turned to Braden. "Sir, your witness is in your hands. You are responsible to return her to this jurisdiction at the earliest date possible. We're done here."

Bell jerked his sheepskin coat off a brass-and-mahogany coatrack and all but sped out the door. She felt too numb to move, too confused to think straight because it finally struck her when and where she had seen him.

Elliott Braden had been present in Switzerland in the room where she cut her deal with the Interpol official. He'd said nothing, but he'd been there. Watching her.

Panic shot through her. She started to appeal to Dex for help but his face was a blank and a hysterical little laugh burst out of her.

What was she thinking? He was in on it all, and she was terribly afraid he had just stepped aside and let her be given over to the Interpol collaborator Matt had stayed on to catch.

A man who would as soon slit her throat as look at her.

WEDNESDAY MORNING Matt drove along a back country road in his rented Bronco, keeping a sharp lookout along the roadside for J.D., who according to plan, would have driven into town near dawn.

Matt chose the site and arranged to rendezvous by Global Positioning System coordinates in the most deserted location possible. They couldn't afford to be seen by Hanifen or whoever he might have patrolling the area.

He slowed to less than twenty miles per hour as the GPS readout approached the designated coordinates, then passed them. He had just taken his eyes off the road to reset the unit and double-check his position when he heard a thump at the rear of the Bronco. He put on the brakes.

J.D. came up along the passenger side in a crouch

and ducked into the SUV. "About time you got here."

"Beggars and choosers," Matt cracked, pulling ahead now, shifting up into third. "What'd you use for transportation?"

"An FBI loaner out of Sheridan. I left it stranded off a dirt road about five miles back." He sighed heavily and looked hard at Matt. "Pull over a minute, would you?"

His pulse scattered, but he kept driving. There wasn't a likely place to stop. "What is it?"

"Pull over."

His scattered pulse began drumming as he drove the Bronco off-road and came to a stop. He turned, leaving one hand on the wheel. "Spit it out, J.D."

J.D. grimaced. "They've got Fiona."

Matt's left hand tightened on the wheel till his knuckles shone bone-white. He could hear his own heart beat now, as well or better than he could feel it pounding. "Who's got Fiona?"

"The bad guys."

His head was thick with denial and disbelief. "I know that. She's in the Johnson County jail."

J.D. shook his head, his lips compressed. "Last night that was true. This morning there is no one in the Johnson County jail."

Matt told himself to keep calm, told himself there must be an explanation, but his chest hurt something fierce. "How do you know?"

"Fiona was sent a bouquet by her mother. A freaking bouquet, can you imagine?" He swore. "Sorry. I was in town scoping out the territory when this delivery truck drove up to the sheriff's office. A kid got out with the flowers, went in, turned around and came right back out, still holding the flowers. I intercepted him, asked him if I could buy them. He was a little shook up that he couldn't deliver, but the sheriff's deputy told him there wasn't any Fiona Halsey there.''

"So you're telling me somebody just waltzed into the Johnson County jail in the middle of the night and took her out of there."

J.D. nodded unhappily. "I took a long shot and walked back across the street and marched myself in to the clerk of the court. She said there had been an emergency hearing after midnight and Judge Bell had ordered the prisoner transferred out of this jurisdiction."

Matt drew a long breath, exhaling sharply, reverting to the oldest trick in his book, which was to act as if nothing and no one mattered to him. Not personally. He didn't quite pull it off. "Did you get a look at the transfer order? See who took her? Get a description from the clerk?"

J.D. nodded. "His name was Elliott Braden."

Matt began to chew his lip. Rage wasn't far off the mark. Interpol agent Elliott Braden had been sitting at the planning table with Garrett and J.D. all this time. He was The Fraternity collaborator himself. Now Braden had Fiona.

J.D. looked hard at him. "Don't BS me, Matt. I've been there, remember? And Garrett, for that matter."

He returned the flinty stare. "Where's that, J.D.?"

"You think I won't say it?"

"I think maybe you'd better not."

"Tough. The answer is, in bed with the woman I was trying to keep safe," he snapped, pulling no punches. "Tell me you're not, tell me I'm mistaken. Go ahead. I've been wrong before."

"You've been wrong—"

"But not this time."

"No." He turned back in his seat, shoved the clutch to the floor and tore back onto the road. From the way his chest hurt, if he hadn't known better, he'd have thought he was having himself a heart attack, but he did know better. He was keenly aware that he was doing with the Bronco what he had done on horseback with Pilsner when Fiona had high-fived the juvenile delinquent Robbie. "Not this time."

"GOOD MORNING, sunshine."

Fiona woke with a splitting headache, barely able to open her eyes for the pain rocketing through her head. Covered with an afghan, her body ached as well, but it was the tenor of the voice greeting her that sent chills down her spine.

Braden. She couldn't see him, but she knew.

She remembered the chopper, the fear that had streaked through her, a crack on the head with what had to have been the butt of a handgun. She must have been carried from the chopper and dumped onto the sofa in the hunting lodge. She closed her eyes. If she dared move, the pain in her head would make her throw up.

"Feeling a little on the ragged side this morning?" Braden goaded.

The throbbing increased. Various rejoinders shot around in her skull, but she wouldn't give him the satisfaction.

She pushed the afghan aside and battled her way through the nausea to a sitting position. From the cor-

ner of her eye, she saw him lounging in one of the
easy chairs at the end of the sofa.

He looked casually elegant in black slacks and a
black turtleneck. In his hand, trailing from his long
fingers, was a glass filled with orange juice.

She realized how thirsty she was. As if reading her
mind, he got up and poured her a glass as well.

She didn't want to take anything from him, but she
needed it desperately. "Hemlock?"

He laughed and returned to his lounge chair.
"Wouldn't it be wonderful if things were that simple
for you?"

She swallowed down half the glass of juice.

"There's a good girl. We need you clearheaded
now."

She stared at him. "Maybe you should have
thought of that before you knocked me out."

"Oh, my. Feisty even in the midst of a very bad
episode." His eyes, black as coal, narrowed. The
threat seemed overwhelming to her, and she felt pan-
icky. "You don't want to make me angry, Fiona."

She jacked up her courage, drawing her body taller.
"What do you want from me?"

"Nothing more than the pleasure of your company.
Soon enough your lover will come running to your
rescue, and then I shall have what it is I really want."

Her chin went up. "I doubt it."

"You think he will succeed, then?" Braden
laughed, a ruthless sound that gnawed at her confi-
dence. "We shall see. He has, you know, been known
to fail."

Her throat convulsed again. She fought back
against nausea that went beyond what her headache

could account for. When had he failed? "Is Braden your real name?"

"Elliott Braden is...an alter ego, so to speak. An identity I assume when necessary. But I will tell you my name is Sloan Roszelle. I assure you, it is quite a well-known and highly respected name in the inner circles of the international law enforcement community."

Her eyes flared. He laughed. "Poor Fiona. I see by the panic in your beautiful face that I have shocked and offended your sensibilities. How can this be true? I see the question in your eyes. A dirty cop. Quite an American institution. I don't know why I should so easily transcend your worst nightmares." He got up to leave. "If you care to freshen up a bit, feel free."

He walked out of the great room, laughing softly to himself. She forced herself up and went to the plush master bedroom where she could lock herself in. She turned then against the door and sank to the floor clutching her throbbing head in her hands. Silent sobs tore through her body. No way in hell would Roszelle know how obscenely close he had come to seeing her crumble. He would use her to bait Matt into a fatal ambush.

She dragged herself into the shower and turned the water on full blast so her own worst-case imaginings might be drowned out.

She stood under the pounding streams of hot water. Within a few seconds the bathroom door slammed open and a man, a local employee of the feed-and-grain store she frequented, threw open the shower door, grabbed her by the wrist and flung her out onto the tile floor.

"Get out," she shrieked at him, grabbing desperately for a towel hanging from a wooden butler.

He snatched the towel away from her. "No can do, sweetheart. Wouldn't wanna see you try to hang yourself."

Crouching on the floor, she covered her bare breasts with her arm, wrapped the other arm about her waist and gave him a murderous look. "Give me the towel."

"Don't you know? You're on a suicide watch."

Chapter Fourteen

Matt spun a U-turn at the first possible widening in the road and drove like a madman in the direction of the Bar Naught. He frankly didn't give a damn anymore whether Dex spotted him or not, but it was more important than ever not to be careless now, and Dex still had a deputy posted at the turnoff. He told J.D. his plan, started to give him directions to the ranch house.

"I think I can figure it out, Matt," J.D. interrupted him. "Take it easy. I'll be there inside twenty minutes and we can figure out what the hell we're going to do."

"I can tell you what we're not going to do."

"Call Garrett in?"

Matt nodded. "No way is he leaving Kirsten at a time like this. Not to mention the fact that Braden is obviously intercepting our messages." J.D. didn't argue, which made Matt testy. "I mean it, J.D. He turns up here and I will personally whoop your ass."

"Yeah? You and what army? Besides, he's already on his way. You know Kirsten wouldn't stand for him bailing on you."

"This doesn't make me happy," Matt snapped, but

he didn't have time to argue. "Are you ready?" he asked, scanning the highway ahead and behind them, then suddenly shouting *"Go."*

J.D. released the latch, shoved open the door and rolled out. Matt swung wide left and hard right to bring the door closed before he came within view of the deputy standing guard.

He pulled to a stop and gave her a brisk wave. She held up a hand and did a once-around to make sure there was no one with him. He drove on into the ranch yard, shut down the engine so suddenly that the SUV jolted, and hopped out.

Fiona consumed his thoughts, and pretty much had a stranglehold on his stray emotions. The thought of her in the hands of the dirty Interpol agent made his gut churn.

He unlocked the back door for J.D., then went straight to Everly's computer and booted it up. Surprise, surprise. A message awaited him, signed by Elliott Braden.

Guiliani: The princess and I await your arrival at the hunting lodge. At 7:00 p.m. Come alone, come on horseback, come unarmed. I will know if you have defied these simple rules. Braden.

Matt sank into Everly's chair, the same one in which he'd held and made love to Fiona. His heart landed in his throat. He had not only been in bed with the woman he had promised to protect, he was in love with her—and he had been from the moment she shared that high-five moment with Robbie gentling the mustang.

How had he chosen his tactics so witlessly? How could he have believed that she would be safe if he allowed Dex Hanifen to take her into custody? He should have called in federal marshals, but he hadn't wanted to tip his hand or do anything to upset the delicate balance he had with Dex. Now it was Fiona's life upping the ante to high-stakes poker in a game where there were no rules.

Matt had to hand it to him. Braden had made an incredibly bold move, first revealing the existence of an Interpol collaborator, and then in stealing Fiona and leaving his name. He was *himself* the collaborator whose identity he pretended not to know, baiting Matt into going ahead even after Fiona turned over the evidence she had stolen.

He began to pace, needed to salvage his self-control. He had been suckered by Braden, the ultimate insider, the dirty cop perfectly positioned in worldwide law enforcement to dabble in police business around the world, scouting what actions were being planned and taken against The Fraternity members.

Braden allowed them to keep operating, to keep selling weapons and hiring out assassins, profiteering in the tens of millions of dollars, costing tens of thousands of deaths, innocent and not so innocent alike.

The Fraternity members would not be showing up on the Bar Naught, he knew. Not ever.

What he could not quite grasp was the why. Braden had any number of chances to neutralize whatever threat Matt represented—all he had to do was to call off the summit on the Bar Naught. Instead, he'd urged them to go forward. And the only reason that made any sense to Matt was that Braden had it in for Fiona over everything else.

Dex Hanifen may have handled the details, but it had to have been Braden who came up with the strategy for The Fraternity's protections—knocking off Kyle Everly and framing Fiona for his murder. When that failed, he sent a sharpshooter after her. And when that failed, Braden lied to manipulate events till he had a chance at her himself.

Which left Matt to question her truthfulness again. Why, above all else, did Braden want her silenced? And if he had her in his clutches, why fool around with Matt?

He heard J.D. rapping on wood to signal his presence. He came into Everly's study. Matt turned to the computer, printed Braden's e-mail and handed it over.

J.D. studied the sheet. His look hardened. "There's no way he'll know I'm there."

Matt exhaled slowly. "Yeah, there probably is. He's got the local constabulary in his back pocket, not to mention enough TruthSayer bastards to deploy over half the damned county."

"They haven't dealt with me yet. Remember, the late unlamented Kyle Everly and I grew up in country a lot like this. You better believe we played war games in the mountains." He paused. "It only takes one slacker getting bored with his assignment, Matt, to show up as the weak link. You know that as well as I do. I'll get through, I promise you that."

"I hope you can," Matt answered, flinging himself out of Everly's chair. "I'm out of here. I'm not going to do this on Braden's timetable."

J.D. grinned. "I like it already. How much time can you shave off?"

"If I leave right now, I should be there by five, five-fifteen. Just before dark."

"A couple of hours ahead of time, then?"

Matt nodded. "I'll need it." He'd never personally

made a bomb and put it on a timer. There was a first time for everything.

J.D. followed Matt out to the barn, and while he helped saddle up Pilsner, they constructed a plan. Since he couldn't follow on horseback without risking being seen, J.D. would recruit the DEA chopper that had ferried him from Seattle to drop him in under cover of darkness. And at a distance not to be heard at the lodge, which meant a grueling trek through unfamiliar terrain before J.D. could break through Braden's defenses.

Matt checked Pilsner's cinch one last time, then took off his ankle holster and handed his gun to J.D. "Guess this is it."

J.D. socked him on the shoulder. "What d'you say we go do this thing and you ride off into the sunset with the princess?"

He grinned. "Ann and Kirsten are gonna love this. I love this." He held his thumb and fingers three inches apart and drew a banner in the air. "Guiliani Bites The Marital Dust."

Matt stepped up into the stirrup, threw his leg over and settled into his seat. "Who said anything about marriage?"

"Shoot, boy. You've got a passel of learning to do."

"Yeah." But until then a total crapshoot was all they had for a plan. And his last remaining doubt. He checked his watch. He had to leave. The question remained.

Why Fiona?

HE RODE AT A PACE Pilsner could sustain in the long uphill ride to the hunting lodge. He took the long way around again, so that he could come down the mountain to the bunker and not up. He figured any lookouts would be focused in the wrong direction.

His hours in the saddle took their usual grueling toll but gave him time to map out in his mind what he had ahead of him to do. He didn't make it before dark, but he encountered no one to stop him.

He tethered Pilsner a hundred yards from the bunker, ran crouched for eighty yards, then dropped to the ground and crawled on his forearms like G.I. Joe across the rocky terrain to the door of the armory. The time was five-fifty. His wedge was still in place at the hinge.

He knocked it out with the butt of his hand and walked right in the disabled door. Making straight for the crowbar he'd used to open the crate of semi-automatics, he flipped on the lights bold as you please, retrieved one, loaded and put the weapon aside while he searched for the components of a couple of timed bombs. He would make one for a decoy, another set to go off half an hour later, both armed. And then he would ride up on the dot of seven as Braden had decreed. If J.D. didn't make it in time, Matt would need the mother of all distractions. He set to work at three minutes after six.

At six-thirty, his bombs concealed and time frame evaporated, moving silently back down the hallway toward the outer door, he heard a vicious thud from above him, and a scream that made his blood run cold.

THE FEED-AND-GRAIN STORE clerk had let her take a flannel shirt from Everly's closet to cover herself. The tail skimmed the top of her thighs. She had no un-

derwear at all. He'd locked her in the stark room outfitted to billet assassins-in-training, complete with
bunk beds, but it had been stripped of all linens and
blankets, even pillows in which she might try to
smother herself.

She had laughed hysterically. Did he think she
couldn't hang herself from the frame of the bunk bed
by the sleeves of the shirt more easily than smother
herself?

She had spent hours there alone when feed-boy
threw open the door and told her it was six-thirty.
Nearly show time. Roszelle wanted her up and
dressed and ready to go.

She ignored him.

He took a German Luger from a holster hanging
from his belt and shoved the short barrel tight against
her temple.

"Do it, feed-boy," she snarled. "Go ahead and
pull the trigger." Instead, he grabbed her shirt by the
placket and jerked down so hard that the fabric tore
away and she hit the floor again.

She screamed and lashed out at him with her legs,
a sweeping blow that took his legs out from under
him. He crashed to the floor and his gun went flying
across the bare wooden floor toward the door. She
dove for it and almost reached the Luger when Roszelle's booted foot came down on the gun.

He stood smiling, amused, with a length of cream-
colored satin over his forearm. A small paper bag of
an exclusive Paris boutique filled with toiletries hung
from his fingers by its silvery cords. "Fiona, my dear,
you have my complete admiration. But then I must
say, you've surprised me again and again with your
resourcefulness. On Mykonos, in Paris, again in Ge-

neva, and yet again on your own turf. The list is truly quite impressive.'' He spared a less pleased glance at feed-boy.

She drew herself into a crouch, ready to spring at him with his attention diverted, to gouge out his eyes if she got high enough, or land a blow at his groin if she failed. She'd just lost track of the snarling feed-boy, who launched himself at her shoulder and leveled her again.

''Enough!'' Roszelle snapped. He kicked the Luger out into the hall and jerked his head at feed-boy. ''Get out.''

She pushed herself up through pain shooting in her shoulder and jaw and her head, and curled her legs beneath her to cover herself.

''We'll have no more of this, princess,'' Roszelle warned her as he sank to his haunches and reached out to her.

She jerked away. ''Don't touch me.''

He smiled, held out the satin gown and the toiletries. ''I've brought you an exquisite dressing gown. Why don't you see how you like it?''

She recoiled with a sudden sickening realization. Roszelle wanted her to wear the sexy garb to enhance the illusion before Matt that she was intimate with Roszelle.

Impatience grated in his cultured voice. ''Fiona, have you any wish at all to see your lover alive again? I will have him blown off his horse before he arrives unless you stop this ridiculous behavior and get dressed.''

Her throat closed. ''He will never believe this,'' she hissed. ''*Never.* He might believe that I would betray him for the ranch, but never for you.''

"Is that so?" His facade of civility snapped. He lashed out and jerked her by her hair so hard all she could see were stars. She screamed and fought, bit into his hand and drew blood, but he dragged her head toward him so that his hot breath touched her ear. "Then I will simply avail myself of what is his by force, won't I?"

But in Roszelle's split second of fury and inattention, a horrendous inhuman roar exploded into the barracks room. Matt grabbed Roszelle with both hands and hauled him off her by sheer force, throwing him aside in time to wheel around at her scream and force up the barrel of the machine gun wielded by Dennis Geary, who had just entered the room.

Matt threw a deadly punch and kneed Geary as bullets ripped into the ceiling. Geary dropped the machine gun as he clutched himself and crumpled to his knees. Matt snatched up the weapon, and had them both in his aim when feed-boy dashed in from behind. She screamed to warn Matt again, but too late. Feed-boy brought the butt of his Luger crashing down onto Matt's head, and he dropped, unconscious, to the floor.

Tears of rage streamed down her face. Barely aware of the three men bellowing at each other, she scrambled to Matt's side. But feed-boy shot at the floor beside Matt, missing his head and her hand by no more than a couple of inches. She froze in her prostrate position and became aware of Roszelle rising up with a furious barrage of epithets, demanding to know how Guiliani had gotten past Geary and his cohorts.

He grabbed the Luger away and the feed-boy skit-

tered out, only to call triumphantly that the door leading up from the bunker was thrown wide open.

Geary groaned and got to his feet. From the look
on Roszelle's face, Fiona thought he would kill her
and then Matt on the spot, but he turned in his cold
fury to go and investigate with Dennis Geary what
other havoc Matt might have unleashed.

She heard the lock clicking shut on the barracks
room door again, and she knew with a sickening certainty that it would have been too unsatisfying for a
man of Roszelle's ilk to kill them both and be done
with it.

AT 6:00 P.M., one hundred and two miles away, J.D.
prepared to make the jump from a chopper on loan
from the DEA into the forested canyon on the other
side of the mountain from the hunting lodge. Garrett
was on-site at the private hangar facility, coordinating
and feeding J.D. and his team information as fast as
Garrett could talk.

The FBI Hostage Rescue Team had done a flyover
of the lodge in a superquiet craft loaded with the most
sophisticated heat-sensing and detection equipment in
the world. There were scouts placed, as Braden had
intimated, around the hunting lodge, but there were
only four of them.

A corridor through which J.D. could elude detection himself had been marked out on a topographical
map.

A satellite had been chosen, as well, for its place-
ment in the heavens in the necessary time frame, and
priority access given over. The Global Positioning
System, which relied on the triangulation of satellite

beams, would not be interrupted by the satellite moving out of position.

J.D. would wear a receiver in his ear and be guided, along with two HRT agents, by Garrett according to their own constantly changing positions.

"The flyboys," Garrett was saying, "think there is a possibility that one man is doing periodic checks on the outside of the lodge. The analysts say the likelihood is this individual is also the pilot of the chopper."

J.D. and the HRT agents, both snipers and a chopper pilot as well, had been extensively briefed. Their options ran the gamut from disabling Braden's helicopter to replacing his pilot to dropping Braden in his tracks to blowing the chopper out of the sky. They would have to make the decisions in the field according to what they found.

As they walked into the windstorm beneath the blades of the chopper, Garrett gripped J.D.'s shoulder. "Bring him back alive, okay?"

A PAIN LIKE HE HAD never known ricocheting through his head, Matt could not hear. He thought he must be dead, thought he must have died and gone to hell for the anguish on her face and the tears streaming down.

Oddly, he could feel her fingers, faint as butterfly wings on his face, her thumbs lightly, desperately stroking his eyelids, his cheeks, his lips. He knew she was trying to keep him with her, begging him to stay alive. Didn't she know he was already dead?

Don't you dare die. I love you. Don't you dare die.

But still he couldn't hear her, and he knew that meant he was dead. A black maw opened up around him again, and he was curiously aware that his eyes rolled back in his head. And that if he went down again, he wouldn't make it back up.

He wanted to hear her. Had to hear her. He fought to escape the clutches of certain death. He wanted her too much. Deserved her. Needed her. Loved her. It wasn't his time to die.

And if he ever got out of this, if he managed to cheat death just this one last time, he would not leave her again. Not ever.

And then, he could see the light. As if the decision to recognize his own feelings freed him, he could hear again. Slowly he raised a hand to the bleeding knot on his head. He came fully awake, and the pain roared in to reassure him that he was still alive.

His head cradled in her lap, her burnished golden hair falling near his face, he had other, sweeter bodily indications that he was indeed among the living. He thought of the line of poetry from the Bible J.D. and Ann had used in their wedding vows. *Set me as a seal upon thine heart.* He wondered why it took such a vicious blow to his thick head to clear the debris and see that was all he wanted. To be set as a seal on her heart, to have her set as a seal on his.

He looked up at Fiona's tearstained face. One would never have known his thoughts were not where his words suggested. "Where's Braden?"

She backhanded her tears and smiled brilliantly at him. "You just never let it go, do you?"

You'd be surprised. He cleared his throat to clear his head, but the pain wouldn't go so easily. He meant to tell her he wouldn't be leaving her again, but he didn't get it all quite out. "Never say never, princess."

She swallowed her grateful sob. "He's gone looking to see what else you've got in store for him. Matt, listen to me. He told me 'Braden' is an alias—an agent he created. His real name is Sloan Roszelle. Does that mean anything to you?"

His eyes focused on the cut on her temple and the bruise surrounding it. "He hurt you."

"Matt, listen! Sloan Roszelle. Think—"

"He hurt you."

She began to cry. He cared more for her than he cared about the name of his enemy. "He's a worm."

"I'll tear out his heart."

She smiled through her tears. "Ooh, be still my heart."

He scowled. Or would have, if it didn't hurt so damned bad. "Are you mocking me, princess?"

She shook her head. Her tears showered him with love, her smile with joy. "I wouldn't dream of it."

Her fingers touched the gash on her temple. "Actually it was feed-boy who did this."

"Feed-boy."

"Uh-huh." She couldn't stop smiling or crying, or looking at him as if the sun rose and set in his eyes. "Feed-boy. He works at the feed and grain—"

Her explanation was cut off by Braden thrusting open the door. He towered above them, legs spread like a colossus. "I'm so glad you've found some amusement in all of this."

Fiona tried to shelter Matt with her body, but Matt hauled himself out of her lap, into a sitting position, as Braden stepped aside and let Geary and the feed-boy by.

Braden had regained his composure. Her heart sank. He ordered his flunkies to haul his guest into the great room, then turned on his heel and walked away.

The pair started in after Matt with murder in their eyes. Geary was still mincing his steps.

"There's nothing more dangerous than a man with nothing to lose," Matt warned. He was without a gun to their maxed-out automatics, but both of them stopped short of his reach. He struggled to his feet, and the pain sent him right back down to his knees, and still he got up again. "Touch either one of us and I will kill you."

He waited for Fiona to precede him. She grabbed up the silk robe to cover the shirt that reached only to her thighs. At the brink of passing out again, Matt followed her, leaving the two thugs in his pathetic dust to snarl at each other. He had no idea what power they thought he held over them.

He caught Fiona's shoulder once to keep himself on his feet when the blackness swarmed up again. He found himself by some grace in front of the couch before his head reeled again and he sank down beside Fiona. Her hand on his shoulder was the only thing that kept him upright.

He forced himself to note the positions of Geary and Fiona's feed-boy, then to seek out Braden's form in a chair opposite the couch. He trained his scant focus on the deadly eyes of his enemy.

"Ah, Mateos," Braden mocked. "We meet at long last. I must say, you've all but ruined my day."

Mateos. He stared at the slug of a man. A deep, uneasy feeling roiled up inside him from some wholly instinctual well of regrets, but he couldn't focus long enough to identify the source of his unease. He feigned a shrug. "It's a start."

"Abortive," Braden agreed, "but a start nevertheless. We found your entry into the bunker. And disarmed your handiwork." He gave an admiring nod. "Both of them."

Matt blinked. "There are three, Braden."

For an instant, fear flared in the Interpol traitor's eyes. Then he thought better of it and restored his smile. "Such a worthy opponent. I'll tell you what. When I see you getting nervous for Fiona's lovely neck, I will look after my own." He got up to pour himself a shot of brandy. He rolled the dark liquid around and then inhaled the scent. "You disappoint me, Matty-boy. The blow to your head must have dimmed your wits."

Matty-boy. Fiona's fingers dug into his shoulder at about the same instant that his muddled thoughts began to come clear. Matty-boy was the nickname of the son of Alex Karamedes.

"And it is not Braden," he added, "though I have employed the role from time to time. I would have thought, if your own memory failed you, lovely Fiona would have told you by now. The name is Roszelle. Sloan Roszelle."

Then his poor battered steel trap of a mind slammed shut on the truth. Sloan Roszelle was only a name Matt had seen on the chart of officials at the very highest levels of Interpol. One degree removed from the pinnacle.

The guardian angel of Alex Karamedes's enormously profitable trafficking in priceless antiquities. Now, sixteen years later the guardian angel of The Fraternity. And it wasn't Fiona he wanted but Matt himself.

This was personal, a long-smoldering vendetta.

This was Sloan Roszelle cornering the international market in illegal arms, and at the same time, exploiting a golden opportunity to exact his revenge against Matt.

"I see by the sickly color that adorns your flesh, Mateos, that you have finally arrived."

A bitterness rose up in his throat he thought he could not endure. "What do you want, Roszelle?"

"What would you say might compensate me for the monstrous disrepute you caused me? How many millions of dollars? Do you know how many years it required to recoup the lifestyle to which I had become so accustomed? Sixteen years I have waited for such a moment as this. And you wandered with such finesse into my trap. Once I learned that *you* were the man who would be king of Kyle Everly's domain, I was most eager for Interpol to cooperate fully with the United States Department of Justice."

Matt gritted his teeth, a hedge against the pain screaming around in his head, a protection against saying the words that would send this madman over the edge.

"You ordered the murder of Kyle Everly," Fiona accused.

"Why, yes! I have found your local contingent of TruthSayers quite amenable to my causes. Sheriff Hanifen and his deputy, Crider. Monsieurs Geary and Schockly here. Mr. Norville. The Honorable Henry Bell—oh, and—"

"Cut the roll call, Roszelle," Matt snapped, sick to death of Roszelle's bragging. He had timed Everly's murder to coincide with Matt's arrival on the Bar Naught, and with that murder also took out a half a dozen birds with one stone.

Roszelle had been able to eliminate a powerful competitor and send a message, like the shot heard around the world, that would keep the rest of Everly's cohorts in line and ensure they would never show up on the Bar Naught.

They would wait instead, unwitting, for their arrests.

"What do you want now?" Matt asked.

Roszelle dosed his sneer with a swallow of brandy. "Well, let me see. The arrests have already begun around the world of the various hapless members of La Fraternité. You see, Mateos," he goaded, "even without your interference the world would still have been restored to a safer place."

"Until you replace them all with your stoolies."

"*Bon mot,* Mateos! My sentiments exactly! And for you? I would have contented myself with your deaths, until your bit of tail here added insult to injury." He regarded his bloody hand.

Fiona began to shake.

"You must die, of course. You are, to me, the most dangerous man left alive. There are others who may suspect who and what I really am, but I can deal with them. As for you, Fiona, your inevitable grief over Mateos's death might assuage my pique. But as a bit of a grace note, if you will, I have decided on a further complication for you." He addressed Matt. "Once you are dead and gone forever, it will be our lovely Fiona who will be held accountable. I should imagine Fiona Halsey may well become one of the most wanted—dare I say, vilified—fugitives on the face of the earth."

A bolt of fear for Fiona shot through all Matt's

pain. "Who's going to believe Fiona Halsey would do this?"

"Alone?" Roszelle stopped short and arched a brow. "Why, no one, to be sure. She must have been acting in concert with someone—but who? With the murder of Kyle Everly hanging over her head, the fact that she lured you to your death, here of all places at the hunting lodge her father built—" He broke off, tsking. "The issue of her accomplice will fade away to nothing. Have a little faith, Mr. Guiliani. Nothing has been left to chance. Ms. Halsey's history with Pascal Lariviere, not to mention her stormy relationship with Everly, will assure her fate.

"Elliott Braden will cease to exist. And as for me? I have a great deal of respect for Garrett Weisz and J. D. Thorne. I suppose I shall have to retire to a place where there is no extradition."

He sighed as the clock on the mantel gonged the eight o'clock hour. "Mr. Geary, if you please. Go warm up the chopper."

Geary slung the weapon back and left out the front door. Roszelle trained a Luger on Matt and the feed-boy, his automatic. "Let us proceed to the cellar. Fiona, my dear, why don't you lead the way?"

She hesitated too long. "Move it, Fiona," Roszelle warned, waving the gun at Matt's lower torso, "or your lover will suffer the very painful loss of his masculinity before he dies."

She began to tremble violently, and moved toward the cellar door. Matt fell in behind her and started down the stairs. "You'll never get off the ground."

"Oh, I think I will." He flipped on the lights and ordered Matt to keep a proper distance from Fiona. "You, Mr. Guiliani, will remain behind, so that you can warn anyone who might be lying in wait to spoil our getaway that Fiona is on board.''

She reached the bottom of the stairs and kept going, through the door that led into the cinder-block halls. Roszelle was a professional, knew all the tricks and kept back far enough that Matt could not turn and try to disarm him.

But Fiona tripped near the end and fell to her knees. Roszelle fired to keep her going, the blast magnified a thousand times in the confines of the underground bunker.

Instinctively, Matt held out his hands and turned to watch Fiona. Her hands clamped tight against her ears, she dragged herself up from the floor and started walking again, her posture brittle and terrified. He followed, his heart thudding, his mind searching desperately for a way out. She hauled open the door into the branching corridor and then the tremendous noise of the chopper revving up boomed through the bunker.

The heavy steel door at the end of the corridor opened on the outdoors, and as Fiona pulled it open, a blast of frigid air knocked her down. Matt bent to help her get up and then he felt the heel of Roszelle's boot come crashing into his back, leveling him with the fresh assault, the sudden devastating blow to his kidneys. He fell to his knees, felt the pain rocketing through his torso, but he fought to stay conscious as he pitched forward and his prone body stopped the door.

He heard Fiona's scream, sensed her flying at Roszelle with a murderous cry. But he socked her across the face with the Luger, lifting her off her feet. She landed in a heap beside him as Matt felt the cold ring of steel clamp around his wrist and dimly, as if from miles away through a gamut of hellish pain, he recognized the cuffs.

He hurled his body back, fought the dragging by his arm, but to no avail. Roszelle hauled him out the door, into the lashing winds, and hoisted Matt's arm with inhuman strength to lock the other cuff to the outer door handle.

He must have started on Fiona, then. Her screams were wisps in the wind, useless cries of rage. Matt forced himself to think, to stay conscious, but all he could see was Roszelle's legs taking huge strides through the dark night toward the chopper, and Fiona's, resisting him and kicking all the way.

Roszelle threw her bodily into the door of the helicopter and hopped aboard himself, and Matt watched in horror as it began to lift off the ground, and then all his senses cleared and sharpened to an unbearable intensity. He heard J.D. shouting, "He's down, he's down," then bullets fired to get the attention of the pilot and a voice over an electronically boosted megaphone commanding, "Set down or be shot down. Now!"

With his arm unnaturally twisted, locked tight to the door, he spotted at a distance of fifty yards the man in position to take out the tail rotor and force the chopper down. The shooter elevated the rocket firepower to his shoulder, and Matt knew then that the threat was not idle.

They had to have seen Fiona fighting her captor, but the chopper would be taken down, and Matt began to scream "No! No!"

The chopper lifted thirty feet up into the air. Roszelle appeared at the edge of the door as a spotlight hit him from another source on the ground, but he had Fiona tight against him, a human shield.

Armed with a semiautomatic, he shot from the hip, raining down a cloud of bullets at Matt, chewing a hideous path on the steel door.

The voice boomed again over the megaphone. J.D. hurled himself from out of the dark to Matt's side, and with a sidearm blew away the links of the cuffs, freeing Matt's arm. He was still screaming "No!" when it appeared, as if in slow motion, amid another hail of bullets, that Fiona dropped to the floor of the chopper and lashed out at Roszelle's legs with her bare feet.

Scrambling, his semiautomatic waving wildly, spraying bullets behind him, the evil Roszelle was hit by the HRT marksman and fell from the copter, dead as he crashed to the ground.

Over the pain still battering his head and body, Matt scrambled to his feet as the chopper gyrated and crashed to the ground.

He knew Fiona hadn't fallen out like Roszelle, but he couldn't see her, couldn't tell if she'd been hurt or maimed, or God forbid...worse. His heart pounded. His head throbbed beyond endurance, but he lit out running, fearing that the chopper would go up in a fiery explosion and Fiona would be caught in an inferno just like the one that had destroyed her beloved Soldier Boy's spirit.

He couldn't lose her now, couldn't lose the woman brainy, brave and gutsy enough to be his one true match on God's green earth.

The chill night air reeked of spilling fuel. The chopper blades torqued and tore into the earth, spewing dirt and fallen pine needles like a tornado. Matt ran toward the twisted wreckage, choking, battling his way past the men who had come with J.D. to their rescue. Men who tried to hold him back. Nothing would, no mortal man. Dimly aware that they were calling in reinforcements and fire crews, Matt would get to Fiona or die trying.

He tripped and fell hard to his knees, got up and in a nightmarish panic, watched as Fiona rose up and struggled out of the open chopper door as the spilled fuel ignited. She screamed for Matt and hurled herself toward him, the belt of her robe torn loose, its edges fluttering behind her like the wings of an angel. The blast knocked her another ten feet from the chopper, out of danger, but she fell to the ground as if caught in the back by the deadly flying debris.

He reached her a split second later, crouched low and rolled her up into his arms, carrying her still farther away to the limits of his endurance. He sank to his knees on the ground, cradling her close to his own battered, spent body.

She struggled to come to in Matt's arms. She knew she'd escaped with her life, but the incredible blast of heat that had thrown her also left her temporarily deafened. Her eyes fluttered open, and she saw Matt's face, his fierce love for her carved in his hard, relentlessly masculine features. She couldn't hear him, only knew that his lips shaped the endearments and pleas she'd longed to hear.

Princess. Tears eked out of the corners of his eyes. *No one but you.*

I love you. Tears fell onto her cheeks that belied his tough-boy expression, gave utter credence to emotions he had oh-so-recently begun to feel.

She had never felt any emotion sweeter than this,

more precious in the midst of unbelievable carnage, than in the instant his tears left tracks on his chiseled cheeks, spilled and bathed her own.

A tiny baptism of credence.

She reached up to stroke his bloodied cheek with her hand. "I love you, Matt. I love you." She couldn't even hear herself, but she could see in his eyes that he heard. "I was so scared Roszelle would blow up the armory and you—" Unable to hear her own words, she couldn't finish the thought. She gulped. Her lips pressed tight, but her chin quivered. "I was so scared."

He shut his eyes, those beautiful long lashes tear-soaked, and lowered his mouth to hers. And however cracked and dried both their lips were, no kiss would ever mean to her what this one conveyed. Matt Guiliani had found his match in her, in a backwater girl with distant relatives in Buckingham Palace who had eyes only for him.

After a few moments he began to laugh in sheer, crazed joy through their kisses, and fell back. They tumbled together, laughing till it hurt, down the small incline.

Epilogue

"The pilot, Geary, must have been killed by the bullets. The chopper began to gyrate like crazy. And you've gotta know, Christo-man," Matt said, holding Garrett's enthralled little boy on his lap, "that my heart hit rock bottom, because Fiona was still on that bird when the engines choked and died and it fell out of the sky by itself."

They were sitting together, sideways on a sofa in the delivery waiting room, all three of them, spooned together, Matt in Fiona's arms, Christo in his.

The cheerful sunlit room seemed filled with what had become to Fiona, in a matter of their first moments together, family. J.D. and Ann and, when he wasn't prowling the halls in search of vending machines, their son, Jaz. And Matt had been telling Garrett and Kirsten's son of their big adventures for a couple of hours to keep him entertained while they waited for Christo's baby sisters to be born.

Her arms wrapped tight around Matt, his body cradled between her long legs, Fiona watched over Matt's shoulders as Christo clapped a hand over his mouth and twisted around in Matt's lap to make sure she was okay. "What happened then, Uncle Matt?"

"Then—"

He was interrupted by Garrett bursting through the doors into the delivery room lounge. "The babies are born!" Garrett crowed, whipping off his paper scrub hat and tossing it into the air. Everyone cheered wildly. The men high-fived one other. Fiona thought the whole affair must be terminally embarrassing for Jaz.

Garrett came next to the sofa, where Christo was jumping up and down now. He sank to his haunches. "You want to come meet your baby sisters, Christo-man? We're gonna call them Hannah and Made-leine."

"Ah, Dad—"

Matt shared a look with Garrett. "It's okay, Christo. I'll still be here when you get back."

"And then you'll tell me the rest of the story?"

Matt promised, and Christo did a flying leap to Garrett's arms. He shook hands quickly with his two best friends and touched a kiss to Ann and Fiona with his finger, then swung Christo up on his shoulders and ducked through the doorway.

Jaz tossed aside a magazine he'd been flipping through, trying to act as if he hadn't been listening and couldn't care less about the story Matt was telling. He got up and stretched his lanky body and jerked his head at Matt in the direction of the elevator. "You got a minute?"

"For you, Jaz, I guess."

Fiona watched Jaz half loping away in his massive, elephant-legged pants, T-shirt and ball cap worn backward. Matt gave them all a shrug and followed the boy. Fiona's heart knocked about, seeing the boy in the man she was in love with.

They had time for only a couple of exchanges. At the end Matt caught the kid's scrawny teenage neck in the crook of his arm and shot a thumbs-up to her, and to Ann and J.D. Jaz snagged an elevator and went looking for a soda. Or an escape.

Matt reclaimed his place on the sofa, beside her this time.

He looked to her as if he might really need a place to escape to as well. She combed her fingers through his hair. "What did Jaz want?"

He looked back over his shoulder at her. "Wanted to know if maybe he could come to the Bar Naught sometime this spring and see what Miss Halsey does with them mustangs."

Tears sprang into her eyes. "Oh, Matt. I would love that."

"Since he's opened the door for that kind of, um, request…Miss Halsey—" He broke off and fished something out of his jeans pocket. An antique diamond ring set in platinum with a dozen tiny diamonds all around. "This belonged to my grandma." He took her hand from his neck and slipped the ring onto her finger. "Do you think maybe I could come back to the Bar Naught? Forever?"

A brilliant smile shone through her tears and she gave him her answer.

"I do."

Where the bond of family, tradition and honor run as deep and are as vast as the great Lone Star state, that's...

Texas families are at the heart of the next Harlequin 12-book continuity series.

HARLEQUIN®

INTRIGUE

is proud to launch this brand-new series of books by some of your very favorite authors.

Look for

SOMEONE S BABY
by Dani Sinclair
On sale May 2001

SECRET BODYGUARD
by B.J. Daniels
On sale June 2001

UNCONDITIONAL SURRENDER
by Joanna Wayne
On sale July 2001

Available at your favorite retail outlet.

HARLEQUIN®
Makes any time special ®

Visit us at www.eHarlequin.com

HITT

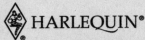

Harlequin truly does
make any time special....
This year we are celebrating
weddings in style!

A Walk Down the Aisle
WEDDING CELEBRATION

To help us celebrate, we want you to tell us how wearing the Harlequin wedding gown will make your wedding day special. As the grand prize, Harlequin will offer one lucky bride the chance to **"Walk Down the Aisle" in the Harlequin wedding gown!**

There's more...

For her honeymoon, she and her groom will spend five nights at the **Hyatt Regency Maui.** As part of this five-night honeymoon at the hotel renowned for its romantic attractions, the couple will enjoy a candlelit dinner for two in Swan Court, a sunset sail on the hotel's catamaran, and duet spa treatments.

MAUI
the Magic Isles™
Maui • Molokai • Lanai

To enter, please write, in, 250 words or less, how wearing the Harlequin wedding gown will make your wedding day special. The entry will be judged based on its emotionally compelling nature, its originality and creativity, and its sincerity. This contest is open to Canadian and U.S. residents only and to those who are 18 years of age and older. There is no purchase necessary to enter. Void where prohibited. See further contest rules attached. Please send your entry to:

Walk Down the Aisle Contest

In Canada
P.O. Box 637
Fort Erie, Ontario
L2A 5X3

In U.S.A.
P.O. Box 9076
3010 Walden Ave.
Buffalo, NY 14269-9076

You can also enter by visiting www.eHarlequin.com
Win the Harlequin wedding gown and the vacation of a lifetime!
The deadline for entries is October 1, 2001.

HARLEQUIN®
Makes any time special ®

PHWDACONT1

HARLEQUIN WALK DOWN THE AISLE TO MAUI CONTEST 1197
OFFICIAL RULES
NO PURCHASE NECESSARY TO ENTER

1. To enter, follow directions published in the offer to which you are responding. Contest begins April 2, 2001, and ends on October 1, 2001. Method of entry may vary. Mailed entries must be postmarked by October 1, 2001, and received by October 8, 2001.

2. Contest entry may be, at times, presented via the Internet, but will be restricted solely to residents of certain geographic areas that are disclosed on the Web site. To enter via the Internet, if permissible, access the Harlequin Web site (www.eHarlequin.com) and follow the directions displayed online. Online entries must be received by 11:59 p.m. E.S.T. on October 1, 2001.

   In lieu of submitting an entry online, enter by mail by hand-printing (or typing) on an 8½" x 11" plain piece of paper, your name, address (including zip code), Contest number/name and in 250 words or fewer, why winning a Harlequin wedding dres would make your wedding day special. Mail via first-class mail to: Harlequin Walk Down the Aisle Contest 1197, (in the U.S.) P.O. Box 9076, 3010 Walden Avenue, Buffalo, NY 14269-9076, (in Canada) P.O. Box 637, Fort Erie, Ontario L2A 5X3, Canad

   Limit one entry per person, household address and e-mail address. Online and/or mailed entries received from persons residing in geographic areas in which Internet entry is not permissible will be disqualified.

3. Contests will be judged by a panel of members of the Harlequin editorial, marketing and public relations staff based on the following criteria:
   • Originality and Creativity—50%
   • Emotionally Compelling—25%
   • Sincerity—25%
   In the event of a tie, duplicate prizes will be awarded. Decisions of the judges are final.

4. All entries become the property of Torstar Corp. and will not be returned. No responsibility is assumed for lost, late, illegible, incomplete, inaccurate, nondelivered or misdirected mail or misdirected e-mail, for technical, hardware or software failures of any kind, lost or unavailable network connections, or failed, incomplete, garbled or delayed computer transmission or any human error which may occur in the receipt or processing of the entries in this Contest.

5. Contest open only to residents of the U.S. (except Puerto Rico) and Canada, who are 18 years of age or older, and is void wherever prohibited by law; all applicable laws and regulations apply. Any litigation within the Province of Quebec respecting the conduct or organization of a publicity contest may be submitted to the Régie des alcools, des courses et des jeux for a ruling. Any litigation respecting the awarding of a prize may be submitted to the Régie des alcools, des courses et des jeux o for the purpose of helping the parties reach a settlement. Employees and immediate family members of Torstar Corp. and D. L. Blair, Inc., their affiliates, subsidiaries and all other agencies, entities and persons connected with the use, marketing o conduct of this Contest are not eligible to enter. Taxes on prizes are the sole responsibility of winners. Acceptance of any priz offered constitutes permission to use winner's name, photograph or other likeness for the purposes of advertising, trade and promotion on behalf of Torstar Corp., its affiliates and subsidiaries without further compensation to the winner, unless prohibited by law.

6. Winners will be determined no later than November 15, 2001, and will be notified by mail. Winners will be required to sign a return an Affidavit of Eligibility form within 15 days after winner notification. Noncompliance within that time period may resu in disqualification and an alternative winner may be selected. Winners of trip must execute a Release of Liability prior to ticke and must possess required travel documents (e.g. passport, photo ID) where applicable. Trip must be completed by Novemb 2002. No substitution of prize permitted by winner. Torstar Corp. and D. L. Blair, Inc., their parents, affiliates, and subsidiarie are not responsible for errors in printing or electronic presentation of Contest, entries and/or game pieces. In the event of printing or other errors which may result in unintended prize values or duplication of prizes, all affected game pieces or entri shall be null and void. If for any reason the Internet portion of the Contest is not capable of running as planned, including infection by computer virus, bugs, tampering, unauthorized intervention, fraud, technical failures, or any other causes beyon the control of Torstar Corp. which corrupt or affect the administration, secrecy, fairness, integrity or proper conduct of the Contest, Torstar Corp. reserves the right, at its sole discretion, to disqualify any individual who tampers with the entry proces and to cancel, terminate, modify or suspend the Contest or the Internet portion thereof. In the event of a dispute regarding an online entry, the entry will be deemed submitted by the authorized holder of the e-mail account submitted at the time of entry Authorized account holder is defined as the natural person who is assigned to an e-mail address by an Internet access provi online service provider or other organization that is responsible for arranging e-mail address for the domain associated with submitted e-mail address. **Purchase or acceptance of a product offer does not improve your chances of winnin**

7. Prizes: (1) Grand Prize—A Harlequin wedding dress (approximate retail value: $3,500) and a 5-night/6-day honeymoon tri Maui, HI, including round-trip air transportation provided by Maui Visitors Bureau from Los Angeles International Airport (winner is responsible for transportation to and from Los Angeles International Airport) and a Harlequin Romance Package, including hotel accomodations (double occupancy) at the Hyatt Regency Maui Resort and Spa, dinner for (2) two at Swan Court, a sunset sail on Kiele V and a spa treatment for the winner (approximate retail value: $4,000); (5) Five runner-up priz of a $1000 gift certificate to selected prize outlets to be determined by Sponsor (retail value $1000 ea.). Prizes consist of or those items listed as part of the prize. Limit one prize per person. All prizes are valued in U.S. currency.

8. For a list of winners (available after December 17, 2001) send a self-addressed, stamped envelope to: Harlequin Walk Dow Aisle Contest 1197 Winners, P.O. Box 4200 Blair, NE 68009-4200 or you may access the www.eHarlequin.com Web site through January 15, 2002.

Contest sponsored by Torstar Corp., P.O. Box 9042, Buffalo, NY 14269-9042, U.S.A.

PHWDACONT2